Walter Wager, a grad Harvard Law School and a
former Fulbright Fell
diplomatic advisor to
editor at the United
Playbill and *Show*. A
articles to sixteen ma
dagger novels under
documentaries for th
Information Agency. o
the American Society of Composers, Authors,
Publishers.

Also by Walter Wager:

TELEFON

WARHEAD

SWAP

TIME OF RECKONING

Walter Wager

Sledgehammer

Futura Publications Limited
A Futura Book

A Futura Book

First published in Great Britain by
Futura Publications Limited in 1979

This book is dedicated to
George Nobbe, Jim Bryans, and
Don Fine – for their encouragement –

– And to Jay Topkis, for friendly counsel

– And to my daughter Lisa – because she likes to read

ISBN 0 7088 1457 1

Printed in Great Britain by
Hazell Watson & Viney Ltd
Aylesbury, Bucks

Futura Publications Limited
110 Warner Road
Camberwell, London SE5

CHAPTER ONE

Shortly after 11 p.m. on the balmy evening of May 21, Mr Edward R. Barringer, a slight white-haired man whose cunning and boldness were a matter of official record in certain sealed files of the Government of the United States, emerged from his gray stucco house at 54 Crescent Drive in Paradise City. He walked slowly, almost awkwardly, to his car at the curb. Mr Barringer had a pronounced limp, a glass left eye, twenty-six false teeth, a battered tan attaché case and the keys to a green 1966 Ford convertible. In accord with the request of the local Chamber of Commerce, a fully ripe moon was shining over Paradise City, and Mr Barringer nodded in approval as he got into his car. Then he placed the attaché case on the seat beside him.

'This is going to be easy,' the fat-faced assassin in the doorway across the street thought cheerfully. He had no way of knowing that Edward R. Barringer had been a skilled practitioner of the violent arts himself, had adroitly slain three policemen with knife and wire garotte before finishing his senior year at Harvard. Mr Barringer did not talk about his savage past, for as a working journalist he much preferred to write about the present.

So the white-haired little man with the limp retracted the canvas top of the convertible, sniffed the jasmine-scented evening and inserted the key in the ignition. He turned it, stepped on the gas pedal. Then he was dead. A jagged blast of fire and sound broke open the night, and smoke and flame erupted from the wrecked convertible as the bomb detonated. Mr Barringer perished instantly, crushed and seared in the sudden savage convulsion of fatal force that hurled his corpse thirty feet down Crescent Drive. His long years of terrible nightmares were ended.

But that was not all that the four sticks of dynamite achieved. Nearby windows shattered, epithets soared and lights flashed on all through the comfortable residential neighborhood as outraged taxpayers reacted indignantly to this unseemly interruption of the Late Movie on WPAR-TV – one of those wonderful old Bette Davis films in which everybody has brain tumors and smokes a lot. Four blocks from the explosion, Mr and Mrs Arnold Fellows vigorously debated whether a Russian satellite had fallen on Paradise City, while across the street former Sanitation Commissioner Willy Ed Rawlins drafted a press release on teen-age hooligans. Four maiden ladies conducting a seance over on Stonewall Jackson Boulevard decided that it might just possibly be the end of the world and sensibly put in a person-to-person call to the Reverend Billy Graham. A sixteen-year-old blonde who was baby-sitting in a house on Magnolia Drive fainted, but at least nine sober citizens remained cool enough to telephone the police, the fire department and the local commander of the American Legion. Somebody even called the City Desk of the Paradise City *Trumpet*.

Then it was only minutes until the sirens sounded and the cars arrived and the photographers' flash guns cut away the darkness and any shreds of normalcy left on Crescent Drive. By this time, however, the stocky slayer of Edward R. Barringer was two miles away in a noisy tavern trying to make a telephone call over the combined din of the Jefferson Airplane and a roomful of dedicated bourbon drinkers. It was not easy to communicate above that wholesome American uproar, for the jukebox alone was putting out sound waves fierce enough to drill teeth.

'It's done,' the man who had installed the bomb announced curtly.

He mentioned no names, places, deeds.

He was a professional and he knew all about wiretapping.

'That's what I said,' he insisted. 'There'll be no more trouble, because it's *completely* finished.'

But it wasn't.

Not at all.

Mr Edward R. Barringer was dead all right – but there was still Dr Andrew F. Williston. Dr Williston was not known in Paradise City, but he could be extremely violent and dangerous. As a matter of fact, he had once machine-gunned seven men before breakfast and then robbed an armored car of a $110,000 payroll that same afternoon.

As long as Dr Williston was alive, it wasn't *nearly* finished.

CHAPTER TWO

The letter reached New York City on the morning of May 28, but Dr Andrew F. Williston didn't collect it until four that bright afternoon when he turned in the final grades to the Registrar. It was a lovely, lazy spring day on Morningside Heights, and pink Barnard girls in yellow miniskirts fluttered by in coveys like the plump pigeons that swooped over the domed Low Library in the warm May sun. They were fine, slim, young women, clean and open-faced and laughing and sure of the eventual triumph of folk-rock and educational television over the massed forces of evil. Restless and a little unsure of themselves, small lonely clusters of Columbia College seniors bravely joked and smoked and remembered on the stone steps of dormitories – wondering about the future 'outside' as they waited out the last strange days until graduation. The final semester was over.

And Andrew Williston, a gifted Associate Professor of Psychology who'd be a full professor in another year, was very glad that school had ended. The tall, thin, crew-cut scholar was tired – wan from the Manhattan winter and vaguely bored with the comfortable but repetitive ritual of the academic life. As he strolled across the campus, he couldn't be sure whether this fatigue came from the monotony of lectures, quizzes, term papers and conferences – or was it the *wild* thing again? Was it the old hunger for excitement and danger? It didn't matter, he tried to reassure himself, for tomorrow he was leaving for the wooden farm house in Vermont – the quiet, airy place on the peak they called Terrible Mountain. He'd been born there, and because he was the last of the Willistons it was his. He knew that he would be safe there.

Dr Williston smiled as he thought of the house on Terrible Mountain, looked up just in time to avoid bumping into two Japanese graduate students and walked on to his office in Schermerhorn Hall for a final check of the mail box. The letter was waiting, a square cream-colored envelope with no return address. He scanned it as he left the building, and then sat down on the steps to light a cigarette and open the letter.

But there was no letter, only three clippings from a newspaper named the Paradise City *Trumpet*.

The first announced that *Trumpet* columnist Edward R. Barringer had perished in an explosion caused by a bomb attached to the starter of his car.

The second reported that Captain Benjamin Marton, chief of the Paradise City Police Department, had personally searched the wreckage and Barringer's stucco ranch house at 54 Crescent Drive in an attempt to find some clue to the reasons for this shocking murder. Seven hours of meticulous and scientific examination had failed to produce a single shred of evidence as to who might have wanted to slay the journalist – or why. The authorities had no idea of who planted the dynamite, but the investigation would continue.

The third clipping was an editorial eulogizing Ed Barringer as a fine dedicated newspaper man and a splendid human being.

Williston stood up in the warm sun and shivered, suddenly remembering the night they had blasted their way into the police station to rescue Barringer. He closed his eyes and saw it all again – the snow-covered streets, the moonlit square – and four grim men huddled in the back of an ambulance. It was incredibly real, with the coppery taste of fearful fury flooding his mouth in the moment of recollection. Now the fear turned to hate, not the blazing rage of the indignant academician but the cold focused enmity of the professional gunman.

Now he knew what he had to do.

The little man was dead.

The little man was dead – and somebody had to pay the bill.

Suddenly it was like the Old Days when he carried the sub-machine gun and was angry all the time.

Williston puffed on the cigarette as he looked into the envelope again, but there was no note and no clue as to the sender. Yet the message in the clippings was clear. Get the others, and come with your guns and knives and other implements. Come swiftly with bomb, bullet and blade to avenge the little man with the limp. Come to this strange place, where you must find *them* and kill *them*.

It was obviously not a one-man job. He would have to call the others. They were scattered now – living very different lives – and perhaps they wouldn't want to come. No, he had to believe that they would, to base his plan on that. The beginning of a plan was already forming as he slipped the envelope into his jacket pocket. First they would need weapons and money, he reasoned soberly, and that meant the smiling hunter.

That meant P. T. Carstairs.

CHAPTER THREE

Parker Terence Carstairs, a household word like Drano and Elizabeth Taylor, was, is, internationally famous as an extremely rich and utterly handsome sportsman who commutes between Earl Wilson and Leonard Lyons via the men's room of the bar at the George V in Paris. 'Sportsman' is a gracious phrase for males either too wealthy or too lazy – or too stupid – to work regularly. P. T. Carstairs is both bored and lazy, too blasé even to play at his role of jet-set celebrity with much passion. Nevertheless, because he has a vast fortune, wavy blond hair, excellent teeth, wonderful taste and almost no morals at all, he remains the joyful toast of the wire services and the second most eligible bachelor in the United States. He is actually the first most eligible because the supposed 'champion' has been arrested three times in his mother's dresses and will obviously never marry, but the society columnists prefer to ignore this disconcerting idiosyncrasy.

P. T. Carstairs is, beyond doubt, a bonafide celebrity. Every patriotic American – and quite a few Britons, French, Japanese, Italians and Latins – knows that Mr Carstairs inherited more than $26,000,000.45 from his late father and that P. T. collects fine old guns, beautiful young women and sleek Italian racing cars. He collects diligently and impressively, as *Life* and *Esquire* and *Paris-Match* have reported at length.

He collects superbly.

Some of his racing cars are beautiful and several of his women have been Italian, but all of his guns are really extraordinary. He keeps them in a spacious gallery in a large town house in Manhattan just off Fifth Avenue on 71st Street, and he shows them to good-looking females before dinner. This is a 'bit' with him. Some men do the flowers-and-champagne bit, and some do the long-hair-and-sandals bit – with bells – and some do the social-karate-at-the-drive-in-movie bit. With P. T. Carstairs, it was 'Come by for supper and look at my antique firearms' – and they usually came. He did a big breakfast business too, as might be expected.

Mr Carstairs, whose chilling proficiency with a variety of single-shot and automatic weapons had once earned him the nickname of 'The Widow Maker,' was a very civilized man. In the twentieth century it is possible to be a homicidal marksman and still be considered a civilized man. Mr Carstairs was a man of taste and breeding. He took a shower every day and saw his dentist twice a year, and he never invited girls under twenty-one no matter how pretty or hungry or animal they were. He never asked other people's wives or women who talked too much or those given to drink or irksome scenes, rules which eliminated 91 percent of the female population right there.

That made life simple and easy, and he liked it simple and easy. On the evening of May 28, the fair lady who had come to visit was a blond Swedish ballerina, a proud, healthy woman with large blue eyes and a dancer's body of supple steel. She'd met Carstairs at a wonderful party in Rio in February and immediately decided that it was highly desirable to see his guns. Now it was three months later and she had two perfect martinis glowing within her hard flat stomach – and the night was full of charm and promise.

It was five after eight; she had already seen twenty-six of the finest, rarest, costliest pistols in the world. One of the six known Cookson repeating flintlocks made by Glass of London in 1775, a silver inlaid Battazanti of 1700, even a 1550 German over-and-under wheellock – each a museum piece. He had a Spanish miguelet lock flint blunderbuss, a Model 1777 Charleville French army pistol and even a .54 caliber 1806 Harper's Ferry model. There were also a number of wicked-looking little derringers and belly guns popular with riverboat gamblers of nineteenth-century America. He knew the history of each weapon, told it beautifully with a wealth of anecdote and jest that would shame a Southern senator.

'And *this* is the pride of my collection,' the millionaire announced with an irresistible smile as he pointed to a battered old .44 caliber six-shooter in a glass case.

'I beg your pardon, Mr Carstairs,' the tall balding butler began from the doorway. The second most eligible bachelor in the United States nodded affably, confident that whatever it was it wasn't going to interfere with his plans for the evening.

'I'm sorry to interrupt, sir,' the usually cool manservant continued uncertainly, 'but there's just been a most extraordinary telephone message for you. The person who called claimed that it was a matter of life and death.'

Carstairs grinned pleasantly like some good-humored tiger, finished his drink in a single gulp. The Swedish dancer could see that he was amused.

'And what is the message, Rodman?' the gun collector asked.

The liveried servant sighed, shook his head as he took the piece of paper from his pocket to scan it again. 'It may be a game, sir, in which case I'm terribly sorry,' he apologized. 'If I got it correctly, it reads as follows. Quote: Uncle Charles has lost his pen. Come to the farm. Thursday at nineteen. Condition black. Close quote. I asked who was calling,' the butler assured his employer, 'and was told that I should say Marie Antoinette.'

'But it was a man,' Carstairs announced.

He wasn't guessing. He knew.

'Yes, a man. Is it a game, sir?' the puzzled butler asked.

'Well, *I* think it is,' the millionaire gun collector replied slowly and thoughtfully, 'but I don't suppose that very many people would agree with me – and most of those who would are dead.'

The ballerina blinked, wondering when he would make sense of it all. Carstairs walked to the sideboard and poured two more of those martinis. He put down the Orrefors pitcher, paused for a moment, considered, smiled again. 'Uncle Charles has lost his pen. Well, well, well,' he reflected to nobody in particular as he carried the drinks to the lovely blond woman.

'Petie, Petie – what does this mean?' she asked.

The collector smiled that wonderful *Life–Look–Paris-Match* cover smile with all those excellent teeth, and then he shrugged those splendid shoulders disarmingly.

'As the man said, the matter is simply life and death, my dear, he replied. 'That's all there is to it – nothing more.'

He took three steps toward the wall, stopped. When the millionaire said 'Thank you, Rodman,' the butler departed on cue and Carstairs considered whether he should remove the green metal trunk. She wouldn't guess what it contained, he judged, so he pressed the molding on the paneled wall. Suddenly – just like the old movies – there was an opening. He reached into the hole, took out the dusty metal trunk as the woman watched.

'Let me explain,' P. T. Carstairs proposed with an odd look that managed to combine grimness and mischief. 'I don't have an Uncle Charles, but I'm extremely concerned about his pen. I thought that I'd lost it – forever – some years ago, but good old Marie Antoinette found it. That's why I'll be going away tomorrow.'

'But you promised to come to see me dance tomorrow night,' she protested.

This was going to require just a bit of handling; but it would be no problem, for if there were three things in the world that P. T. Carstairs could handle effortlessly, two of them were women. He knew precisely what to do.

'I'm sorry, dear,' he said truthfully as he leaned over and kissed her. Then he looked into her luminous eyes, shook his head in unconcealed regret. There was no nonsense about this warm worldly woman, no nonsense and an unabashed animality that was clean and attractive. He kissed her again, much harder, pressing her tight and caressing her tenderly as her body started to move against his. Her eyes were wide open, remained that way throughout the next eighty minutes as they made love. They didn't get to eat until nearly 10 p.m., and when they finished their brandies shortly after midnight they made love again. The radiant smile on her face as she fell asleep beside him was still glowing the next morning at eleven when she awoke, saw him seated on the edge of the bed – watching her approvingly.

Kisses, touches, morning greetings.

'You're really going?' she asked.

'Matter of being responsible. No choice,' he assured in matter-of-fact tones.

'You're a strange man,' she judged without complaint.

'Perhaps, but I used to be much worse. As a matter of fact,' he confessed wryly as he studied her lush beauty, 'I was, in my youth, a highly successful bank robber, thief and criminal.'

She laughed. American humor was so delightfully grotesque.

'I'm not joking,' her handsome love insisted. He stroked her shoulder, and her eyes opened wider as she took a deep breath. 'I'm not kidding a bit; I worked with one of the smartest mobs in the business for more than three years.'

Through the open bedroom door he could see the green metal trunk and he thought about Sammy. Marie Antoinette was certainly no fool, Carstairs admitted to himself without hesitation, but if this was really as important and difficult as the millionaire intuitively guessed, then they'd need Sammy Gilman. It wouldn't hurt to have the wild Italian along either.

CHAPTER FOUR

Samuel Mordecai Gilman, a short sturdy man with gray eyes and a talent for numbers, looked out the window at the array of glowing neon tubing and automatically began to compute the light bill of the big hotel half a mile away. He couldn't help it, being mathematically inclined and endowed with a memory that retained all sorts of odd facts, including the rate schedule of the Las Vegas Electric Company. Remembering all this data served no particular purpose other than to keep his mind off the nonstop clutter that was life in Las Vegas. Even for a metropolitan pleasure dome dedicated to diversion, this city offered too many stimuli in endless irrational sequence. As a matter of fact, he reflected, there was no sequence at all.

Gilman thought about the scores of whirring wheels and the heaps of colored chips and the all-night dentists, the $39.95 'instant wedding chapels with an orchid for the bride,' the squadrons of little red MGs and the platoons of big blond chorus girls and the peculiar twenty-four-hour days in which people ate breakfast at 3 p.m. and nobody noticed. Everything was going smoothly all the time, 365 days a year, so you could never tell when to brush your teeth or pick up a girl or get divorced. However, the weather was good and the pay was excellent and the cheese cake was almost as satisfying as that in New York. No air pollution, no violence in the streets, no parking problems and a lot of fine-looking women who had – in the words of Frank Loesser – perfect teeth and no last names.

Mr Gilman hit the adding machine again, smiled when he saw the total. He had been, of course, right. He could have found the gadget if he'd bothered to search, for he was very close to being an electronics expert, but it pleased him that he could prove the 'rigging' mathematically. He enjoyed being right.

He was always right – well, almost always. He'd been right about the armored car and he'd been right about the train job and he'd calculated the payroll messenger's schedule right down to the second. He'd been wrong just once, the night everything had gone to pieces and Barringer was arrested. That hardly counted – being the work of an informer, who no longer counted. 'The Widow Maker' had attended to that with a .38 Smith & Wesson special. Carstairs had always preferred revolvers to automatics, Gilman recalled absent-mindedly.

At that moment, Harold Dorelli entered the fourth-floor office and broke into Gilman's reverie. Dorelli, whose dark impassive face resembled that of a forty-five-year-old George Raft, stood about six inches taller than the film star. Dorelli was neither an actor nor a gangster, the latter being quite important in the righteous state of Nevada where men with criminal records are not licensed to manage gambling casinos. Dorelli's employers included several individuals with impressive underworld credentials and a lot of cash – the Cleveland Boys. Casino manager Dorelli worked for the Cleveland Boys, and Gilman worked for Dorelli.

'What did you find? Does it check out?' Dorelli demanded.

'Almost to the penny,' Gilman replied. 'As I told you last week, somebody's using an electronic gizmo to fix the Number Three wheel. It's been paying out seventy-five hundred to ninety-five hundred more per night for ten days now, and that's no accident.'

Dorelli nodded.

'You don't believe in accidents, do you, Sammy?'

'No, especially when it comes to gambling. I believe in mathematics, in averages, in scientific predictability – and so do you. If you didn't,' he reminded his employer, 'you'd be in another business.'

Samuel Mordecai Gilman was, of course, right.

Without being unpleasant about it – but still inevitably right.

'Could one man do it from the outside, or would he need help from one of our people?' the manager of the Desert Delight wondered slowly.

'Harold, our machines are equipped with the latest and most sophisticated defensive devices, and you know it.'

The stocky Californian was, as usual, right. There had to be, an 'inside man,' an accomplice on the casino staff. That meant that the two individuals and their electronic 'gizmo' had to be eliminated, but Dorelli wasn't going to talk about those details with Gilman. They had an understanding on this subject; acts of violence or law-breaking were never to be discussed. Something quite violent and illegal was going to happen to the ambitious adventurers who had dared to steal some $89,600 that belonged to the Cleveland Boys, but Gilman preferred to ignore that.

'You owe me one hundred dollars, Harold,' he reminded his employer.

Raised on the Las Vegas code in which welshing on a bet is worse than matricide or bed-wetting, the manager of the Desert Delight paid the wager instantly. He should have remembered that, he thought with a frown as he removed the two $50 bills from his pocket. It was when he put the silver money clip back that he felt the folded telegram.

'Wire for you,' Dorelli announced as he dropped the yellow Western Union envelope on the desk beside the adding machine.

Gilman tore open the envelope, read – and then reread – the message from Marie Antoinette. The surprise in his face was unconcealed; he wasn't prepeared for *this*. All *this* had ended a long time ago. He glanced at his stainless-steel Omega, saw that he had only twenty-one hours to get *there*. There was no question of not going, not if Uncle Charles' pen was involved.

'Bad news, Sammy?'

'I don't know – but I'll have to go East right away.'

'How long will you be gone?'

The Californian shrugged noncommitally.

'I suppose that Artie can look after things for a week or so,' Dorelli reckoned aloud. 'Say, is this trouble? The wire?'

Gilman paused to light a short Canary Island cigar, puffing twice on the luxurious Don Diego before he replied.

'I would think so,' he answered. 'The odds are – and I go with the odds – that this particular person wouldn't have sent that particular telegram unless there was very big trouble.'

'You need some money?' volunteered the casino manager, a true Las Vegas thoroughbred who could barely conceive of any problem that cash or a woman wouldn't cure.

The man who was always right nodded his thanks, shook his head.

'Not money – a gun. Don't look so startled, Harold,' Gilman advised with a wry, sad, amused smile. 'Just because I'm so cerebral and statistical now doesn't mean I didn't used to be a first-class outlaw in my tarnished youth – a real two-gun pistolero. We were quite an organization, rough as any mob you ever saw in a B movie and ready for anything. We even knocked over a police station.'

The manager of the Desert Delight gaped.

'In our day, we were the best in the business,' the gray-eyed Californian recalled. 'Quick, tricky, bold – and a little crazy. We even had an acrobat on the team, a big swinger from Boston named Tony Arbolino.'

If Arbolino was alive and out of jail, Gilman mused as he puffed on the cigar, he'd be getting a wire too. There was no need to calculate the odds on that, however. It was a sure thing.

CHAPTER FIVE

Tony Arbolino looked down the stairway swarming with armed police, and he laughed. He raised the sub-machine gun to squeeze off two more bursts, listened to the shattered thunder and laughed again in the best Jimmy Cagney tradition. He was well aware that there was nothing funny about this situation, but this was the peculiar way in which he made his living. The police were shooting back. No, he thought as he dodged behind the massive girder, this wasn't nearly as much fun as the Old Days with Williston and P.T. and the others. The stakes had been much higher, the opposition much more deadly. That had been the Big League, the Biggest.

The police had five or six lights glaring up at him from the warehouse floor, trying to pick him out on the narrow metal catwalk as they fired insistently from a dozen points below. There wasn't much time left; they were closing in swiftly. Now the explosions of the machine guns and revolvers were nearly deafening, and big catlike Tony Arbolino tried to remember exactly how he was to get out. He let off three more short bursts as he went over it quickly in his mind. They'd planned his exit quite carefully and in detail; it was a good scheme even if not too original. Arbolino noticed that the men in blue were putting on quite a show, especially the handsome blond 'hero' who was leading the pack up the steps. That pretty boy was probably the lead in a class play at grade school when I was killing police with Andy Williston, Arbolino reflected as he squinted in the blinding beam, and now he's a 'star.'

A tear-gas shell bloomed suddenly on the catwalk.

It was about time, and Arbolino emptied his magazine with a defiant curse as he retreated. Gasping and choking in the swirling fumes, he staggered to the fire-escape exit and flung open the door to let in the fresh clean night.

There it was – safety.

At that moment, the handsome yellow-haired policeman reached the top of the stairs and fired. Crucified by intersecting spotlights, Tony Arbolino shuddered, stared for a long moment as he struggled to keep going and finally toppled off the roof. The shooting stopped.

'Cut!' shouted the director, and the set buzzed again with half a hundred conversations. Make-up men rushed to the sweating blond star and script girls turned pages and two starlets who never wore brassieres puffed out their chests like pouter pigeons when they saw a *Life* photographer approaching in a covey of white-on-white press agents. Nobody but one assistant director, who was practically nobody, paid any attention to Arbolino as he landed in the safety net and bounced.

The A.D. waved in approval, flashing a 'thumbs up' sign. The smiling stunt man swung himself up and over, landing easily on his feet with the resilience of a professional athlete. He was just that, a lithe hard professional with medals as a distance runner, gymnast and judo champion. He had played at much more dangerous games in the past, but these grim sports he never mentioned here in Hollywood. In this city, he was known simply as the best stunt man in the business.

Taking out the telegram again, he coughed out the last of the imitation tear gas and mopped his brow with the towel that some thoughtful production assistant had left draped over the net. The wire from Marie Antoinette had arrived just as he'd left his home three hours earlier, and now he had a feeling that he wouldn't sleep in his own bed again for a long time. It was fortunate that his role in the film was completed, for he had to go home to pack. He was glad that there was money in the bank, that Maria was the sort of wife who would understand that he had to go even if he couldn't spell out the precise reasons. He couldn't have told her if he wanted to, he thought ruefully.

No, he had no real idea as to what the telegram was all about – but tomorrow night he would be at the farm to meet them. They would all be there. Just as sure as little apples and summer rain and the way Maria smiled contentedly in the morning, they would all be there.

And the killing would probably start all over again. He couldn't predict how the others might feel, but he certainly didn't look forward to it. He'd lost his taste for that other life so long ago, and now he had a wife and two children who depended on him. Well, at least he was in excellent physical condition. Maybe the killing wouldn't be necessary, he reasoned as he strolled toward the dressing room.

Maybe it would be different this time.

CHAPTER SIX

'Look again,' the big-headed man whom they called 'Little Johnny' ordered in soft merciless tones.

He was a large dark man with the shoulders of a stevedore, which he had been at seventeen, and if it seemed incongruous to speak of him as 'Little Johnny' it was no more senseless than the widespread U.S. custom of calling king-sized males 'Tiny' or addressing the most vicious corrupted bitches as 'Baby.'

'Look again,' he insisted.

It was midnight and the roulette wheels and cash registers were clicking joyfully in the Fun Parlor, but all was not well in Paradise City. Mr John Pikelis, who owned both the Fun Parlor and effective control of Paradise City, was ill at ease. He wore a $300 suit and a permanent smile that had all the charm of a durable-press shirt, but his cutting black eyes showed focussed irritation.

'I tell you I went over his whole place ten times, Johnny – from top to bottom and inside out. We tore it to pieces,' beefy Ben Marton repeated nervously. The fifty-year-old police captain stood flat-footed and awkward on the thick cream-colored carpet, listening to the dim hum of the powerful air-conditioner and sweating like a day laborer in the noonday sun. Police Chief Marton was afraid of Johnny Pikelis, an attitude that was no mere male menopausal tantrum but was soundly based in reality. In Paradise City, only an idiot or an ignoramus would view Pikelis without fear.

'Look and look and look – until you find it,' the underworld chieftain commanded. The press – not the local papers, of course – had often called Pikelis a racketeer, but that was as understated as describing Adolf Hitler as 'aggressive' or that astonishingly buxom German 'actress' at 20th Century-Fox as 'friendly.' He was unquestionably and notoriously Number One, head of the criminal organization that dominated all of Jefferson County. He'd hacked and hammered, bulled and battered his way up from the docks – breaking everyone and everything in his path – and now he was used to having his way. Even though he now lived in this plush penthouse and had all the poise that goes with $4,500 worth of the best dentistry, he still thought like a man with a baling hook.

'Look ten times more, Ben, and don't stop until you find whatever that sly little bastard hid,' he told Marton in tones that were almost imperial. The city spread out below was his empire in many ways, his life-and-death power being only one facet of his total dominion. 'We shut up Barringer, but we've got to find that evidence.'

'But, Johnny—'

'He wasn't any childish hot-air artist, Ben,' the ganglord announced. 'If he said that he had evidence against us, he damn well had it.'

The balding flawed policeman sighed.

'Maybe it was burned up in the car?' he suggested.

Pikelis studied him for several seconds, wondering how it was possible for a grown male to be so corrupt and ruthless for so long and still remain so innocent and weak. Suddenly he appreciated how two of his private 'heroes,' Mussolini and Batista, had been let down by similar incompetents. Hitler and Napoleon had been much better served by their staffs, but it was probably unrealistic to expect that sort of efficiency in a medium-sized Southern city on the border of Florida and Georgia.

'I'll spell it out in small simple words, Ben, and you listen just as hard as you can,' Pikelis grated. 'I took over this city twenty years ago, built an organization. My organization runs this city, and we're all rich. To stay rich and to stay out of jail, we're breaking laws and cracking skulls and once in a while we still have to kill people. Despite all the state and federal cops, the investigations, the big magazine exposés and the nasty TV specials, we're still in business. But if we don't get our hands on Barringer's evidence, everything and everybody is in trouble. Maybe finished. That doesn't mean just your nickel-plated badge, Ben. It could mean the electic chair.'

The police chief grunted, calculated swiftly. Even as he stood there damp and tense, he realized that whoever held that missing evidence might also hold control of Paradise City.

'I'll give it another look, inch by inch. I'll rip the walls out,' he promised with guarded sincerity.

Pikelis stood up, walked from the armchair to the expanse of glass 'picture window' that offered such a fine view of his city. 'When you find it, don't forget to bring it up here to me,' he advised. 'The last fellow with the big wrong ideas about it ended up in smelly pieces on the sidewalk at Crescent Drive.'

'I'll keep that in mind.'

'Write it on your desk calendar, Captain.'

Marton blinked assent, started for the door. His hand was on the knob when the underworld ruler spoke again.

'Give it that genuine Robert E. Lee try, Ben. Until we find it, not one of us can rest easy. Nobody's safe. You got that clear? Nobody!'

When the police chief left, Pikelis lit a long Jamaican cigar and considered whether Ben Marton might not require an 'accident' himself before many weeks. A man in power – the top man – could never afford to trust anyone completely, he ruminated. It was part of the price of power. The head of U.S. Steel and the man in the White House probably had the same problems, he realized sadly as he blew a perfect blue-gray smoke ring that hung in the air like some work of transient pop art. Several seconds passed before the cool current billowing from the air-conditioner destroyed it.

Undaunted, he blew another.

CHAPTER SEVEN

It was seventeen o'clock when P. T. Carstairs stepped off the Eastern shuttle plane at National Airport across the Potomac from Washington, and some forty minutes later Mr Philip Collins paid a bellboy half a dollar to leave Room 515 at the Hay-Adams. There are a number of hotels where employees will leave a room for a smaller sum, but the Hay-Adams is a superior establishment where standards of service still prevail. By the time the man who called himself Philip Thomas Collins had unpacked, it was nearly 1800. That was the way he'd been trained to think. Six p.m. was 1800 and use a simple alias whose initials match those on your luggage. There were no markings at all on the small green trunk that sat beside the now empty leather suitcase. It had been illegal to move the contents of the metal foot locker across state lines, but that had not troubled P. T. Carstairs, who had broken so many laws so many times that he had long since stopped counting.

The room was cool, a pleasant contrast to the clotted miasmic heat of the steaming city outside the building. June in the District of Columbia is never a comfortable experience. It is nothing like April in Paris or Autumn in New York or Springtime in the Rockies – or any other hit tune. It will never make the charts. It is much too hot and clammy to be romantic, and the beat is simply terrible. It is actually a depressing soggy plop unsuitable even for a waltz, and only those with a good deal of verve or a permanent Civil Service position are likely to endure it.

Full of verve, Carstairs washed his hands and face before he ordered a bottle of cold Carlsberg beer and sat down to think. Despite his playboy demeanor, he was an excellent thinker – which was one reason that he was still alive with all his limbs and organs intact. Another reason was the fact that he was an incredible shot with the police and military hand guns of eleven nations. In the 1970s, this is a survival skill as important as the ability to lie to the press, tell obscene jokes or drive in heavy traffic.

When the beer arrived, Carstairs bribed another employee of the Hay-Adams to go away and then sat in single splendor sipping the excellent Danish brew. This wasn't as potent as the '18-B' that the Carlsberg people sold in Europe, but it was very good and it helped the time pass. At fourteen minutes after 1800, he checked his weapons – the metal touchstones that proved *it* was starting again. Both guns – the heavy Magnum .357 in the quick-draw belly holster and the little .32 with the stubby silencer that rested in the canvas sling under his left arm – were loaded. Each had a round in its chamber, so he could now leave for the farm. The millionaire walked out of the hotel at 1821, precisely on schedule.

The rented car was waiting. As he drove through the humid metropolis toward the bridge that would take him to Virginia, he speculated as to what the trouble might be. He was sure that it was trouble, for otherwise Marie Antoinette would not have called about the pen. He flicked the car radio on as he guided the Rambler across Constitution Avenue with its long low row of 'temporary' buildings housing parts of the Navy Department, and he hoped that the trouble would be interesting. Grand Prix races and Swedish ballerinas were fine as a regular diet, but after all these years a little *real* excitement – some *challenge* – seemed terribly appealing.

It was going to be dangerous, he told himself smugly.

It *had* to be.

At 1900 minus ten, he turned the Rambler off the main highway and he smiled in recognition. He still remembered the route, the area – every bit of it. Four minutes later, he grinned again when he saw the familiar stone posts that still bracketed the driveway to the farm. It hadn't been a working farm even then but a fashionable girls' finishing school with stables and a big barn behind the main residence hall. He halted the vehicle just off the back road, decided that the rendezvous point would probably be the barn. They had planned so many raids from barns, but this was the one that had been their first headquarters. Carstairs stepped out of the Rambler and started walking – warily.

It was still twilight, but the thick stand of trees blocked out most of the rays of the disappearing sun. Carstairs advanced some two hundred yards through the gray-blackness with his linen jacket unbuttoned and one hand resting lightly on the butt of the .32; he heard the whistle. Recognition and reaction were instantaneous.

'Sur le Pont d'Avignon.' He nearly shivered.

The old French folk song did that to the jaded jet-setter; he couldn't help it. He crouched instinctively in a reflex reaction as automatic as those of Pavlov's conditioned dogs, and he softly whistled back the next two bars of the simple melody.

He was at war again.

Squinting into the growing darkness, he watched a tall figure emerge from the thicket of trees and shadows – a figure that was almost a shadow itself. The stranger beckoned, and Carstairs followed without question. They kept to the dark places until they were a few yards from the barn, still large and redolent of hay and needing a coat of paint. It was only then that the second most eligible bachelor in the United States saw the face of his guide clearly. It was Andrew F. Williston, who sometimes called himself Marie Antoinette.

Still silent, they entered the barn and Williston closed the door before switching on a rectangular electric 'lantern' which he placed on the cement floor. They looked at each other with open curiosity for several seconds, gauging and judging and wondering, before each sighed and they shook hands. Suddenly the tall thin teacher flipped open Carstairs' jacket and saw the two guns.

'Still heavy,' Williston muttered.

'And they're loaded, Sonny.'

The psychology professor shook his head.

'They ought to lock you up,' he announced. 'Have you a license for this hardware?'

The wealthy gun collector arched his eyebrows.

'Andy, you know I have. I've got licenses that you never even dreamt of – to carry trench mortars, fly jets, conduct puberty rites and teach modern dance in the State of California. Dog licenses, fishing licenses, an international driving license and even one from Liberia that authorizes me to carry a blowgun on religious holidays.'

Seeing that Williston was unimpressed, the millionaire extracted his own wallet to show the New York City Police Department gun permit for the Magnum. The teacher's eyes moved to the smaller .32, which Carstairs cooperatively half drew from its shoulder holster.

'That's an assassin's gun,' Williston observed grimly. The meaning of the silencer left no doubts. 'They don't give any goddamned license to carry any goddamned assassin's gun, not even to well-connected rich boys who went to Yale with the mayor.'

Carstairs shrugged, flashed those fine teeth boyishly.

'You're right. It is an unlicensed weapon, and it is an assassin's tool,' he confessed with no visible remorse. 'I brought it along in case there was somebody we had to assassinate.'

The humor of the 'sportsman' had not changed.

Violence, crime and killing were still all jokes.

'Did you bring any *machine guns*?' Williston demanded sarcastically.

'A couple, but I left them in the hotel. Don't look so hysterical, Andy,' his former comrade urged. 'I only brought the machine guns because I thought we might need them. I didn't know what you had in mind.'

You could write an entire textbook about this man, the psychology teacher reckoned.

'If I follow your logic,' Williston reasoned aloud, 'you brought the machine guns in case there were some people we had to machine-gun, right? Just like the assassin's pistol, right?'

Carstairs nodded. It all made perfect sense to *him*, so why was the lean, boyish Vermonter so bitter? Weapons had never affected Andy Williston like this in the Good Old Days. The second most eligible bachelor in America was about to point this out when the two men heard the sound.

Somebody was approaching the barn.

'Nineteen hundred – on the dot,' the professor announced after a quick glance at his watch. Carstairs didn't answer, but drew his Magnum – the .357 blooming in his fist as in some conjurer's trick.

It had to be Sammy Gilman. He'd always been on time, on schedule – to the second. You could always count on him for mathematical precision and pure logic.

'Cover the door – but no shooting,' Williston ordered crisply as he extinguished the light. 'If it isn't Sammy, or Tony, just slug him. That's all.'

In the blackness, the millionaire smiled at the way Williston had taken charge again just as if the years had never passed – just as he had in the Good Old Days when the five of them were hunted day and night. The simple fact was that in any crisis the Vermonter was an instinctive leader, naturally quick, sure and cunning. It was a gift, like Carstairs' talent for handling guns and women.

With a slight squeak, the door opened to admit a shaft of fading sunlight and Samuel Mordecai Gilman. Williston closed the portal, relit the lantern – and the three men shook hands solemnly. It was almost as if each of them was surprised that the others were still alive. Statistically – on the basis of actuarial tables – they should all have died a long time ago, and they knew it. But they didn't know what the others had been doing in the past few years, so the next five minutes were consumed in these exchanges. The psychology professor watched and waited, curious as to who would ask the other question first.

It was not cool cool P. T. Carstairs.

'Well . . . the telegram . . . what is it?' Gilman finally wondered aloud.

'I don't want to go through it twice,' Williston explained, 'so let's wait until Tony arrives.'

'Don't wait any longer,' boomed a strong voice from the darkness of the hayloft behind them.

The three men spun to see the muscular stunt man drop to the floor with the easy resilient spring of an acrobat. 'I've been up there for an hour,' Arbolino confessed. 'Came in over the roof from the back to look things over – just in case. Just in case the wire didn't come from Andy after all.'

The smiles, handshakes, appraising glances, warm greetings were repeated. 'Now that the *paisan* is here the only one to wait for is the little guy,' Gilman pointed out – but Williston shook his head.

'Eddie isn't coming. He's dead,' the teacher explained in a harsh, hurt voice. 'Somebody put a bomb in his car last week.'

The gun collector's eyes gleamed.

Yes, *it* was starting all over again.

'Who did it?' Carstairs asked softly.

'I don't know – yet.'

'Where?' Gilman pressed.

'Paradise City, on the Georgia–Florida line.'

'Why?'

'They didn't say.'

'Maybe we ought to ask them?' Arbolino proposed in a voice edged with stainless steel.

The teacher nodded.

'That's exactly what I had in mind,' he replied. 'That's why I called you here.' He lit another cigarette, wondering what he'd do if they wouldn't help.

'Not one of us would be alive today if it hadn't been for Eddie Barringer,' Williston began grimly. 'We were hot stuff back in 1943, OSS "Jeds" who chuted into Occupied France to organize Maquis groups for guerrilla warfare. We blew bridges, knocked off armored cars, wrecked troop trains – we even grabbed a Wehrmacht payroll. We were big wheels in France ten months before Normandy, until something went wrong and the Nazis caught Eddie. He took it all for forty-seven hours, the whips and the pincers and the soldering irons and the electric shocks and the water treatment. Forty-seven hours, and he didn't break. He didn't tell them where to find us.'

Williston didn't have to finish the ugly story. They all remembered how they had slipped through the German checkpoint in the ambulance, shot their way into the police station, cut down eight – or was it nine? – Gestapo men, and rescued what was left of Eddie Barringer. Five weeks later, Carstairs had slain the informer who'd betrayed Barringer, and nine weeks after that the massive Allied Expeditionary Force fought its way ashore in Normandy. It was September before Barringer reached Walter Reed, but the Army hospital's best doctors couldn't give him back his left eye and his teeth and his toes. Then the war ended and they were no longer 'Jedburghs,' the code term for the OSS teams dropped into Hitler's Europe. Before long, the Office of Strategic Services itself had been carved up by Army Intelligence and the State Department – and the 'Jeds' scattered as they returned to civilian life. But these 'Jeds' – this team – was alive only because one man had endured forty-seven hours of endless agony.

There were no words to describe their debt to Barringer, but the four men in the barn had no need for words.

The debt must be paid.

The teacher studied the others' faces, waiting.

'Paradise City – that's a mob town,' the man from Las Vegas thought aloud.

'Sure . . . sure, the Senate Rackets Committee gave it a big splash a couple of years ago,' the stunt man recalled. 'It was in all the papers.'

Williston nodded.

'Eddie worked on the morning paper in Paradise City,' he announced,' and maybe the mob boys didn't appreciate what he was writing.'

Carstairs was smiling now. He knew what was coming.

But what about the others?

'We're not senators and we're not the FBI and we don't control any newspapers or television networks,' the tense teacher continued. 'And it wouldn't do much good if we did because Paradise City has been exposed more times than Ursula Andress' cleavage – and with less result.'

The awful debt to the little man had been eating at him for a long time, and now it was a sharp-toothed animal whose mother was guilt and whose father was vengeance. He paced up and down as he spoke, not quite certain how to tell them.

'What are you selling, Andy?' Gilman asked.

'We can only do what we know how to do,' Williston replied as the yellow-haired millionaire flashed him a mocking 'V' for victory signal with the fingers of his left hand.

'You'd better say it straight out, Professor,' Carstairs advised.

'All right. We were trained to infiltrate enemy-occupied territory, organize resistance movements and wage a dirty secret war of sabotage, guerrilla attacks and subversive propaganda.'

Samuel Mordecai Gilman blinked, frowned.

'If you're thinking what I'm thinking you're thinking, I think you're *foux* – crazy,' the mathematician interrupted in a voice that was only half jesting.

'We know how to crack safes, tap phones, dope drinks, forge papers and steal secrets,' Williston pressed on grimly. 'We've got to do what we know how to do.'

'Then you're saying—'

'I'm saying, Tony, that we should consider Paradise City to be enemy-occupied territory – that we should assume false identities and infiltrate it, that we should collect or steal evidence and organize a Resistance movement to bust the whole city and the gang that runs it wide open.'

'The full OSS treatment?' the stunt man wondered.

'The whole bit. We'll be a self-contained unit, just as we were in Nazi-held France.'

It was hardly necessary to calculate the odds, the man from Las Vegas thought. The odds were all wrong.

'Crazy . . . it's crazy. You really think that you can get away with this in the States?' Gilman demanded bluntly. 'Four angry men, practically stark naked, without equipment, money, guns or anything resembling a Maquis or an Underground? Without any organization or government behind them? It was one thing to have the whole damned OSS to arrange air-drops, weapons, funds, reinforcements. This will be a very different deal. I don't think that even Errol Flynn or Lee Marvin would buy it.'

Williston dropped his glowing cigarette on the cement floor, ground the embers out under his heel. Gilman was right, but the teacher couldn't help that.

'It just doesn't add up, Andy,' the mathematician insisted.

'We've got to pay our bills. I don't know any other way. Are you with me, Sammy?'

'We'd never get away with it, Andy. We'd end up dog meat.'

'Are you with me?' Williston repeated.

Gilman shrugged.

'I'm with you . . . you maniac.'

Arbolino thought of his wife, his two dark-eyed daughters and his home. Then he remembered what Barringer had looked like when they carried his unconscious body out of the Gestapo headquarters.

'I'm with Sam,' the stunt man announced slowly.

The three turned to Carstairs, who smiled again but said nothing.

'Speak up, Petie,' Arbolino urged impatiently.

'What for? Ask the professor. He knows where I stand.'

'He's in,' Williston confirmed coldly. 'He can't help it. He enjoys this sort of thing.'

They were committed. They didn't shake hands or take any oaths, but they were unequivocally and totally committed.

'I don't suppose that I have to point out that we've got to avoid all unnecessary violence,' Williston said a moment later with his eyes fixed on the gun collector. 'As Sammy mentioned, we're in the States and this is what passes for peacetime. Is that clear?'

'Absolutely, Professor,' Carstairs answered in a voice so earnestly sincere that he had to be mocking.

It was time to go, to disperse, to reassemble elsewhere, to start the planning and training and collection of equipment. It all had to be done so carefully, so wisely, so professionally. There would be no second chances, no OSS or Maquis to rescue them.

'We begin "security" right now,' the tall teacher announced. 'Let's not leave any traces here. Police up the cigarette butts, matches, everything.'

They picked up anything that might reveal their unauthorized meeting in this barn, the place where their OSS careers had begun when the farm was a clandestine training area so many years ago. It was a girls' school again, but somehow the intervening years had vanished.

They were at war once more.

It had started.

As they started toward the door, Arbolino paused abruptly and turned to face the man from Las Vegas.

'What are we going to call this thing, Sam?' he asked.

'This thing?'

'The whole deal. The operation has to have a proper code name if we're really doing it OSS style.'

Gilman pondered, nodded toward the teacher. He was in command again. Let him name it.

'Let's keep it simple,' Williston proposed. 'We're out to demolish a large and well-built totalitarian organization, to smash it to bits. Let's call the operation Sledgehammer.'

Then, one by one at thirty-second intervals, they walked out into the warm moonlit night, and Professor Andrew T. Williston closed the door behind them.

CHAPTER EIGHT

Without bugles, drums, flags, editorials, patriotic songs or even a statement by Allen Ginsberg, their secret war began. Each of the four drove back to his hotel alone, carefully observing the speed limits to avoid any contact with the police. Each of them spent the night in the room he had rented, for it would attract attention to do otherwise. And when Arbolino wanted to telephone to his wife that he'd be away for a while, he walked to a drugstore two blocks from his hotel to call from a public booth. He had not desire for the long-distance call to appear on his hotel bill, even though he too was registered under an alias. Hotels kept records, and the four conspirators were men who must leave no meaningful traces. In the language favored by Soviet espionage professionals, they were already living like 'illegals.'

On the next morning, each of the four men paid his bill – in cash – and left Washington. It was all planned; each had memorized the time and place of the rendezvous. They would meet at the millionaire's isolated hunting lodge deep in the woods of New York State's Adirondack Mountains. With 290 acres of land and no other house for nearly three miles, privacy for Phase One of Sledgehammer was assured. Each of the quartet came separately – the stunt man by bus, Williston in his 1966 convertible, Gilman on the New York Central and Carstairs on a Mohawk Airlines flight that put him down at Albany. It was the gun collector who arrived in the area first, rented a Chevrolet panel truck and waited. There was no strain in this, since the teacher had worked out the schedule quite carefully with Gilman.

At 4:10 p.m., America's second most eligible bachelor watched the man from Las Vegas emerge from the Albany railroad station and start walking west. A few moments later after observing that no one seemed to be noticing or following Gilman, Carstairs drew up in the truck and called out a casual greeting.

'Give you a lift, Mort?' the man behind the wheel offered.

'Thanks. Guess my wife forgot again,' the man who was always right answered with proper husbandly irritation.

Gilman was not married, not now. He had been – for nearly six years – to a rather intelligent and gifted painter named Judith, a warm, giving woman who could find compassion and acceptance for almost anyone except a man who was always right. They hadn't taught her that at Bennington, so she'd left with the three-year-old boy and eventually remarried – an easygoing rancher who made lots of mistakes and told her that he needed her. Gilman missed her and his son, and sometimes when he was very tired he realized how wrong he'd been to be right all the time.

But he wasn't thinking of this as the Chevrolet rolled away from the city toward The Inferno that warm afternoon. They had named the hunting retreat The Inferno because it would be through their hard word and suffering there that they meant to reach Paradise. An hour after the truck reached the lodge, Williston picked up Arbolino three blocks from the Albany bus station and pointed his convertible down the route that the gun collector had helped him memorize. It was 7:05 when the tall, thin teacher turned off onto Carstairs' private road, the journey easy and soothing as the car radio spun out the sounds of old Lena Horne albums and the stunt man chatted about his wife, daughters and life in Hollywood. About two hundred yards in from the highway, Williston saw the barbed-wire fence and the heavy steel-mesh gate and he stopped the car.

Without a word, he handed Arbolino the key that Carstairs had provided. The stunt man opened the padlock, swung back the gate and followed the car through onto the estate. Then he closed the gate, reached through to click the lock shut according to plan. Everything was going according to plan, and ten minutes later the four men sat facing each other in the big timbered living room of the lodge. The two vehicles were parked out of sight in the shed behind the large old house, and the green metal trunk rested on the flagstone in front of the fireplace. Each of the committed quartet had a drink in his hand and a hundred questions in his mind.

Carstairs spoke first.

'Welcome to my humble hut,' he announced archly in his capacity of host, ignoring the recent *New York Times* article that had described the magnificent seven-bedroom house as a '$280,000 masterpiece that is both tastefully simple and luxurious.' He sipped the iced liquor, continued. 'This is a place that my father built in 1927 to get away from it all – a charming euphemism for the fact that my mother was sweet but alcoholic,' he explained.

He looked at Williston, wondering how the psychology professor might react to this confession.

'I never knew you had a mother, Pete,' the teacher parried.

Williston didn't want to, didn't have to hear about Carstairs' troubled family or childhood traumas. They were all only too clear in his behavior, career, hobbies and life style.

'We've got two hundred and ninety acres up here, eighty of them woods, plus an excellent shooting range that I installed four years ago. For the automatic weapons and high-powered rifles,' the millionaire added nonchalantly.

'Automatic weapons?' the muscular stunt man questioned.

'He's gun nutty. You know that,' Williston said in quietly bitter tones.

P. T. Carstairs tugged at the chain linked to his belt, found the right key in the cluster and bent over to open the green metal foot locker.

'Automatic weapons,' the gun collector announced succinctly.

Three 1944 German nine-millimeter machine pistols of the MP40 model.

Two modern L2A3 British submachine guns, chambered to take the NATO standard round.

Two of the .45-caliber M3 submachine guns with silencers, the General Motors product that OSS used during World War II.

Three of the new short-barreled Israeli submachine guns, Uzi nine-millimeter parabellums with wooden stocks.

One of the Soviet Army's standard nine-millimeter Stechkin machine pistols.

One Swedish 'Carl Gustaf' submachine gun, the Model 45 with the folding steel stock.

'This is all extremely illegal,' Gilman announced with elaborate gravity, 'and the FBI will not like it.'

'Let's not tell them,' proposed Carstairs.

Arbolino and Williston stared at the extraordinary display of weapons, exchanged glances that were identical in significance. *This* was not normal. Their host was not normal. Of course, Sledgehammer wasn't a job for the normal, but this private arsenal seemed to hint at some mental or emotional flaw that could prove dangerous to the entire operation.

'I suppose you've got more?' the teacher speculated.

'Smaller stuff. Revolvers, carbines, a couple of sniper rifles with real good scopes. Got a Bushnell "Phantom" marksman's scope that works beautifully with my Smith and Wesson K-38 target pistol – and a few odds and ends.'

How crazy was he? That was the question.

'No bazookas?' wondered Williston.

'Nobody I know drives tanks, Andy. I'll put one on the shopping list.'

Maybe he wasn't crazy. In an era in which teen-agers suck on LSD-impregnated sugar cubes to 'blow' their minds – perhaps permanently – and California school principals smoke marijuana and police use electric cattle rods to disperse civil-rights demonstrators, was there anything crazy about collecting automatic weapons? With Vassar girls wearing chains around their waists and Congress cutting antipoverty funds and Che Guevara acclaimed as the Jimmy Dean of the guerrilla warfare enthusiasts, Carstairs' hobby might not be so strange after all.

'Okay. Okay, we've got plenty of guns and we might need them,' the tall, thin teacher acknowledged. 'But we also need training – a lot of training. Mentally and physically, we're in no shape to take Paradise City.'

The husky stunt man nodded.

'We'll build an obstacle course, like the one they had at the Farm,' he proposed.

'We've got a firing range and plenty of ammo, so you can polish your shooting,' chimed in the second most eligible bachelor in the United States.

'We're going to need a lot of wire-tapping, bugging and radio equipment, Sammy,' Williston warned. 'Can you get it and can you still handle it?'

The man from Las Vegas nodded, explained that it would be relatively simple to buy the miniaturized electronic gear in Manhattan – if sufficient money was available.

Arbolino laughed.

'Petie's loaded,' he reminded Gilman. 'He's got trunksful – according to *Time* magazine.'

The mathematician sighed.

'I never read those left-wing journals,' he confessed. 'What about you, Andy? What will you do in this operation?'

'R and A, which suits my scholarly nature. Somebody has to prepare the research and analysis studies so we'll know what we're getting into. We'd be imbeciles to move in without a detailed report on enemy strength, dispositions, organization and leadership. I mean a full order-of-battle study on the mob that rules Paradise City.'

Gilman nearly smiled. If the gun collector was eager to return to violence, there was something in the lean psychology professor that responded almost as passionately to the intelligence collection aspect of the mission. Williston's eyes, voice, eager alertness, all communicated a special enthusiasm. The stocky man from Las Vegas had learned to 'read' people in the gambling casinos, and right now it was very easy to read the oddly boyish teacher.

Sledgehammer, on the other hand, would not be easy.

Gilman said so.

'With all the guns and gadgets, money and training,' he warned thoughtfully, 'it's still going to be a very hairy operation. There'll be no resistance reception committee waiting at the drop zone. In effect, we'll be "jumping blind" into what Special Forces teams now call "denied territory." '

Williston shook his head in disagreement.

'Oh . . . no, I guess I'm wrong about that,' confessed the man who prided himself on being right. 'Andy's right. We have one contact in Paradise City – the nameless citizen who mailed Andy the clippings.'

'So we've got an agent there,' reasoned Carstairs, 'and all we've got to do is find him – if he's still alive.'

One person among the 110,000, plainly afraid and obviously someone who knew about Eddie Barringer's career in the OSS so many years ago. As Williston reflected on this, there was a sudden crash of thunder and an embarrassingly dramatic flash of lightning. In an instant, a powerful downpour hammered menacingly upon the lodge's roof and the storm was upon them.

It rained for hours.

CHAPTER NINE

Match dissolve.

That's a film term for a standard motion-picture transition, say, from the face of a clock in a police chief's office to the face of another clock in the senator's bedroom.

Match dissolve to Paradise City.

It rained all that night in Paradise City, a gentle, steady fall that dripped softly from the trees and clouded the streets with dim rolling walls of warm mist. The local television station was off the air and the night clubs were closed and the last blank-faced men had left the brothels, for it was 4:20 a.m. and almost everyone was asleep. Two countermen in Arnie's All Night Diner listened to a long-distance trucker tell a dirty joke that four other drivers had already recounted in the past week, and the countermen prepared to laugh out of pity and commercial sociability.

Five police cars roamed the empty streets in fixed geometric patterns, floating slowly through the drizzle like yellow-eyed ghosts as they mechanically patrolled their assigned routes. A score of uniformed foot patrolmen yawned and sighed as they walked their silent beats, drowsy and unafraid. They knew that there would be few, if any, armed burglars or desperate junkies to battle in the mist. This was a well-run town, and 'Little Johnny' didn't tolerate free-lance competition. Paradise City had no room for small-time thugs, for petty crime was uneconomical and irritated the taxpayers, who didn't mind being inmates of Pikelis' zoo so long as they were not disturbed. Every hoodlum in the state knew better than to work this town.

The price was too high. The first time that they caught you in Paradise City you might get off with a fractured jaw and a couple of kicks in the lower abdomen, or a pair of broken wrists if you were a car thief. Pickpockets usually had their ankles smashed with clubs, leaving them free to ply their trade elsewhere after they had departed but still emphasizing the Paradise City ground rules. Captain Ben Marton had a sense of humor that wasn't quite Mort Sahl's, but then his audience wasn't quite the same either. As for narcotics peddlers, there simply weren't any because Pikelis simply wouldn't tolerate anything that could attract federal attention. After the 1966 discovery of the badly burned trio from Miami, nobody tried to sell dope in Paradise City – not even once.

As for other illegal activities, an independent entrepreneur might possibly get away with his life the first time he was caught in Paradise City. But the second time that the local cops caught him, they'd shoot him in the belly two or three times and then stand around watching him die. This was reported as 'resisting an officer' in most cases, although sometimes – to keep the statistics in line with national averages for towns of this size – such deaths were recorded as auto-accident fatalities or, for variety's sake, suicides. The obliging coroner was the mayor's brother-in-law. Whatever quaint fiction was inscribed on the death certificate, everyone agreed that being 'gut shot' was a painful way to go and very few people risked it anymore – which was the idea in the first place. Larry Lewis, the 260-pound hoodlum whom the AF of LCIO bounced out in 1962, used to chuckle that Paradise City was truly a closed-shop town.

In the small hours of this rainy morning, Lewis was asleep beside a blond 'model' from New Orleans who'd recently become an 'exotic dancer,' and Mayor Roger Stuart Ashley sprawled unconscious after a losing battle with a fifth of Jack Daniel, and Little Johnny Pikelis was dreaming in his penthouse. He dreamt of a splendid society wedding for his twenty-three-year-old daughter who'd soon be returning from a year in Paris. There would be lots of flowers, all kinds of flowers, and imported champagne and a nineteen-piece Meyer Davis band. The fact that pretty Kathy Pikelis wasn't even engaged in no way reduced the beauty of the dream.

In the entire town, only ninety or one hundred people were awake as the big clock in the Municipal Hall steeple showed five o'clock. One of these sat by a sixth-floor window, smoking a cigarette and staring out at the wavering wet wall of mist that masked the harbor a mile away. The room was dark, and there was silence for a long moment before the record player clicked again and the subtle George Shearing album dropped into playing position. The music was very, but not wholly, relaxing.

The clippings had been mailed.

Now there was nothing to do but wait.

Just wait and hate and wonder and pray.
Would they come?
Would it be soon?

CHAPTER TEN

When the four committed men awoke in the lodge the next morning, they went about the chores that they had so carefully divided among themselves the night before. Cooking the ample breakfast was Arbolino's assignment – this week. One or another of the quartet would prepare each meal so long as they remained at this training base, for Carstairs had sent his caretaker off on a month's paid vacation so that the sixty-year-old 'outsider' would not see the unusual activities involved in getting ready for their secret war. 'Maximum security,' Williston had said firmly, and that compelled the exclusion of anyone not involved in Sledgehammer.

After breakfast, Gilman and Arbolino set to work constructing the simple body-building devices and the obstacle course. Ropes to climb and swing on, barriers to scale or vault, routes to trot or sprint – all the basic items to build wind and stamina and animal power. While they were working, the teacher and the second most eligible bachelor in the United States drove into Albany – in separate vehicles – to purchase the supplies. They bought in small quantities. Williston went to one Army-Navy store near the Negro section of the city to procure fatigues, boots, work shirts, coveralls and other clothing items for himself and Gilman. Carstairs shopped for himself and Arbolino at another 'surplus' store thirty blocks away. They assembled a month's supply of food by dividing their purchases among five supermarkets, two delicatessens and four groceries.

'If a man walks into a single store and buys three hundred dollars' worth of food, they're going to remember that at the shop,' Gilman had warned.

He was, of course, right. Everything had to be inconspicuous, ordinary, routine. That was the theme that the man from Las Vegas had repeated so many times as he'd reminded them of comrades and allies who'd died for breaking that rule. No big purchases, no checks. Buy in cash, in small bills. Take everything with you. It would be most inconvenient to have deliverymen arrive at the lodge when the automatic weapons were hammering in target practice. Think ahead. Be careful. They'd been over it all fifty times. Always have a plausible 'cover story' for everything. When Carstairs had sent his caretaker away, the millionaire had hinted that he needed absolute privacy because some beautiful – perhaps famous or married – woman was arriving. That was entirely believable, and the loyal employee could be counted on to keep the secret – as he had several times in the previous decade.

And with all the deceptions and precautions, there was still danger, the second most eligible bachelor in the United States thought as he pointed the truck away from the city. Here he was in his own country, land of the free and home of democracy – thousands of miles from any dictatorship or secret police – and he was at war. All police and public authorities were to be avoided, and he had to be alert and wary every instant. Under Williston's security rules, they couldn't even carry guns outside the barbed-wire defenses of The Inferno. It was strange – but exciting.

When he reached the lodge, the millionaire found Williston and the others packing food in the freezers and kitchen closets. The thin boyish Vermonter had gotten back first; he was always first. After all the boxes and packages were unloaded, the men who could not forget Edward R. Barringer changed into loose-fitting fatigues. Now they were ready to go to work, to finish the obstacle course and training devices. It was hard sweaty labor in the bright clear sun, chopping trees and digging ditches and sealing rough-barked, sweet-smelling fir trunks to rig lines. By sunset, they knew how far from being battle-ready their bodies were, and they sensed how much strenuous work would be necessary to re-condition four men in their forties into anything like the quick, tough 'Jeds' they'd once been. The stunt man and the wealthy sportsman-athlete were in the best condition, Williston next and the Las Vegas mathematician the furthest from combat-fit. When they sat down to dinner that night, they agreed that there was much to do before they could go into action against the enemy.

They were already using military terminology – again. The house was 'headquarters' and Paradise City was 'the target area,' and their talk focused on 'infiltration routes' and 'field security procedures' and the foe's 'order of battle.' Within forty-eight hours after the caretaker left, they had achieved a rigid training schedule that left them feeling tired but purposeful by each sunset. The days were long, beginning at six a.m. with an hour of calisthenics before breakfast and then a jarring sixty minutes on the obstacle course before the distance trotting started. They were panting, drenched with acrid sweat by the time they dived into the icy lake for a mile swim. Later it would be two miles, and the afternoon marksmanship drills would move on from hand guns to rifles and automatic weapons. They ate a lot, cursed a lot, laughed infrequently and slept long and deeply.

Their bodies began to respond, to remember, to revive. After a week, they started to walk differently, to breathe differently and move with traces of the old animal alertness. Now Arbolino could add daily instruction in judo and karate, a basic course in knife-fighting and the half-forgotten but still familiar tactics of 'dirty' unarmed combat. The ugly tricks were coming back to them day by day; hour by hour. The four men who had long since put all this aside were remembering how to stun, hurt, cripple, kill. Although he didn't mention it, Arbolino was surprised at the exceptional skill and energy – almost ferocity – that the professor showed in this work. It was as if some hungry beast inside Andy Williston was being unleashed – something dangerous and angry and savage. It was clear that his body had forgotten very little despite the long peaceful years of scholarship and teaching, for he was fighting expertly by reflex – by instinct – within two days.

In the third week, the ammunition began to run low and it was agreed that Carstairs would drive down to buy more in Newark, where the laws and regulations weren't as rigidly enforced as those in adjacent New York City. Williston left with him to start the research on the 'target area,' a complex project that could take months but might be completed much more quickly if he could farm out parts of the work to three intelligent graduate students whom he knew needed money. Upper New York State is a lovely place in mid-June, and even with their minds busy planning secret violence the two former OSS agents were soothed and seduced by the green hills and rolling fields so alive in the late spring sun. The two nondescipt men in light windbreakers drove south along the six-lane highway in the rented panel truck, eying the splendid landscape and talking about what lay ahead and each wondering whether the other could be relied upon when the crises came.

They would surely come.

Carstairs turned off Manhattan's West Side Highway at 125th Street, dropped the teacher near the Columbia campus and continued down Broadway to the Lincoln Tunnel that extended beneath the Hudson River bottom to New Jersey. Williston left his tan canvas suitcase at his small Riverside Drive apartment, looked down briefly at the ships – he loved ships and water – and proceeded to his office to find the addresses of the three graduate students. It was quiet on the campus now, a welcome change after the demonstrations and violence of the spring semester. How long this steamy tranquility would last was another matter, he thought as he dialed the number of the man whom he wanted as his first recruit.

Marvin Asher.

Asher, Baker, Carlson – it was as easy as A,B,C.

The money provided by the second most eligible bachelor in the United States made it that simple. Marvin Asher, Thomas Baker and Eric Carlson were delighted to do research on Paradise City for $750 each, and not one of the three graduate students showed any suspicion that the funds weren't actually coming from 'the new Ford Foundation race and crime in the South study' that Professor Williston mentioned. The thought of $750 for two weeks of concentrated work was more than enough; for the same money they would have investigaged masturbation patterns among Apache Indians or the impact of lobbyists on the Massachusetts legislature or the divorce rate among Miss America winners since the death of Woodrow Wilson. A charming redhead who'd been Andy Williston's girl for a year after his wife died in 1960 was now a senior researcher at *Time*, and she was willing to go through the magazine's files to provide additional material and information on the notorious town where Barringer had been murdered. She still liked Williston; he was very likeable in so many ways. He had been a strong, honest, excellent lover – and he might be again.

It was a very different motive that caused Barry Corman to mail up from Washington the printed transcripts and exhibits of the 1962 and 1965 Senate Rackets Committee hearings on Paradise City. Corman, best of the bow-tied and crew-cut administrative assistants to an ambitious Michigan senator, had studied under Williston and had received a Fulbright grant largely on the basis of his teacher's enthusiastic letter of recommendation. It wasn't just that Corman owed him a favor – although he did and was enough of an instinctive politician to know that debts must be paid – but Corman admired and respected Andrew Williston. This was useful. Ordinarily, a letter requesting copies of hearings would bear fruit in eight or ten days. Williston had his, via special delivery, nineteen hours after he telephoned.

The second most eligible bachelor in the United States was equally successful, although the trip to New Jersey had proved a minor disappointment. Purchase of bullets for the hand guns and rifles had been uneventful, but the bald gunsmith who'd previously been able to supply machine-gun ammunition explained that 'the heat's been on since the Kennedy thing, and even the Boys are running short on this stuff.' If the Boys – a fun-loving group united in sincere conviction that Al Capone had been a better businessman than Henry Ford – were low on clips for *their* automatic weapons, the situation was obviously difficult. However, resourceful P. T. Carstairs had an alternate source in reserve – the bartender at a Greenwich Village nightclub named the Balls of Fire, where the drinks were $1.50 each, the 'exotic' dancers $50 and the barbecued spare ribs terrible. But the bartender had a friend who knew a man whose brother-in-law was a longshoreman, a galaxy of social relationships that might not have thrilled either Dr Margaret Mead or Professor Kenneth Clark but which finally provided 9,000 rounds of machine-gun ammunition for the British L2A3s plus 6,000 for the .45-caliber U.S. weapons.

It was all stolen and they all knew it, and nobody mentioned it – not even once. Carstairs' three dozen $20 bills did almost all the talking; the rest of the conversations consisted of grunts, inane pleasantries and delivery instructions. It was heavy, bulky. The handsome sportsman also knew that it was dangerous. Within an hour after the ammunition was loaded into the rented panel truck, he was driving north at a law-abiding fifty miles per hour en route to The Inferno.

The truck returned to Manhattan three days later, with Samuel Mordecai Gilman at the wheel. He was looking tanner, leaner, tougher and even more purposeful than usual.

'I suppose I could have mailed down my little shopping list,' he told Williston over lunch at a very good Chinese restaurant on 125th Street near Broadway, 'but I'm a terribly wary and fussy fellow and I'd rather buy this gear myself. I want to see *exactly* what I'm buying.'

'Pass the shrimp,' the teacher answered.

'You think I'm compulsive, don't you, Andy?'

Williston shrugged.

'You think I'm compulsive,' Gilman insisted.

'No, not really, but I think you're hogging all the shrimp.'

The man who was always right pushed the dish toward his friend, sighed.

'All right, I'm compulsive – especially about details,' admitted the man from Las Vegas.

'It's not such a bad thing, Sammy.'

'No, you don't understand. I was raised that way, trained like that.'

The psychology professor ladled more of the shrimp onto his own plate, nodded.

'Please don't tell me terrible stories about your terrible childhood,' he requested. 'Not here, anyway. I'm a dead loss without my couch.'

'I've got to be right, perfect. My parents – both teachers – brought me up like that. That's why I have to do things myself – to make sure they're done right.'

Williston smiled sympathetically.

'As compulsions go, yours is one of the more useful ones,' he assured his friend. 'It's a lot better than starting fires or exposing yourself in the subway. You get things done, and that's worth a lot of Brownie points. You're clean, efficient and know the words of every lyric Cole Porter ever wrote – so don't brood about your compulsions.'

'My father—'

The thin Vermonter broke in, aiming his fork as if it were a classroom pointer.

'Was a difficult man. But *you're* not, just a bit fussy. I'm counting on that. We're all counting on that, on you,' Williston assured him. 'Without your special talents, your precision – yes, your occasionally irritating compulsion – we wouldn't have a chance.'

Now it was Gilman who smiled, a grateful but oddly haunted smile.

They finished the meal as the man from Las Vegas explained where he meant to purchase the radio and electronics equipment, the shop on West 46th and the two stores far downtown near Chambers Street. These purchases, like the earlier ones in Albany, would be spread among three different stores so that the unusual size of the total order would be less noticeable. Nine of the newest solid-state 'walkie talkie' radio sets, four for use and five to serve as replacements. Each set weighed only three pounds, had a range of more than a mile. They were the sturdiest, most compact and most expensive – the best that P. T. Carstairs' money could buy. These 'walkie talkie' units were the first items on Gilman's shopping list.

There were others that were more costly.

Item: one AM radio transmitter made up of two suitcase-size components that could be fairly easily concealed, a voice- and code-sending rig with a range of 500 miles.

Item: one telescoping antenna for use with that transmitter.

Item: three FR-11 jammers easily adjustable to neutralize certain short-wave frequencies, including those used by many police radio networks.

Item: eight different sorts of 'bugs,' wire-tapping and electronic surveillance gadgets ranging from a miniature FM transmitter no larger than a silver dollar to a long-range 'shotgun' that could pick up voices at 200 yards.

Item: four tape recorders, all the modern voice-actuated models, including a $1,900 Swiss 'Nagra,' a Uher 400 and a tiny 'body model' designed to be worn in a holster inside a man's jacket.

Item: five of the cigarette-pack-size 'bug' detectors, Japanese gadgets that were set to sweep the frequencies often used by concealed transmitters.

Replacement batteries, spare parts, an electronics technician's tool kit – Gilman bought them all with the prudence of a supply officer outfitting an expedition into the remotest corner of a New Guinea jungle. The gear completely filled the rear of the panel truck, leaving no room for the still-to-be-purchased infrared equipment or safe-cracking torches with their bulky acetylene tanks.

'Tony'll have to pick the rest of it up when he buys the trailer,' Williston calculated as they locked the cargo compartment.

It was 5:40 p.m. on a boiling summer afternooon in Manhattan, and the heat and the traffic and the exhaust fumes and the humidity combined in a conspiracy so offensive that it might have seemed deliberate. Any well-adjusted New York City paranoid would have judged it deliberate if not outright malicious, Williston thought as the truck inched northward up Eighth Avenue, and there were obviously quite a few paranoids nearby. Most of them seemed to be driving the vehicles that surrounded the Sledgehammer truck, he pointed out to Gilman at a red light at the corner of 32nd Street.

'Easy on the persecution complex,' the man from Las Vegas advised while he mopped the soot from his brow. 'Remember, you're the psychologist, not the patient. *They're* the paranoids.'

'Even paranoids have real enemies,' the teacher jested wryly.

The light changed, and this time they covered almost an entire block before the traffic stopped them. Drenched with sweat and oppressed by the choking wet heat, the two worn men exchanged weary glances.

'Even a paranoid wouldn't be crazy enough to drive in this, Sammy,' Williston judged. 'Let's park the truck near my place, shower and eat and then you can start for The Inferno at about ten when it's cooler.'

'You're very practical for an egghead college professor who never met a payroll,' Gilman complimented in arch accord.

The Columbia teacher chuckled.

'For a man who's always right you've got a short memory,' Williston corrected. 'I met at least one payroll – with you, and a tommy gun. Remember?'

The Wehrmacht payroll.

Swift, savage, sure.

Williston had been like a surgeon on that operation, cool and competent and professionally indifferent to the sight of blood. Violence had been an instrument, a tool, a matter of course for all of them in those days. They'd been young and the Nazis had been evil, and everything had seemed so clear and simple.

A long time ago.

'I remember the payroll,' the gray-eyed mathematician announced. 'We were pretty wild back then – young and wild.'

'Barely house-broken,' Williston agreed.

'Gilman wondered, eyed his friend at the wheel.

'It's going to be different this time,' the man from Las Vegas said in a voice that was as much question as promise.

'I sincerely hope so.'

The fountain was splashing at Columbus Circle and the fountain was splashing as they drove north on Broadway past the Lincoln Center complex, but the two men felt no relief until they entered Williston's air-conditioned apartment on Riverside Drive. Showers, chilled beer, a simple dinner of cold chicken and fruit all helped. A few minutes after ten, they each put on fresh clothes and descended to the side street where the truck was parked.

A thin swarthy man, perhaps twenty-five or twenty-six, was sitting on the steps of a brownstone a few yards from their vehicle. Williston and Gilman were nearly abreast of him before they realized why.

Lookout.

He was the lookout for two other men who were trying to jimmy open the lock on the truck's cargo compartment.

'Take the lookout!' snapped the Vermonter as he moved forward.

The thieves turned, saw Williston coming at them and swore.

'Stay away, Mother!' warned the big one with the jimmy.

'You'll get hurt!' promised the other thief.

His left hand moved; a switch-blade knife blossomed.

At that moment, the lookout bolted and Gilman turned just as Williston dodged a swinging jimmy that was intended to split open his skull. The teacher feinted, faked a punch with his left hand and dropped low under a second swoop of the steel tool. Then a number of things happened very quickly and in stunning but utterly logical succession – logical to any alumnus of the OSS hand-to-hand combat or 'silent killing' course.

It was effortless, classic, right out of the textbook.

Within thirty seconds – perhaps twenty – the man with the jimmy was lying on the sidewalk. His wrist – the hand that clutched the burglar tool – was broken, his collarbone was smashed, his head was bleeding from two places and he was retching helplessly from the awful blow to his stomach. The man with the knife had been circling warily for an opening, but now he saw his ruined partner on the cement and he panicked.

He rushed in blindly, holding the switch blade high.

'Andy!' Gilman warned.

The lean teacher spun, dropped agilely into that graceful crouch – and hit. The knife flew. Hit. The man screamed as a numbing blow paralyzed one arm. Hit. Something broke. Hit. Teeth and jawbone splintered. Hit. Williston was using his hands like hammers, but with the precision of a homicidal surgeon. He knew exactly what he was doing, or at least he was doing exactly what he'd been trained to do. It was almost as if the whole thing was choreographed and terribly well rehearsed.

Suddenly Gilman realized what came next in the karate sequence.

'Andy! Don't kill him! Don't!'

Williston hesitated, and the man slumped into the filth of the gutter. The teacher looked around, sighed.

'I wasn't going to kill him,' he assured his friend. 'I admit that I was fighting by reflex, all right – not bad after all these years either – but I certainly wasn't going to kill him. I'd have to be crazy to do that.'

Gilman looked down at the two bodies, searched the larger man's jacket and found what he'd expected – his 'works.'

'Just as I thought,' announced the man who was always right as he held up the hypodermic. 'Junkies – needle commandos out looting cars and trucks for anything that might bring cash to buy drugs.'

Williston nodded. 'Stupid,' he said softly. 'Stupid to park the truck here because the area's full of junkies, and stupid to hurt those two that badly. I'll have to watch that, I guess. P.T.'s supposed to be our homicidal maniac-in-residence – not me.'

Then he looked up and down the street cautiously.

'Time to go, Sam,' he advised. 'We don't want to explain these two battered bastards to the police.'

They shook hands, and a few moments later Gilman drove off on the first leg of his journey back to the upstate hideout. It was an uneventful ride up the New York State Thruway, pleasantly cool at sixty miles an hour. Gilman reached The Inferno shortly before 3 a.m., approximately half an hour before a restless, thoughtful Professor Andrew Williston was finally able to fall asleep in steamy New York City.

CHAPTER ELEVEN

Just before noon on the following Friday, the unlisted telephone at The Inferno rang and Carstairs answered it.

'This is Doubleday's,' a male voice announced. 'You asked us to phone you about those Civil War picture books you ordered.'

'You get them all?' the gun collector asked.

'Yessir, and we're sending them air express as you ordered. They should arrive at the Albany airport on the Allegheny flight due in at six-ten tonight.'

'Could I have the invoice number?'

'Certainly. 322, 9199, 7755.'

'Thank you for your splendid service,' the second most eligible bachelor in the United States declared courteously as he terminated the call.

Then he turned to Arbolino.

'Andy's on his way. Flying up late this afternoon. We're to pick him up at the airport at six-ten,' Carstairs reported.

'How did he make out?'

The millionaire smiled as he flashed a V-for-victory sign with two fingers.

'Home run. Got it all, he says. Everything's groovy.'

The expression on Williston's face when he entered the lodge that night seemed to confirm Carstairs' judgment. The men who greeted him looked tan and fit, but the gleam in his eyes was purposeful pride.

'My R and A trio did a good job,' he said as he put down the large Naugahyde suitcase and tapped it approvingly. 'Labor of love, you know.'

'I thought it was money – my money,' Carstairs teased.

'Love. Pure love. There's nothing like the romance between hungry graduate students and the prospect of cash,' the teacher explained. 'It's an awesome passion, totally consuming. Romeo and Juliet, Caesar and Cleopatra, Richard Nixon and his dog Checkers – all nothing by comparison. You'll see after I've had some dinner.'

He changed into the coveralls that were their uniform, ate quickly and questioned the others about their progress. At 8:05, he finished his excellent espresso and opened the suitcase. It was loaded with green-bound Congressional reports, plastic-covered memoranda in multiple Xerox copies, three bulging folders of clippings and photographs plus a blue-gray looseleaf notebook.

'Preliminary situation estimate for Sledgehammer,' he announced crisply as he opened the notebook. 'A brief summary and analysis of data on the target area and enemy forces dominating that area.'

His partners leaned back in their armchairs, Gilman and Carstairs puffing on cigars and the stunt man simply listening.

'Paradise City is a community of approximately one hundred and ten thousand people – according to the last census – and is the largest city in Jefferson County. The population is seventy-nine thousand whites and thirty-one thousand blacks, and neither the civil-rights movement nor desegregation of schools or jobs or housing has made any significant progress here. Just token stuff; we'll go into that later. The city has a small but busy port – mostly coastal shipping and some fishing – but the main industries are a G.E. electronics plant, a synthetic textile mill that's part of a big outfit based in New York, and a cannery. Vice and gambling are also large, thriving under the rather dynamic and efficient management of the criminal combine that controls the city.'

He paused to catch his breath.

'This organization also controls the municipal government, which is nominally headed by Mayor Roger Stuart Ashley. Take a look.' Williston urged as he extracted a photo from one of the folders and handed it to Gilman. 'He claims to be descended from Jeb Stuart, the Confederate general, but if that's true the family's descended pretty far.'

'A drunk?' the man from Las Vegas estimated.

'Bourbon for breakfast. Aged fifty-nine. Dresses like a Princeton graduate of the nineteen-thirties, which he was. Lots of oratory and no guts. A tiger at bridge, though.'

'As a Southern gentleman should be,' the millionaire commented.

Williston eyed him coldly.

'You'd better let *me* do the talking and *pay attention*,' he ordered, 'because I'm going to ask questions later . . . As I was saying, this criminal group also controls the local police department – there's a crooked captain named Ben Marton who looks like a pig and lives accordingly – and they own much of the stock in the newspaper, the radio station and the TV station. For our purposes, the mass media are in hostile hands and are being used by the enemy for propaganda designed to discourage any resistance.'

'Labor unions?' wondered the stunt man.

'This mob – the combine – includes the thugs who've dominated the local unions for the past fifteen or twenty years. The hoodlums and their phony locals were expelled from the AFL–CIO eight years ago for racketeering – but they're still in business. Wages in Paradise City are eighteen percent lower than those in the rest of the state,' Williston reported, 'and anybody who argues can end up in the Jefferson County Hospital – if he's lucky.'

Arbolino nodded. 'A wonderful place to raise kids,' he reasoned solemnly.

'I'm glad to see that you're getting into the spirit of the thing,' Williston replied. For the next seventy minutes, the lean professor explained the structure of the criminal syndicate, talked about 'Little Johnny' Pikelis, his key associates and the many ways in which they methodically milked the passive city as if it were a defenseless cow.

'There's a lot more information here,' Williston announced as he gestured toward the pile of documents, 'but before we get too involved in those details I'd like to present my first situation estimate of the over-all problem. Here it is, in a nutshell.

'One: Inasmuch as democracy and self-government are basic in the United States and Paradise City is within the U.S.A., it appears that this city has been infiltrated and occupied by agents of a foreign – that is, totalitarian – organization. Morally and politically, the criminal group controlling Paradise City must be considered wholly *un-American*. These foreign aggressors have succeeded in taking over every branch of local government, in part because of the indifference of the indigenous population and in part because the aggressors were skillfull and ruthless in their use of both force and bribery.'

The parallel was too obvious to ignore.

'France – nineteen-forty,' Gilman muttered.

'Exactly, and the similarity ought to cheer you up. To continue with the estimate:

'Two: Therefore, if we are to be realistic we must consider Paradise City to be an enemy-occupied town that is totally dominated by a paramilitary fascist organization of criminals and corrupt police. For our purposes, the local police must be considered similar to the Milice, the Vichy police who collaborated so brutally with the Germans from ninety-forty-one through nineteen-forty-four during the Occupation.'

Something extremely ugly glowed in the gun collector's eyes. He remembered the Milice – clearly.

'Bastards. They were all bastards,' he recalled.

'Yes, they were. Three: As for the Pikelis criminal syndicate itself, its power and methods and superior position force a comparison with the Gestapo. As the Gestapo dominated and used the Milice,' the teacher explained, 'so the Pikelis group dominates and uses the Paradise City police. From this evaluation, we see that Pikelis himself is functioning as the Gauleiter – the head of the fascist apparatus in the region with the same life-and-death powers that Hitler's gauleiters exercised in conquered territories.

Fantastic.

Even though it made sense it was all fantastic, Arbolino thought to himself as he listened to the presentation. Almost as strange was the cool, sensible voice in which Williston was presenting this extraordinary material, just as if it were simply another lecture in 'Psychology 1 – An Introductory Survey.'

'Four: The fascist occupation forces now dominate both political parties, and today these parties are largely sham organizations within Jefferson County. Within Paradise City, Mayor Ashley and all senior officials must be viewed as collaborators – either bought or intimidated. As already outlined, mass media are in enemy hands and Paradise City – like any other town garrisoned by a foreign force – has no recourse to public opinion. No help can be expected from the state government or state police, since the Pikelis group has reached an accommodation with key politicians based on regular 'delivery' of the Jefferson County votes.'

The man from Las Vegas shook his head gloomily.

The odds were even worse than he'd calculated.

'There's more, and it isn't any jollier,' Williston warned.

Gilman shrugged. 'It's all a bad dream,' he said. 'Just a dream, a terrible dream. I'll wake up in a minute in my little trundle bed in Las Vegas, and I'll find that this entire thing is a nightmare caused by eating too much smoked salmon.'

'Go ahead, Andy,' Arbolino urged impatiently.

'Five: The enemy armed forces garrisoning Paradise City, uniformed and civilian, number between one hundred twenty and one hundred sixty men, and their support organization probably includes five hundred or six hundred paid collaborators. The garrison is well equipped with modern weapons, operates a fleet of fourteen police radio cars plus the usual criminal investigation laboratory. In the absence of any Resistance organization, it must be assumed that the occupation forces have the skills, equipment and organization for effective counterespionage and counterinsurgency operations. So far as we know, there is only one person even considering active opposition – the anonymous individual who sent the clippings . . . Now we get to The Problem.'

He glanced up, saw that P. T. Carstairs was still smiling.

The gun collector wasn't the least bit troubled or discouraged.

'Six: The Problem: to infiltrate covertly the enemy-occupied area that is Paradise City, now totally dominated by a foreign fascist organization; to ascertain and exploit the weak points in this paramilitary organization; to build, train and equip an effective Resistance movement that will cooperate in a vigorous campaign of espionage, sabotage and psychological warfare; to splinter and destroy the fascist organization; to identify and punish the person or persons responsible for the death of Eddie Barringer.'

With his eyes half closed and his internal computer automatically filing the data, Gilman puffed on one of P. T. Carstairs' excellent Canary Island cigars and gently nodded in agreement.

'A fair and realistic estimate of the situation,' he judged.

'It's better than that,' the husky stunt man chimed in briskly. 'It's a *great* situation estimate, but the trouble is that the situation itself stinks. They've got us more than one hundred to one, Andy.'

Williston listened silently to their reactions to his carefully factual report, conscious that they were all betting their lives on his appraisal of the situation and dangers. Now he looked at the second most eligible bachelor in the United States.

'We're outnumbered,' the millionaire admitted, 'but we've got plenty of the best equipment and weapons. Besides, we'll never have to shoot it out with their entire force anyway. Guerrilla warfare, not pitched battles, is our bit. We'll know them but they won't know us, so it could be fun.'

'You have an odd sense of humor,' observed the man from Las Vegas as he tapped the ash off his Don Diego. 'An excellent house brand of cigars but a most peculiar notion of fun. I hope you won't take it amiss if I suggest that you have your head candled at your earliest convenience. They may find two yolks – or perhaps an entire mushroom omelet.'

Carstairs smiled.

'Scared, Sammy?'

'You bet your silk Sulka shorts I am.'

'Franklin D. Roosevelt said that we have nothing to fear but fear itself,' the gun collector admonished, 'and I'm with him.'

'He's dead – and I don't want to be. Not this year anyway.'

'All right,' Williston said loudly.

The others turned to look at him.

'All right, let's cool the small talk. It's too late for that now; we're committed,' he reminded them. 'Let's start reading and memorizing these reports and dossiers – now. You guys have a lot of homework to do.'

They walked to the table, each reaching for one or two folders.

'You going to give us a quiz on Friday, Professor?' Carstairs jested.

'Study it all carefully, Pete,' advised the teacher. 'Don't skip a word. To paraphrase an old Cold War slogan, better read than dead – which is what you'll be if you make any mistakes in Paradise City.'

The four men scattered around the large room, began to read. The second most eligible bachelor in America started with a biographical profile of Pikelis, studied the photo of the 'gauleiter' and then smiled when he saw a picture of the racketeer's lovely blond daughter. Katherine Ann Pikelis was extremely pretty. She was twenty-three, the report noted, and living in Paris.

The report was quite comprehensive, even listing her address in the French capital.

It omitted one fact, an item no outside researcher could have been expected to unearth.

Kathy Pikelis was booked on the next morning's Air France flight to New York.

CHAPTER TWELVE

The new routine at The Inferno began the next morning. They left the obstacle course for practical exercises in jimmying locks, cutting glass, tapping telephones, concealing microphones and using subminiature electronic devices for recording and/or broadcasting. They cut the calisthenics and the shooting to an hour each to leave time for studying the details – physical and human – of Paradise City.

They tacked up large street maps on walls in the living room, dining room, library and kitchen. They carefully memorized the locations of the City Hall, the Police Headquarters, the Fire Department 'central,' the Paradise Power generating plant, the gas company's control station, the telephone exchange, the water control facility, town incinerator, railroad station, bus depot and garage, harbor police dock, television and radio transmitters and studios, commercial airport and nearby Air National Guard field, the *Daily Trumpet*, the G.E. plant, the Loeb Textile mill, the Blue Star Cannery and the three decent hotels. The enterprising Paradise City Chamber of Commerce had proudly put everything it could think of on the map. This was very useful.

There were other maps, sketches and diagrams. These had been secured, bought or stolen.

Architects' plans of the police and telephone buildings, the television and radio station.

Sketches of the municipal sewer system and underground tunnels for phone and power cables.

Detailed drawings of the city's electric generators and their installation. Photos of Paradise City police cars, banks and the Fun Parlor – Pikelis' largest gambling club.

The four men questioned, tested, helped one another. They read and reread the dossiers on the mayor, Captain Ben Marton, Pikelis and the underworld leader's key aides. Collectively, these men ran a city of 110,000 presumably free Americans the way a housewife runs a vacuum cleaner – coolly sucking up everything in sight.

The ex-Jedburghs also had to learn – everything – about other men, extraordinary men so new that they didn't exist yet.

These new people were to be invented, designed and produced, original creations similar to those that movie industry press agents used to manufacture when nature, heredity, environment and God failed a major Hollywood studio. The men who would covertly invade Paradise City would need much more than glamorous names and expensively capped teeth, however. They required new but ordinary names, new 'lives' for cover stories and documents to verify the lies. Each also needed a tolerably good reason for coming to Paradise City. Details – there were so many details, and each had to ring true. Place of birth, father's name, mother's name, schools, military records, jobs, girl friends, wives and children, medical history, bank accounts, friends, hobbies, clothing tastes and personal life style – not one of these could be overlooked or minimized.

They were inventing people, a sport widely engaged in during the second half of the twentieth century but rarely played for such final stakes. After the life stories had been debated and refined, they turned to the documents needed to support these synthetic sagas. The Social Security cards were easy to procure – with the cooperation of a Carstairs-owned glass company – and then driver's licenses in those false names followed after the investment of a few long-distance telephone calls and several hundred dollars. There is a legitimate business in phony driver's licenses in many states – well-established and flourishing if not entirely legitimate. Next bank accounts were opened in various cities under the various names, producing imprinted checkbooks that added the authoritative blessing of great American financial institutions to the deceit.

More false papers.

More of the latest electronic and infrared gear.

More training sessions.

Now it was time to go.

June 14 had been Flag Day and June 15 Father's Day and June 21 the first day of summer. July 6 was D-Day for Sledgehammer, the day that the invasion began. Without armadas of gray-hulled landing craft, swept-wing fighter-bombers or heavy transport planes packed with paratroops, the carefully planned operation was launched – quietly. It was so silent that neither the Voice of America nor the alert Huntley-Brinkley news-gathering team noticed or mentioned it, and you couldn't decently blame Walter Cronkite for missing it either. It just happened. July 6 was a Monday, and every

Monday, Wednesday and Friday a National Airlines jet arrived from Atlanta at 5:05 p.m. and left at 5:20 for Jacksonville. July 6 was another hot summer day in Paradise City, bright and humid and almost cloudless. The National flight was one minute late.

As a result, H-Hour – in the parlance of the Pentagon – was 5:06, when a moderately pretty stewardess flashed her moderately sincere smile as six passengers left Flight 911 at the Paradise City airport. One of these was the point man, the first scout for the invasion force. He was a short, sturdy man who wore Italian sun glasses, a knowing look and well-made gray suit that cost at least $180, perhaps $200. He had a fine expensive tan that was perfectly color-coordinated with his blue button-down shirt and discreet silk tie, and behind the dark glasses his eyes wandered purposefully, noting and recording, as he walked the fifty yards to the modern white terminal.

His name was Stanley Gordon. It said so on his California driver's license, his Social Security card, his Mobil Oil credit card and the two letters in his suitcase – one from a chorus girl named Toni in Las Vegas and the other from his brother in Phoenix.

It was all a lie.

He was no Californian and he didn't have any brothers and he'd never slept with any girl named Toni – in Las Vegas or anywhere else. He was a Phi Beta Kappa from the University of Chicago, but he didn't wear the key. Instead, he carried a silver-clad cigarette lighter with a tiny camera concealed in the base and a 'fountain pen' that fired .22-caliber bullets – one of the unique contributions to Western culture that Britain's creative Special Operations Executive made in 1942 – plus a .38-caliber pistol that nestled within the portable radio packed in his tan canvas two-suiter.

And his name was not Stanley Gordon.

His name was Samuel Mordecai Gilman, and, like his biblical ancestors, he had come to spy out the land.

As he waited at the baggage counter with the other five disembarking passengers, he glanced at his watch – just as they did – and sighed in mechanical impatience – as they did – and noticed the three men peering down from the balcony. He guessed that they were plainclothes detectives keeping track of new arrivals – like the ones who used to work the Dominican airports during the efficiently vicious Trujillo dictatorship –

and he was right. Of course. Next he saw the pair of uniformed police joking with the buxom waitress at the snackbar counter, and he appreciated how meticulously Little Johnny Pikelis was protecting his investments. Then he picked up his suitcase, shivered in the chill of the air-conditioning and joined three other travelers in the limousine that would take them into Paradise City.

The road was a four-lane concrete highway, lined with semi-tropical trees and comfortable middle-class houses plus an occasional fruit-and-vegetable stand. There was nothing poor or cheap or shabby about the unmistakably suburban ten miles between the air field and the city, for this was a solid two-car-per-family Book-of-the-Month Club residential district inhabited by respectable taxpayers. Even though some of them read such New Left periodicals as *Time*, just about everyone tacitly agreed that it was a good thing the little wooden houses of the Negroes were on the other side of town, for those homes were a bit tacky and wouldn't make a proper impression on visitors. Appearances counted a great deal in Paradise City; the Department of Sanitation did a first-rate job.

The streets were clean and traffic moved steadily, the spy observed as the cool limousine rolled toward the center of town. The store windows were attractively decorated, the cars parked were late-model vehicles and the tanned legs of the miniskirted teenagers were as good as any in Miami or Los Angeles. Defying TV and motion-picture tradition, the local police – the Milice to the spy – were neither gross, ugly or sloppy and they smiled just as if they were the 'white hat' good guys instead of tools of the evil villains.

There was the stone-and-glass building that housed the Jayland Realty Corporation, the firm that John Pikelis used as his legal front and through which he reported such of his income as he chose to mention. Williston's research team had unearthed the facts that the lord of Paradise City had been born in 1912, left high school to become a longshoreman, endured four arrests with only one conviction, collected old pistols and played poker well – but his income could only be estimated. It might be as low as $600,000 a year, or as high as $900,000. Either figure was as respectable as this downtown area itself.

The big car eased to a halt in front of the Paradise House, an eight-story hotel incongruously decorated with the façade of an old Southern mansion. This preposterous pillar-and-portico presumption masked the lower three stories of the eleven-year-old building. Mayor Ashley, who secretly loathed mint juleps and found the Civil War – the War Between the States – boring despite its political usefulness, had argued for something more modern 'to express the progressive spirit of our growing community.' He'd suggested this on a Wednesday morning when he happened to be sober, but Pikelis had not been impressed. It was easy enough for Ashley, whose great-grandfather had lost an arm at Chancellorsville and whose spinster sister headed the local branch of the Daughters of the Confederacy, to abandon the magnolia tradition, but Johnny Pikelis was no Southern aristocrat. He had no roots, no identity, in that mistily glorious tradition. He was the son of a hard-drinking Eastern European immigrant who'd been illiterate in all tongues, a total outsider. Pikelis required – *needed* – a classic Dixie mansion with white columns to remind him of the family plantation he never knew, the gracious home that he should have had instead of the roach-infested slum apartment near the docks. Now he lived in the penthouse on the hotel roof, enjoying the splendid service of uniformed black waiters and maids who made him feel that he really was a courtly Southern colonel, just like the one in the frozen turkey pie commercials.

So the Paradise House looked vaguely like an antebellum mansion, vaguely and illegitimately, Samuel Stanley Gordon Gilman thought as he entered the air-conditioned lobby. At the desk he consented to sign his name and pay $16 a day for a single room with bath, and a few minutes later he was taking a shower in the aforesaid facility attached to Room 411. It was all ridiculous, he thought as he stepped out to dry himself, for he was much too mature and clever to volunteer for such a stupid Boy Scout mission.

'I must be crazy,' he said aloud as he reached for a towel.

An improbable mission conceived by an obsessed academic.

'Crazy, crazy, crazy,' he chanted.

Saying it made him feel better, and that made him remember what he had to do. First he put on a light bathrobe, picked up the desk chair and carefully wedged it under the doorknob. Then he checked the two mirrors to make certain that neither masked an observation post or a closed-circuit television camera. Reasonably confident that *they* couldn't *see* him, he began to search the room to find out whether *they* could *hear* him. After all, Williston had reported that this was *their* hotel and *they* probably took very few chances with strangers who flew in from the North. Washington, D.C., was North. J. Edgar Hoover and canny Treasury agents and special investigators for the Senate Rackets Committee were North. Ambitious newspaper and TV documentary teams were North, and so were the merciless Mafia 'families' of New York and Chicago.

North was smart and tough and dangerous.

Pikelis, himself smart and tough and dangerous, knew all that.

He'd be alert, ready.

The man from Las Vegas continued to scan the room, walls, fixtures and furniture. The odds were at least three to one that this room was – in some way or another – wired for sound. Lamps, moldings, the bottoms of the chairs, the TV set and the air-conditioner, the headboard of the bed – zero. The spy paused, remembered that Williston had described Pikelis as 'logical and simple' and snapped his fingers in recognition. It had to be. The man who was always right flicked open his Swiss Army knife's screwdriver, opened the base of the telephone and smiled.

There is was.

Right again.

It was very old-fashioned, if not quaint, to hide a microphone in a telephone nowadays, which was why only a few stubborn classicists would even look inside the instrument anymore. This little eavesdropping device was presumably linked to a nearby voice-activated tape recorder, perhaps some central station used to monitor the entire building. With the same delicate care that he'd used to open the base as silently as possible, Gilman screwed it back on and began to sing.

' "I'll never say 'Never again' again!" ' he crooned as he selected a blue Dacron-and-silk suit from the closet. He hummed as he dressed, and he was still whistling the same tune as he removed the .38 from the radio case and slipped the snub-nosed weapon into the flat linen shoulder holster. Pausing in front of the mirror near the door, he gave his bow tie a final tug of adjustment.

'Groovy,' he judged impartially.

Then he descended to the lobby to find the cocktail lounge, a long, cool, dimly lit room with a dozen tables and a bar topped with black plastic intended to resemble leather. The wall behind the bar was covered with mirrors, and as Gilman lowered himself onto a stool he noticed the reflected images of the very good legs and eye-catching figures of two young women seated at a corner table. Sleek, bright-eyed and smiling, they had 'call girl' written all over them. Gilman recognized the type from Las Vegas, where there were so many pretty professionals with great legs and permanent smiles. It was hardly surprising that Paradise City had its share of Sandies and Bobbies and Terries, the spy thought without rancor.

'Sir?' the slim white-jacketed bartender invited.

'Vodka Gibson – on the rocks, my man.'

The slight shrewd-faced man behind the bar nodded politely. He mixed the drink, filled the glass to the brim and set it down on the shiny plastic.

'Their names are Jerri and Bobbi,' he announced, 'and they make friends easily. I'm not their agent, you understand,' he added a moment later, 'but I noticed that you'd noticed.'

'My, you're a keen lad,' the spy answered between sips. 'And a talented bartender.'

Gilman took another sip, sighed.

'Jerri and Bobbi – I'll bet they're good conversationalists too.'

'On any subject. They read both *Life* and the *Reader's Digest*. Never miss an issue.'

'I'll bet they're terrific on pop art and modern marriage,' the spy announced.

'Out of sight – and you ought to hear them on How Spiro Agnew Found God.'

Gilman finished the drink, calculated for some seventy seconds and decided two things.

'Do it again,' he requested as he pushed the empty glass away.

The man in the white jacket – the button on the left breast read 'Harry' – immediately prepared another vodka Gibson. A moment after he served it, he poured himself a wineglass of Cinzano.

'Isn't the local drink bourbon, Harry?' the spy asked.

'I'm kind of freaky.'

'And not local?'

The bartender shook his head.

'No, I'm a home-town boy – strictly Paradise City,' he corrected. 'I put in a few years down in Miami, but all that chopped liver was too rich for me, so I've happily returned to peaceful Paradise City.'

Gilman reached into his jacket, hoping that he still had one or two of Carstairs' fine coronas. He didn't.

'It's a nice town, huh?' he questioned casually.

The man behind the bar shrugged.

'Land of the spree and home of the knave, Dad. This is Paradise City, Dad – Lootsville by the sea with girls and wheels and deals and Dixie charm. It's been in all the funny papers,' he pointed out, 'and I'd bet eighty-five cents you know all about it.'

'I heard it on the radio once,' Gilman admitted.

At that moment a fat woman in a red dress sat down – almost fell down – at the other end of the bar and waggled her index finger meaningfully. She had obviously consumed considerable alcohol elsewhere, and it seemed quite clear that if she were served any more she would become one of those messy crying drunks in about another hour. The man from Las Vegas was surprised when the hip-talking bartender promptly poured two inches of sweet Southern Comfort for her.

'She doesn't look like Janis Joplin to me,' Gilman observed when the man in the white jacket returned.

'She isn't. She's the wife of a very hard and heavy police captain, and he'd be offended if I didn't serve his beloved.'

'Isn't it illegal to serve somebody that smashed?'

Harry No-Last-Name smiled.

'I could get myself smashed – and lacerated – if I annoyed Captain Ben Marton. Being a lousy swimmer – especially with my arms broken – I have joined the Don't Make Waves cult and found spiritual fulfillment. You dig?'

'I dig,' the spy answered and sipped at the Gibson.

The bartender finished his Cinzano.

'I don't mean to pry, sir,' he began, 'but are you just passing through or will you be staying for our annual Benedict Arnold Birthday Ball?'

It was going nicely.

This foxy, nosy, talkative bartender would spread the word.

'I might stay, if the money's right. I just might do that.'

The man behind the bar considered this for ten seconds.

'You're too hip for a cop and too smart for a hood,' he finally announced, 'but you're no brassiere salesman either.'

'Stickman. I'm a stickman,' the spy lied.

'That figures . . . Vegas?'

Gilman nodded.

'That figures too. You don't talk like a civilian, not a bit. Looking for work?'

'Maybe.'

They had shaped the cover story carefully. An experienced stickman from the big-league gambling tables of Las Vegas should be hired immediately in a place such as Paradise City, and Gilman had actually worked as a croupier for a week – as a lark – when a regular stickman was temporarily incapacitated after a bad LSD trip.

'Vegas?' the bartender reflected. 'Well, if you're good and you're honest – and you'll be dead if you're not – scoot out to the Fun Parlor tonight and talk to Willie Dennison. He's the manager, used to work a casino in Havana when Batista was *el presidente*.'

'Our classiest whoopee center – out on Ocean Road. About two dollars by cab. Whatever you're buying, they're selling. Live a little.'

'May I use your name?' wondered Samuel Stanley Gordon Gilman.

'I do – all the time. Sure, tell Willie Dennison that Harry Booth suggested that you talk to him. Handsome Harry, the rich bartender.'

Then he walked off to serve two husky men in expensive silver-buttoned blazers, middle-aged men who had just joined the call girls. Jerri and Bobbi – the spy couldn't tell which courtesan was which – were smiling brightly, talking and thrusting forward their impressive bosoms as they'd learned customers liked them to. The prostitutes seemed quite animated and merry, pleased that the boredom of waiting was over and cheered by the prospect of earning fifty dollars each.

Gilman finished his drink, put four one-dollar bills on the bar and headed for the elevator. It was time now. He'd given *them* some twenty minutes, which was all they needed if they were on the ball. In his room, he examined the contents of each drawer in the dresser and found what he'd expected. One tie was wrinkled just a little bit less than he'd left it, and the two letters were a quarter inch out of place. They'd searched the room, as he'd planned. Everything was moving exactly as planned, so far. Now he would descend to the hotel dining room for a filet mignon dinner before journeying out to the Fun Parlor.

At 7:20 p.m. on the evening of July 6, the first invader sat down for his initial meal in enemy territory. At 11:04 p.m. on July 8, the telephone rang in Room 302 of the Hotel Park in Charleston, South Carolina, and a tall thin man with tired eyes answered it quickly.

'No, you must have the wrong room,' he said in matter-of-fact tones. 'There's no Sarah Ellen Foster here.'

He hung up the phone, turned to the blond-haired man seated on the bed.

'Well?' Carstairs asked.

'Very well,' Dr Andrew Williston confirmed. 'Sam's got the job. They checked Vegas by phone, and he came up smelling like roses.'

'How nice, if vulgar.'

'Would you settle for Fabergé after-shave cologne?'

The second most eligible bachelor in the United States nodded pleasantly, stood up to start packing his suitcases. The coded telephone message was all that they'd been waiting for, and the two men checked out of the Hotel Park half an hour later. Now that the first spy had successfully infiltrated the Nazi-occupied town, it was time for the second to move into position.

CHAPTER THIRTEEN

Shortly after five o'clock on the steamy afternoon of July 10, a dusty 1964 Ford Panel truck towed a battered house trailer into Crowden's Caravan Camp on Route 121, nine miles beyond the Paradise City limits. A dark muscular man who chose to call himself Phil Antonelli – he'd worked under many names – stepped out of the car into the ugly glare. His face was covered with sweat and dust, and his blue-denim shirt was splotched with dark perspiration stains. The way he licked his parched lips indicated how long he'd been driving through the ninety-degree heat – too long.

'I need space and a shower and a bottle of cold beer,' he told Mr Crowden.

Fred Crowden was a spry, nasty, little man of sixty-four, white-haired and blue-eyed and secretly glad that his scratchy-voiced wife had passed on three years earlier. 'Passed on' was one of his many piously hypocritical phrases; it usually went with a dreadfully distant look of sadness that would have done credit to Kim Novak. He was that awful an actor, as well as a mean little bastard. Hostile, bigoted, dishonest and selfish, he could have been some *Pravda* editorial writer's Ideal American Man.

'Trailer space, shower, beer – we've got 'em all, stranger,' Crowden answered in a voice that reflected his seventeen years of passionate devotion to TV Westerns.

Inside the plywood prefab that was the office, the trailer-camp owner exchanged a bottle of iced Miller's for two of Antonelli's quarters while the new arrival signed the register. There were only nine of the 'mobile homes' parked in his camp, so Mr Crowden welcomed this olive-skinned customer as an additional $6 a day. Yes, the Ford with the Florida plates was worth fourteen or fifteen bottles of beer per day in income. Crowden always thought in wholesale prices for himself. He was convinced that he was a sly, shrewd, successful businessman who could have been a financial titan if he'd only bought Coca-Cola stock in 1926 when his brother-in-law had suggested it. That one blunder hadn't diminished Crowden's self-esteem, however.

He glanced at the register.

'Antonelli – that's an Eyetalian name!' Crowden crowed in cunning triumph.

'Italian-American,' the sweaty traveler corrected.

'Ain't no Black Hander, are you?' the old man probed warily.

The new 'guest' shook his head, thrust his fingers forward for inspection.

'Wash 'em twice a day,' he assured. 'I'm just a fisherman out of Tarpon Springs heading north in the hot season.'

'I know all about them Black Handers,' Crowden continued smugly. 'Same dirty crowd that tried to do in Eliot Ness on *The Untouchables*. Saw it every week and all the reruns too. Black Handers, Marfias – same dirty crowd of garlic suckers.'

Mr Crowden was beginning to wear on the nerves of the man who'd registered as P. Antonelli.

'You know Lucky Luciano or Capone or those other Marfier?' tested the white-haired widower.

'No, but I've got a second cousin who knows Frank Sinatra's dentist. Will that do?'

The squinty-eyed proprietor of the caravan camp peered at him intently for several moments, grunted and pointed to a parking place in the open field. He watched the dark athletic man – he had the build to be a Tarpon Springs sponger all right – climb into the faintly shabby '64 Ford. No, rich Marfier gangsters didn't drive old panel trucks like that and they didn't live in dusty sagging trailers. They had huge cream-colored Cadillacs, and they stayed in the biggest suites at the most expensive hotels where they drank champagne with naked show girls. Crowden often thought about those meaty, laughing girls, the ones he could have had if he'd bought that goddam Coca-Cola stock. Putting aside his visions of splendid young teats and rumps, the old man concluded that Antonelli was ordinary and harmless.

For the eleventh time that week, Fred O. Crowden was wrong. It is true that he wasn't too bright to start with and he'd already imbibed seven bottles of beer since lunch, but even at his best he couldn't have made a larger mistake about either the man or the trailer. One would hardly rate as ordinary a man who has blown up bridges, machine-gunned his way into a police station and slain a score of heavily armed soldiers – some with his bare hands. As for the trailer, the cargo concealed in the secret compartments – the radio transmitter, infrared beams, sniper guns, revolvers, automatic weapons, bugging devices and electronic jamming gear, safe-cracking equipment, ammunition and plastic explosives – was neither conventional nor harmless.

Any FBI or CIA agent could have told Mr Crowden that, but unfortunately none was nearby and the expensive arsenal was expertly hidden. The old man watched as P. Antonelli maneuvered his truck and trailer into the parking place, got out to connect the caravan's rubber hose to the metal water pipe jutting up there. Tony Pete Arbolino Antonelli was glad to enter the trailer a moment later, for his eyes hurt from seven hours of driving in the glaring sun. He was also pleased that he had arrived in Jefferson County and found this place for a base. He'd smelled the beer on Crowden's breath, found comfort in the prospect that the trailer-camp owner would be half tipsy most of the time.

The second invader had infiltrated successfully.

The rest were already on their way.

CHAPTER FOURTEEN

'It's over a month – well over a month, Ben,' Pikelis pointed out as he sipped from the tall glass of tomato juice.

'Damn near six weeks, I'd bet,' he added, looking down at his city eight stories below.

'That's what I've been telling you, Johnny,' argued the beefy police captain. 'If anybody'd got their hands on any evidence that Barringer might have put together, you'd sure have heard about it by now. Somebody would be here with his hand out for money, I'd bet.'

'Somebody like you, Ben?'

Marton's eyes grew even more hooded than usual.

'That's not funny,' he muttered.

'It wasn't meant to be,' Pikelis answered. He smiled a moment later when he finished the juice. 'Great stuff, Ben – made from our own Jefferson County tomatoes,' he reminded the policeman with a trace of mockery.

'Uh-huh.'

'You ought to drink more of it to show your fine community spirit,' teased the man who ruled Jefferson County.

'I stand up for both "Dixie" and "The Star-Spangled Banner," and I never forget your birthday. That ought to be enough, John.'

Marton paused, watched Pikelis begin an assault upon a cheese omelet.

'As I was saying, John,' he continued, 'we haven't found a goddam thing and there's no sign that anybody else has . . . unless it was some tricky Federal agent or Senate investigator.'

'Now there's a cheerful thought for a nice sunny Saturday morning,' Pikelis exploded. 'July eleventh, I'm eating my breakfast peacefully and my good friend Ben tries to ruin the whole damn weekend with talk about the bright boys from the District of Columbia. Listen, Captain, I've got friends up in Washington too.'

Marton nodded silently, aware that this was no time to speak. Not unless he wanted to provoke even greater wrath.

'I've got a tame congressman up there – and some other

people – who keep their eyes and ears open for just this sort of thing, you know.'

The captain nodded again.

'I'm no idiot, you know,' Pikelis rasped.

Marton nodded a third time.

'I spend a lot of money up in Washington – money that keeps us all in business, Ben, and don't you think that I'd know if those meddling bastards up there were after us again?'

He pushed the plate of eggs aside, glared.

'John, I never said they were,' Marton replied softly. 'I'm trying to tell you that I think nobody has the stuff, that either it got burned up in the car or it never existed. I'm saying there's nothing to sweat about, that we've been churning ourselves up for nothing.'

Pikelis finished his coffee, lit a cigar and looked out over the penthouse terrace toward the sea. His large black eyes roved over the Paradise Country Club and golf course, the line of palm trees near the shore. It was a soothing sight, and he found his tension fading as it calmed him.

'Maybe you're right, Ben,' he admitted with a half smile that flashed several thousand dollars' worth of excellent dentistry. 'Maybe I'm wasting your time when you should be out making like a cop, protecting the entire community. Law and order, that's the ticket. Our women and our streets are safe, right?'

'Safer than a helluva lot of other cities. 'Course we have a bit of mischief now and then. Colored girl got cut up over on Larabee Avenue last night, and I'm fixing to do something about it. Yessir, I surely will,' Marton promised.

'She dead?'

'Yeah, all cut up something awful.'

Pikelis blew a smoke ring before he answered.

'I want you to solve that terrible crime, Ben. I don't hold any brief for coddling the colored, but I think we ought to show our dark-skinned neighbors that we're protecting them too. We don't want any more of those smart-ass outside agitators coming in here to stir up our peaceful black citizens, do we, Ben?'

'No, though I'm not afraid of those goddam agitators. We busted them up pretty good back in sixty-two and again in sixty-six, I recall. That uppity crowd won't be back here soon,' the captain predicted confidently.

He was right. The savage beatings would not soon be forgotten.

'Even so, Ben,' Pikelis counseled, 'it looks good if the Paradise City police show some interest in protecting the colored too. It's like paying your insurance premiums. If they're contented, it'll be a lot harder for outside agitators – whenever those damn fools come.'

Marton sighed, rose from his chair.

'I'll get right on it, John,' he promised.

'Good, and don't forget about the "welcome home" party tonight. Nine o'clock. Black tie,' the gangster-executive reminded.

'For Kathy I'll wear a black tie,' the fat policeman pledged.

Pan down and left quickly, tighten on the bus station at 12th and Conant and zoom in for a close-up of the 10:56 arriving from Jacksonville.

That's what any competent not-too-imaginative Hollywood director would have done if he were shooting the scene. Ingmar Bergman or Antonioni might have filmed it differently, but they're foreigners and their pictures are hard to understand anyway. Tight on the door as the passengers get out. First the pink-faced sailor on leave, then the two teen-age girls coming home from the visit to grandma, the lean crew-cut fellow with the briefcase and finally the black couple with their nine-year-old son. Pull back and widen the shot as they stretch, sigh and start to scatter.

Jump cut – fast – to the man with the briefcase as he collects his suitcase and signals a taxi. Williston is passing as Arthur Warren, a poll taker employed by the Southern Public Opinion Corporation to prepare an in-depth study of Jefferson County attitudes on movies and television. There really is a Southern Public Opinion Corporation, has been for six years since a former Columbia sociology instructor organized the firm in Miami. It's a reputable and profitable firm, duly incorporated and regularly tax paying and a perfect front for Arthur Warren. Arthur Warren is real and sober and respectable. He has Hertz Rent-a-Car and Texaco charge plates, a Diners' Club card, a Florida driver's license, a Blue Cross card and a checkbook establishing his account at Miami's First Federal Bank. In his briefcase is a four-page memo from the president of the S.P.O,C. explaining in detail what Arthur Warren is to do. The memo is laced with just enough sociological and academic jargon to be wonderfully boring – but convincing.

With no disrespect to the Paradise City Chamber of Commerce, the heat was unpleasantly excessive and the humidity was oppressive and the total effect was lacking in charm. Arthur Warren was glad to accept the taxi driver's suggestion and took a room in the Hotel Jefferson on Jefferson Avenue. It was centrally located, medium-priced, air-conditioned and drab, the sort of place where shoe salesmen or a visiting basketball team might stay. The best cigar that the lobby newsstand offered was a twenty-five-cent Bering, and the rack of paper-back books featured standard treatises on nymphomania, teen-age orgies, sadistic motorcycle gangs, suburban sodomy and Communist infiltration of the United Nations.

Just an ordinary third-rate hotel, Williston thought as he unpacked his bag in Room 407. When he was finished, he set out to stroll the downtown area for as long as he could endure the clammy heat. The Jefferson Theater was showing one of those vicious Italian Westerns along with a Disney film about a boy and his pet octopus, and the Central – two blocks down the street – was offering a picture about an alienated rock-and-roll musician plus a Japanese science-fiction feature treating a gigantic roach that ate half of Osaka. The papier-maché half, it appeared. High-school girls eyed the new bathing suits in the Herman Brothers' windows, mothers in slacks dragged reluctant children into Weiner's Tiny Tots, and outside the A&P on Carver Street the usual sport-shirted fathers loaded cartons of groceries into station wagons.

The poll taker walked past the secretaries who were debating evening-gown styles outside Paris Fashions, turned left at Larry's Liquors and looked around for some cool refuge in the noon heat. A moment later, he hurried into Hammer's Drug Store – a modern glass-and-aluminum establishment that offered electric clocks, Bar-B-Q sandwiches, aluminum beach chairs, New York Heroburgers, enema bags, the complete works of Agatha Christie and Ellery Queen, four kinds of birth-control pills, ammoniated toothpaste, Revlon make-up, assorted laxatives, diverse anti-dandruff shampoos, eleven different brands of tranquilizers and Hammer's Own Dubble-Thick Frozen Malt in nineteen flavors. As if that weren't enough, it was also too cold.

While he tried to decide between a tuna-tomato surprise on jumbo roll and a bottle of Sominex sleeping pills, Williston noticed a bald bespectacled man in the traditional pharmacist's jacket giving orders to a young clerk. The infiltrator guessed that the man in glasses was Mr Hammer; he was right. Williston sat down at the counter, shivered in the chill of the air-conditioner and concluded that he'd rather risk his digestion than venture out into the midday heat at this moment.

'Tuna-tomato surprise, please,' he told the blond counter girl in the tight green uniform.

She smiled suddenly and then seemed to squirm, making Williston realize that her change in expression wasn't just old Dixie hospitality after all. A grinning male clerk passing behind her had furtively patted her ample rump on his way to the hot-fudge pot, and as Williston realized that this was why she'd smiled he automatically smiled himself. Then he ordered an iced coffee, and the counter girl singsonged his requests to some invisible sandwich maker.

Williston's eyes roved back to Mr David Hammer, who was handing an envelope to a chubby man in seersucker. It was the assassin who had slain Barringer. The psychology professor didn't know this, but he had seen enough convicts in enough prisons to recognize this baby-faced man with the hooded eyes as, almost surely, a criminal psychopath. Luther Hyatt was a criminal psychopath with a taste for violence and maple walnut ice cream, and he was collecting Mr Hammer's weekly dues to the Paradise City Merchants' Security Service. Williston didn't know this either, any more than he was aware of the fact that every merchant in town belonged to avoid broken windows and fractured arms. The pharmacist's unquestioning payment was no reflection on Hammer's courage, but rather a recognition that the local orthopedic surgeons left something to be desired. The research papers prepared by the three graduate students hadn't been quite that thorough, however, so all that Williston knew was that Mr Hammer had given somebody – probably a criminal psychopath – a white envelope. The tuna-tomato surprise arrived a moment later, focussing all of Williston's attention upon its bulging dimensions, thick coating of mayonnaise and gastric menace.

At his first bite, he barely restrained himself from inquiring as to why any tuna sandwich should be polluted with incongruous chunks of pickle and clumps of relish. It was probably some local custom, he reasoned as he forced himself to eat, and even if it wasn't, only a very stupid spy would attract attention on his first day by complaining about Paradise City food. Williston methodically finished the sandwich, drank his iced coffee and left a 15 percent tip on the counter. Mr Hammer stood by the cash register near the door to the street, and Williston carried his money over there wondering whether the pharmacist-owner would say it.

Hammer did.

'Now you come on back, you hear?' he genially admonished in the traditional Southern farewell.

Williston nodded politely, his eyes wandering to the Merchants' Security Service sticker on the register. He walked out into the hot street in time to see the fat assassin collect another envelope from the shopkeeper next door. When the beefy psychopath then reached into the open window of a parked gray Pontiac to extract a pack of Kools, Williston automatically registered the M.S.S. insignia painted on the Pontiac's door and guessed that it meant Merchants' Security Service. It was that uncomplicated, that mechanical.

The spy walked west toward Cherry Street and reached the public library there without any awareness that he was being followed. With only a glance at the bronze statue of the mounted Confederate cavalryman in front of the building, Williston entered the three-story brick library. According to the research paper, it contained 29,000 books, assorted periodicals, back files of the local paper and a head librarian who was the sister of Mayor Ashley. Unlike her brother, she was neither alcoholic nor corrupt nor an ally of murderers. But everyone – with the possible exception of Doris Day and John Lennon – has some human flaw, and Miss Geraldine Ashley's were (1) maidenhood and head at the age of fifty-one; (2) a queasy feeling that a brigade of marijuana-smoking Black Panthers, ferocious, unwashed and heavily armed with Red Chinese weapons, might well be en route from Harlem to ravish all the Caucasian virgins in Paradise City.

Being rather prim, Miss Ashley confided this concern to very few people and she certainly didn't mention it to Andrew Williston when he applied for a library card. In addition to being virginal and prim, however, she was also compulsively prying in a very genteel way.

'I see you're staying at the Jefferson, Mr Warren,' she announced with a tiny nod toward the application form. 'That's a *businessman's* hotel, isn't it?'

'I'm not exactly a businessman – more a social scientist doing research for business,' he answered.

Then he explained about the study of television and motion-picture tastes that the Southern Public Opinion Corporation had been commissioned to carry out in Paradise City and – later – four other communities, two larger and two smaller. He used terms like 'population coefficient,' 'integrated random sample,' 'audiovisual synthesis' and 'evolving leisure market in an automated society' – just as if he assumed Miss Ashley understood them.

'Our client is a major conglomerate with investments of more than ninety million dollars in the entertainment-leisure world,' he confided, 'and these studies are designed to project the post-McLuhan probabilities for a nineteen seventy-nine America with a Gross National Product at least thirty percent higher than today.'

The librarian nodded.

'I knew you'd understand,' Williston continued.

'And you chose Paradise City because—'

'Because a scientific statistical study of the last Federal census showed that this community is an ideal – that is, remarkably typical – example of American cities with populations between one hundred thousand and one hundred and fifty thousand,' the spy lied earnestly. 'We feel that we can learn a lot from this gracious community, Ma'am,' he added in his most boyish manner.

Miss Ashley beamed. Her delightful dimples showed, and for a moment Williston expected her to purr.

'It's going to be a big job,' he predicted gravely, 'and I mean to start right now by beginning to familiarize myself with the television and motion-picture programming offered here during the past year.'

'You'd find it all in the back issues of the paper,' she suggested brightly, 'and we've got a complete file right here.'

As he'd intended, Williston was soon reading through the preceding twelve months of the Paradise City daily. The newspaper carried a lot of advertising, society news, sports reporting, syndicated columns, articles lauding local commerce and industry, and wire-service accounts of riots, violence and urban problems in Northern cities. The films featured at local theaters were almost entirely trash, and nearly every picture had received a fawningly favorable review from the obliging local critic. The published television schedules indicated that the single station – which Williston's researchers had found to be independently owned by a group that included Pikelis – had achieved the near impossible by broadcasting the worst shows of all three networks. Aside from the nightly CBS news, there was practically nothing for an adult to watch.

None of this really mattered to Williston, for his main interest lay in Barringer's columns. There might be – should be – some clue or lead in what he'd written in the weeks before the murder, some hint as to why he'd been killed. Williston read every column for a month before the slaying, but noticed nothing that might provoke violent savagery from the Pikelis organization.

'I'll have to come back Monday and take detailed notes,' he told Miss Ashley when he got up to leave at 4:20.

'We open at noon on Mondays,' she responded.

It was still hot – it must have been more than ninety degrees as he stepped out into the late afternoon glare of Cherry Street – and the furtive watcher who'd been waiting for Williston to emerge was wet and irritated. But he had the calculating cool of a professional, which he demonstrated as he followed the professor-spy back to the Jefferson. Five minutes after Williston entered his room, the watcher entered a telephone booth in the Central Smoke Shop across the street. Thirty seconds later, the phone jangled in Room 407.

'You have a person-to-person call from Miami,' the hotel's switchboard operator announced.

'Okay. This is Arthur Warren. Who's calling?'

'Arthur, this is Stan Clearwater. Been trying to reach you all afternoon,' Arbolino's familiar voice boomed. 'I wanted you to know that the questionnaires are being sent to you in care of General Delivery at the Paradise City P.O.'

'Fine. Good.'

'What's the weather like up there?' the man in the booth two hundred yards away, asked.

'What you'd expect. Hot and steamy, but no worse than Miami, I imagine.'

Arbolino laughed, suggested a cold bottle of Dr Pepper and reminded the pretended poll taker to check in with the Southern Public Opinion headquarters at least once a week.

Clearwater – that was good, Williston reflected as he hung up.

Clearwater, and all afternoon.

The stunt man had been cautiously watching him all afternoon to see whether anyone else in Paradise City was following him, and Arbolino had detected no sign of surveillance. It was a standard OSS tactic that had been borrowed from the French Resistance, old but serviceable. Arbolino was exceptionally gifted in following people discreetly, the lean Vermonter recalled as he peeled off his wet shirt, but it was still disturbing that he hadn't noticed him. That was not good, not adequate.

Gilman would have noticed him.

Ever wary and focussed, Gilman would *surely* have noticed him.

'I'll have to be as careful and compulsive as Gilman,' Williston told himself as he flicked on the television set.

He certainly couldn't count on Pikelis' people being any less skillful than Arbolino in surveillance.

Picture and sound leapt at him suddenly from the metal box, and for ninety seconds the professor gave his attention to the 1949 Grade C 'Western' that WPAR–TV was offering on its Early Show. Williston felt a bit better as he realized that there were a few things in Paradise City on which he could count, after all.

He could count on uniformly terrible local TV programming.

It wasn't much but it was a beginning, and you could build from there.

CHAPTER FIFTEEN

He looked like Gindler.

The room clerk at Paradise House had the same bland face and peering eyes as *Obersturmbannfuehrer* Egon Gindler of the Third Reich's *Sicherheitspolizei*, Carstairs realized as he stepped up to the desk. An *obersturmbannfuehrer* had been a lieutenant colonel and the *Sicherheitspolizei* – SIPO for short – had been Himmler's Security Police, and Egon Gindler had been a prize bastard in that organization of prize bastards. He wasn't anymore, of course. Williston had nearly cut him in two with a sub-machine gun in the ambush right after D-Day.

'Your name isn't Gindler, by any chance?' the millionaire inquired pleasantly.

'No, sir. Hawkins. May I help you, sir?'

The resemblance was uncanny.

He even had the same thin lips and oily complexion as the late *obersturmbannfuehrer*.

'Yes indeed, Mr Hawkins, I'm sure you can help me. My name is P. T. Carstairs,' the second most eligible bachelor in the United States replied, 'and I have carelessly left a small maroon Bentley outside your front door. There are three suitcases in the trunk.'

He paused, smiled that famous smile.

'Yes, Mr Carstairs?'

'In my left hand I hold a set of car keys, Mr Hawkins. Please watch carefully, as I don't intend to repeat this trick until my next appearance on *The Ed Sullivan Show*.'

'Yes, Mr Carstairs.'

He was plainly less intelligent, duller-witted than Gindler.

'I now deposit these keys before you, draw my fine Cross ballpoint pen and prepared to autograph your registration card. Do you know why, Mr Hawkins?'

'You're checking in?' the uneasy clerk speculated.

Carstairs nodded approvingly.

'You're a sly fox,' the millionaire announced as he signed the form. Then he put away his silver-cased pen, opened his wallet and extracted a ten-dollar bill. 'I have no doubt, Mr Hawkins, that you may be trusted to give a piece of this to the keen young chap who parks my vehicle and brings in the luggage,' he continued, 'but I'm also confident that you'll carve yourself a piece as a down payment on wonderful service.'

'We pride ourselves on wonderful service, Mr Carstairs. I assume that you'd like a suite, sir. The Breckenridge Suite – bedroom, sitting room and bath – is forty-two dollars per—'

'Let's not talk money,' the millionaire suggested wryly. 'It's so grubby. Just do your thing, Mr Hawkins, and I'm sure that it will be totally peachy. I'm going to love that suite. I just know it.'

The clerk tapped a bell, sent a uniformed Negro out to the car with the keys. Then he turned, stared at Carstairs intently.

'You're that New York fellow who was on the cover of *Time*,' he accused.

The gun collector sighed.

'You got me. It's all true. I've even been in the Leonard Lyons column, although he misspelled my name,' Carstairs acknowledged. 'The jet set's friendliest sex maniac! The Thing with Twelve Bank Accounts has arrived from outer space! Hide your women and girl children!'

Uncertain whether he was being charmed or insulted, the clerk forced up a feeble grin. They'd had these New York wise guys at Paradise House before, not as rich as this one, though.

'I thought you drove a blue Maserati,' Marvin Hawkins recalled as he remembered the article.

'She's gone, traded her for a couple of rare seventeenth-century pistols and a zinc truss,' Carstairs tossed over his shoulder en route to the bar.

There was nothing impromptu about his remarks or behavior. They had worked it all out back at The Inferno. Since it was unlikely that the well-known millionaire playboy would not be recognized, Williston had argued that they should try to turn Carstairs' fame into an asset instead of a liability. After all, P. T. Carstairs was (1) socially prominent; (2) rich; (3) handsome and unwed; (4) famous for his collection of antique firearms. Any one of these factors should attract the interest of Pikelis, who was (1) socially shaky as a notorious racketeer; (2) wealthy himself, and greedy; (3) father of an unmarried daughter whom he adored; (4) an ardent gun collector who'd surely heard of Carstairs' remarkable hoard of historic weapons.

It would be out of character for the 'glamorous' millionaire to approach the ganglord, so Carstairs had to maneuver Little

Johnny Pikelis into approaching him. That was why the second most eligible bachelor in America had mentioned the seventeenth-century pistols, hoping that word would be relayed to the fellow collector who ruled Paradise City. And while he hoped, he sat in the bar drinking Pernod and water and thought about the Swedish ballerina.

'We don't get much call for Pernod here, Mr Carstairs,' the bartender observed as he put down a small bowl of salted peanuts.

'Omigod, have I committed another awful social blunder?' the worldly infiltrator gasped in mock concern. 'Have I once again offended the good, decent, simple people with my lewd and depraved tastes? If so, I apologize.'

Harry Booth's eyes flickered briefly in amusement.

'If I didn't know that you're putting me on, Mr Carstairs,' he replied casually, 'I'd say that you were putting me on.'

The blond millionaire shrugged.

'Another hideous *gaffe*,' he lamented between sips of the yellow liquid. 'You know, the truth is I only drink this stuff because I love licorice – have since I was the freckle-faced Huck Finn of Park Avenue.'

The anise-flavored liquor was strong, chilling and soothing in a way that seemed to airbrush away all the rough edges of life. Whatever one might say about General de Gaulle's anti-Americanism or bad breath, Carstairs reflected, the debt owed to the French people for supplying Pernod could never be fully repaid. Carstairs looked around the lounge at the half-dozen couples playing knees and preparing for the usual Saturday-night charm contests, realized sadly that these earnest whiskey lovers weren't even trying.

Harry Booth walked away to serve a short, sturdy man with gray eyes who had just entered.

'One for the road,' Gilman ordered without a glance at his partner.

Booth prepared the vodka Gibson quickly.

'Excellent,' the man from Las Vegas judged after the first sip. His eyes wandered around the room, narrowed when he noticed the millionaire.

'We've got a celebrity in the house,' Booth said softly.

'I've seen the face somewhere, Harry . . . Who is he, Sonny Tufts?'

'Parker Terence Carstairs, rich and hip and a famous collector of fast cars, young girls and old pistols.'

Gilman studied his friend at the other end of the bar.

'You think he dyes his hair, Harry?'

The bartender chuckled, Gilman paid his bill and departed for the Fun Parlor as Carstairs signaled for another Pernod.

'That fellow wanted to know whether you dye your hair,' Booth reported with the slightest touch of malice.

'No, but I read *Vogue* at the dentist's sometimes – and that ought to count for something,' the playboy counterpunched automatically.

'Who was that clown anyway?' he added when the second Pernod-and-water arrived a few seconds later.

'Stickman who works out at the Fun Parlor, our main center for games of chance and girls who're sure. It ain't Antibes or even Vegas, but for Paradise City it really swings.'

Carstairs sucked at the drink, put it down and removed a dark cigar from his pocket. Then he pulled out a gold cutter that some woman – was it the passionate Roman contessa? – had given him, neatly snipped out a wedge from the tip and lit the corona. After two puffs, he extracted another expensive cigar from his jacket.

'From me to you, Harry,' he said amiably, 'so we can be friends and you can tell me about the rest of your fair city. There must be more action than just the . . . the Fun Parlor. That's all right for the horny businessman, but where do the grown-ups play?'

The bartender pointed the gift cigar in his hand at the ceiling.

'Tonight they'll be playing upstairs in the penthouse,' Booth confided. 'Mr John Pikelis is flinging a thing tonight – a champagne-and-caviar party for his fair and only daughter – and all the influentials will be there. Nobody in this town would dare miss one of his parties without a note signed by a doctor, they say.'

'What do *you* say, Harry?'

'About him? Nothing. I don't carry that much insurance, and neither does anybody else in Jefferson County. All I can tell you is that he's a big tipper, a keen collector of aged arms – like yourself – and a very dedicated papa of a very pretty brunette who just returned from a year in Paris. Oh yeah, I hear that he's charitable too.'

Carstairs nodded, finished the drink.

'He sounds like a terrific talent,' the millionaire said as he got up to go. 'If only he was colored I could make him a star, a big star! Maybe with his own show – in prime time!'

The bartender shook his head. 'Please, Mr Carstairs, no jokes like that around here,' he advised. 'This isn't Easthampton or Hollywood – just a square Southern city with a limited sense of humor and an even smaller interest in changing race relations. You can tell all the dirty stories you want, but no saucy jests about the remotest possibility any Caucasian could be colored. Please don't.'

'Another terrible blunder?'

'Mr Carstairs, for the sake of your future health and my future tips – please don't.'

The millionaire winked, puffed on his cigar, paid the bar bill and asked about the food and wine served in the hotel's dining room.

'If you're looking for tournedos béarnaise and a '62 Chambertin, I couldn't guarantee either,' Harry Booth replied frankly, 'but the shrimp are good and there's a '64 Chablis that you couldn't knock. That's what they say,' he modified cautiously.

'But you're not committing yourself, right?'

'Mr Carstairs, it's going to take two men in white coats to get me committed.'

When Carstairs sat down in the hotel dining room at 7:55 p.m., he found that the service was deft, the large Gulf shrimp fresh and properly sautéed in garlic butter, and the '64 Chablis more than adequate. This was certainly a lot better than it had been living in the snowy woods all winter with the Maquis, moving often to escape Nazi troops hunting them. At the next table, a waiter was flaming some cherries for a middle-aged couple's dessert, and the gun collector abruptly recalled – no, *saw* – the attack on the German fuel truck convoy on the Route Nationale near Dijon. He saw it so clearly, even the motorcyclists and the scout car leading the convoy and the insignia of the 14th S.S. Panzer Grenadiers on the vehicles.

The first truck going up in flames when Barringer detonated the mine.

The hail of phosphorus grenades.

The cross-fire from the properly placed, correctly concealed machine guns.

The explosions and the shouting and the screaming.

The burning trucks and men.

The smoke and the smell, the panting perfect escape.

'Would you like some strawberries, sir?' the waiter beside him asked politely.

Carstairs shifted his focus and attention immediately, like some television director switching cameras.

'That will be fine,' he replied.

The berries were fine and so was the strong-winy espresso, but neither of these satisfactions quite canceled out the uncertainty as to how he'd make contact with Pikelis. Gilman had warned him that it couldn't be rushed, and the man from Las Vegas was right. Eased by this awareness, Parker Terence Carstairs lit a cigar and signaled for his bill. A moment later, the balding maître d'hotel arrived wearing the maître d's usual polyethylene smile.

'I trust that you enjoyed the dinner, Mr Carstairs?'

'Oh yes, so much so that I'll even enjoy the check.'

The maître d' shook his head, about half an inch.

'It's been taken care of . . . by Mr John Pikelis, sir,' he explained.

Bull's-eye.

'And I thought old-fashioned Southern hospitality was dead,' Carstairs announced. 'That's very nice of him. I'd really like to thank him.'

'You'll be able to, quite easily. Mr Pikelis has invited you to join him at a small party in the penthouse – here in the hotel – anytime after nine this evening.'

'It's after nine now, according to my slim gold timepiece,' the millionaire noted. Then he stood up to go.

'Black tie, of course,' the maître d'hotel added.

'Of course. I shall instantly ascend to don my rumpled tuxedo. Good meal, and your bartender was right about the '64 Chablis.'

The maître d' was plainly puzzled.

'What about the '64 Chablis, Mr Carstairs?'

'You can't knock it. Nossir, you can't knock the '64 Chablis if you've got any taste at all.'

The maître was beaming as Carstairs left, and so was the second most eligible bachelor in the United States. Carstairs' contentment continued after his return to the Breckenridge Suite on the seventh floor, for some thoughtful individuals had unpacked his bags and they'd even pressed the tuxedo. As he shaved, he made the decision – calculating just the way Gilman would have done.

Clean.

No gun.

He would not carry any weapon, not tonight.

At 9:50 p.m., a liveried black butler at the entrance to the sixty-foot living room of the eighth-floor penthouse announced, 'Mr P. T. Carstairs.' The room was buzzing with a score of conversations, but Pikelis heard. He'd been listening, waiting. He interrupted his conversation with Ben Marton and Mayor Ashley to welcome the handsome celebrity.

'I'm John Pikelis, Mr Carstairs,' the graying ganglord said.

'The man who bought the other Cookson flintlock.'

Pikelis grinned, pleased and a little surprised.

'No hard feelings, I hope?'

Carstairs' famous multimillion-dollar smile glowed.

'I may be a bit spoiled, but I'm certainly not piggy,' he answered amiably. 'No, no hard feelings at all. I admire your good taste, as well as your Southern hospitality. Thanks for an excellent dinner.'

P. T. Carstairs wasn't at all spoiled, or pompous, or even world-weary, Pikelis was cheered to discover.

'And thanks for the kind invitation to your party, Mr Pikelis,' the yellow-haired spy added.

'I couldn't do less for a fellow collector,' the racketeer replied.

Then he guided him to Marton and Ashley, who'd been watching.

'Mr Carstairs, I'd like you to meet two of our most important and efficient public officials – perhaps, no, probably our most important and efficient in Paradise City. This is Captain Marton, Chief of Police, and our distinguished mayor, Roger Stuart Ashley.'

As if in some film about the FBI, Williston's neatly typed dossiers on the two corrupt officials jumped into focus and filled Carstairs' mental screen. Actually they appeared side by side in a split-screen effect, hung there for a long moment and vanished as the millionaire reached out to shake hands with Ashley.

'An honor to meet you, Mr Mayor.'

'Welcome to Paradise City. I hope your stay will be a pleasant one,' Ashley replied.

He was a fine-looking man with an aristocratic demeanor and faintly glassy eyes that hinted at considerable drinking. Tiny lines, a few telltale ruptured blood vessels and a subtly ravaged face all confirmed what Williston's dossier had reported.

'If Mr Pikelis' hospitality is typical of the graciousness of Paradise City,' Carstairs assured, 'then my stay should be very pleasant indeed.'

Liveried waiters were circulating steadily among the fifty or sixty people in the large room, and Mayor Ashley accepted a glass of champagne from one of these servants before he replied.

'Without minimizing the friendliness of our fine citizenry, I'm afraid that nothing about Mr Pikelis is at all typical. In his generosity as in everything else, our host is an exceptional person. In determination, imagination, strength – especially strength – Mr Pikelis is unique,' Ashley explained. 'He's a born leader, a natural leader and executive.'

It was difficult to tell whether he was admiring, simply describing or discreetly sneering at the ruthless man who ruled Jefferson County.

'That makes you one of nature's gentlemen, Mr Pikelis,' Carstairs judged.

Pikelis grinned, plainly delighted by the phrase.

'I'm flattered by the mayor's compliments,' he announced, 'since I'm basically a self-made man and Roger's family is one of the oldest and finest in the state. His great-grandfather was a Confederate major, a cavalry major who lost an arm at Chancellorsville.'

It was neatly done. The way Pikelis said 'Roger' made it clear who was the master here.

Carstairs nodded, turned his attention to Marton.

'I didn't mean to be impolite, Captain. I'm pleased to meet you too – especially since I know I'm not illegally double-parked.'

The beefy police chief half smiled, extended a heavy, thick-fingered hand that was both meaty and muscular. It was oddly unpleasant to shake.

'Any guest of Mr Pikelis wouldn't break our parking regulations, at least not so's we'd notice it,' Marton assured. 'You going to be in town long?'

The spy took a glass of champagne, sipped.

'Hard to say. My plans are, as usual, somewhat indefinite.

I've been visiting some old hunting friends who have an estate in South Carolina, and I'm on my way south to Daytona to talk to a driver I may team up with for next year's race.'

Marton shrugged, almost openly indifferent to this rich stranger whom he regarded as a shallow dilettante.

'Of course I hope to stay long enough to persuade Mr Pikelis to let me see his collection,' Carstairs continued.

'That won't be difficult,' promised the ganglord. 'I don't get that many serious collectors passing through here, you know, and I love to show the weapons. My collection may not be anything as big as yours, but—'

'He's got some great old guns,' Marton interrupted. 'I don't go for those antique irons myself. I like something modern and simple and useful, like a thirty-eight Police Special.'

Carstairs sighed.

'That's a workingman's tool, not a collector's item,' he observed.

'Captain Marton is a workingman, a very hard workingman,' Pikelis confirmed with a chuckle. 'Ah, there's our guest of honor, Mr Carstairs,' he announced a moment later.

She was very pretty.

Kathy Pikelis wasn't at all dramatic or glamorous, but she was very pretty. She was a lot prettier and softer looking than she had any right to be, Carstairs thought behind his fixed mask of smile. A vicious racketeer's daughter shouldn't be that lovely, that serene, that innocent in face and eyes. The low-cut Yves St Laurent gown might have been sexually provocative on another woman, but on this one it was simply elegant. Her skin was dark – as her late mother's had been – and her eyes were large and direct, and her voice was gently furred with the soft accents of this part of the South.

They met and they spoke – of Paris and Rome and wines and the pleasures of coming home – and when the trio in the corner began to play they danced. She was graceful, quick and warm in his arms. As if that weren't enough, there was a full moon shining outrageously and Kathy Pikelis smelled subtly of jasmine.

It was all ridiculously romantic.

The scene in the basement of the 17th Street police station was much less romantic. Three patrolmen and a sergeant were systematically hurting Sam Clayton, a twenty-eight-year-old black man who drove an ice truck. They had been wanting to hurt him for several years, ever since the civil-rights organizer from New York had spent a week in Clayton's small wooden house. Now the police were shining lights in his eyes, striking him and pouring ice water over his face and doing many other cruel things that would cause pain but leave few marks. Clayton, a square-shouldered and round-faced man who didn't look the least bit like Sidney Poitier, was neither handsome nor particularly articulate. He moaned and he cursed and sometimes he screamed, because they hurt him a great deal and they wouldn't stop.

They were determined, as they explained, to compel him to confess to the murder of 'that colored girl who got all cut up over on Larabee Avenue.' Equally determined not to confess to a crime that brought the death penalty, angry at the illogic of it all and furious with the senseless agony, Sam Clayton suffered terribly. They wouldn't listen to his explanation that he'd been at the church dance during the period in which the woman had been stabbed, and they wouldn't stop hurting him.

'He's a tough mother,' one policeman said shortly before midnight when Clayton fainted for the fourth time without confessing.

'You got anything better to do tonight?' challenged the sergeant.

A number of obscene and untrue remarks followed, and then the savage and unconstitutional abuse of Sam Clayton resumed. In Room 407 at the Hotel Jefferson, a man who called himself Arthur Warren was preparing a list of 'blind drops' that he'd selected for use by the Sledgehammer team. 'Blind drops' – places where an agent left a message to be picked up by another agent – were hardly the ideal method for a *rèseau*, a network, to maintain communication. A chain of human couriers, preferably including a 'cut out' or two to prevent the entire group from being 'burned,' was certainly quicker. But when a small infiltration team was compelled to operate in hostile territory where it had no local allies and the counterespionage organizations were energetic, 'blind drops' such as hollow trees or the spaces behind loose tiles in a public toilet were often the only way. Colonel Abel of the Soviet KGB had run his New York City *apparat* with 'blind drops,' and the CIA had used them to collect Penkovsky's film in Moscow. Sledgehammer would use them too.

At the Fun Parlor on Ocean Road, Gilman was working at

a roulette wheel as he continued his discreet study of the layout, personnel and security procedures of the tastefully decorated gambling establishment. A number of tastefully decorated young women wandered in and out of a quilted green door at the rear, often with male customers in tow. No one had said it, but by now the man from Las Vegas realized there were private rooms back there. Through the large arch on the other side of the gambling room, Gilman could see the blond head of the singer working with the house quintet. The Art Phillips band was cool and adequate, but the voice of Judy Ellis was much more than that and Gilman's head bobbed in unconscious approval of the way she performed 'What the World Needs Now.' Bacharach and David would have liked what she did with their song, the stickman calculated.

Seventeen miles away at Crowden's Caravan Camp on Route 121, the stunt man sat in his trailer watching his Uher-400 record the broadcasts of the Paradise City police radio. He had reconnoitered – and photographed with infrared camera – the transmitter earlier in the evening, and now he was collecting voices and standard phrases and numbers used to designate various types of 'calls.' He had already figured out what several of the 'signals' meant; in due course he would know them all.

It was going well. On the top floor of Paradise City's finest hotel, the community's most distinguished citizens talked and laughed and drank to honor the homecoming of a notorious racketeer's daughter, and John Pikelis himself beamed at the sight of her dancing with the second most eligible bachelor in America. North America, anyway. Parker Terence Carstairs was also smiling, for Sledgehammer was developing on schedule. The fourth infiltrator had passed – undetected – through the enemy lines and was operating within the headquarters of the occupation forces.

The secret battle had been joined.

CHAPTER SIXTEEN

Sunday.

The next day was Sunday, July 12, as everyone expected.

There were very few surprises in Paradise City, an orderly community where might made right and left was something people read about in magazines and the large complacent center was both quiet and relaxed.

Sunday, traditional day of rest in the Christian world.

Insurance salesmen, physical-education teachers, dental technicians, grocery-store proprietors, switchboard operators, TV repairmen, bookkeepers, junior executives, factory workers, civil servants, bartenders, PTA leaders, whores of all prices and descriptions, ophthalmologists, proctologists and assassins such as porky Luther Hyatt all rested. The police who had been illegally and immorally hurting Sam Clayton rested too – having finally forced him to submit – and their victim slept in hopeless, ruined exhaustion.

July 12, the day that Julius Caesar and Henry David Thoreau were born – some 1917 years apart. It was a good day for rest, but the four infiltrators worked. Williston reconnoitered the areas around the police headquarters, the power plant and Pikelis' Jayland Realty offices while Gilman completed his sketches of the interior and alarm systems of the Fun Parlor. The stunt man developed and studied his photos of the police radio transmitter, and Parker Terence Carstairs awoke at noon to keep his appointment to see the racketeer's antique arms. In an Italian movie, he would have awakened beside some baby-faced nymphomaniac and said something cool as he lit his cigarette. But this wasn't an Italian movie – it wasn't even a Canadian Film Board cartoon – so he awoke alone, washed and dressed and ate a light brunch before his 2:15 arrival at the penthouse. The ganglord's daughter was just leaving to play tennis with some friends at the country club, and Carstairs decided that he'd been correct about her the night before. She was much more attractive and appealing than she had any right to be, as well as intelligent.

'Do you play tennis, Mr Carstairs?' she asked.

'A little – mostly to admire girls' legs.'

It was then that her father guided the blond millionaire to the terrace window, pointed out the club on the horizon and mentioned how good the courts were. Taking the hint, Carstairs suggested that he might drop by there later for a drink after he'd finished examining the gun collection. It was a good collection – not great – and both men enjoyed the connoisseur's talk about rare historic weapons. At four o'clock, Carstairs arrived at the club, where Kathy Pikelis was completing a doubles match with Wanda Ann Ruggles and two young lawyers. Wanda Ann, a large red-headed girl in a small tennis outfit, was the daughter of the president of the Paradise National Bank and she laughed a lot. Somebody had once told her that she had wonderful teeth, so she laughed to show them.

The two young attorneys were less jolly, for their teeth were rather ordinary and they resented the intrusion of the older and more famous stranger. One of the crew-cut lawyers invited Carstairs to play, offered to lend him shoes and a racket. It was more than an invitation; it was a challenge. The second most eligible bachelor in the United States first pleaded fatigue and then lack of practice and then age, after which he blasted the smart-ass attorney in straight sets. Not only straight sets, straight games.

'That was a *mean* thing you did to George,' Kathy Pikelis reproved softly over a drink ten minutes later.

'I'm mean – and sneaky. I don't deny it,' Carstairs acknowledged.

'I'm used to sneaky men.'

'A pretty young woman would be – or should be. Of course, I'm sneakier than most,' he warned. 'I practice sneaky thoughts and sneaky things all the time, so I'm a champ at it.'

She took a cigarette from the pack on the table, and he lit it for her deftly.

'George is quite a good tennis player, you know,' she scolded.

'In my distant youth – back when covered wagons and DC-3s crossed the great plains — I was fortunate enough to be intercollegiate tennis champion,' he confessed. 'Yes, I was spry and dashing and I was widely hailed – nay, acclaimed – as the best goddam college tennis player in the nation.'

She shook her head.

'Poor George,' she sighed.

'I still play once or twice a week to remind me of my boyhood glory,' the sportsman continued.

'You didn't say that you were a champ.'

'I told you I was sneaky – and that hostile youth deserved it anyway,' Carstairs replied glibly. Then he told her a lot of other charming things – quite easily and almost automatically – before they had another drink and he brought her home to the penthouse. That evening, he meticulously examined the Breckenridge Suite and discovered two hidden listening devices – one in the phone and the other in the lamp beside the bed. It was reassuring to know that somebody cared, he reflected as he wondered when and how Williston would deliver the list of 'blind drops.' The radio schedule of times and frequencies had been established and memorized before any of them had left The Inferno, and the standard rules on duration of transmission – fifty seconds – were in force. At 11:51, the second most eligible bachelor in the United States put a blanket over his telephone and unplugged the lamp before carrying his radio into the bathroom and closing the door. Then he turned on the hot and cold taps in the tub.

At 11:52, he flicked on the receiver and tuned it to the first of the five pre-agreed frequencies. He glanced down at the face of his gold Rolex, watched the sweep second hand move steadily past the '4' toward the '5.' As it hit the '6' – precisely at 11:52 and a half, or 23:52:30 if you preferred military time – he heard the stunt man's voice.

'Tampa tower, Tampa tower . . . would you please repeat runway number and landing instructions? Runway Four is clear, right?'

That was it.

Arbolino was reporting that he, Gilman and Williston had arrived and that he presumed the fourth agent – P. T. Carstairs – was also in position.

'This is Tampa tower,' the millionaire heard Gilman reply. 'Yes, Runway Four is clear. Descend to two thousand for downwind leg.'

Total elapsed time on the air: eighteen seconds.

Much too short a conversation for anyone to record or 'fix' with radio-location gear.

Gilman had confirmed that the gun collector was in the hotel, had made contact with Pikelis. Operating from the same hotel, the man from Las Vegas would have to serve as Carstairs' line of communication with the others. The radio telephone in the Bentley was only for emergency use, they had agreed. They had also decided to strike only after thorough on-the-spot 'eyeball' reconnaissance of the area and the occupation-forces defenses.

On Monday, Williston went to work in his role of public-opinion scholar and started his interviews. He began with the genial gross 'critic' who treated television, motion pictures and local 'community theater' and 'classical ballet' for the Paradise City *Trumpet*. He discovered that Frederick U. Kimberley, a large, pretentious man whose cloying after-shave cologne suggested that most of his friends were unfrocked Boy Scout leaders, didn't really care for any of the films or shows that he regularly praised in print but saw no harm in lying. By giving the editor and the advertising department what they wanted, he observed primly, he got what he wanted – a weekly check and an annual trip to New York to report on the theatrical and musical 'scene' and gorge himself in some of those chic French restaurants.

'Of course, I'm busy with my own writing too – my *creative* writing,' he concluded.

'A play, I'll bet?'

Frederick U. Kimberley smirked gratefully.

'Nothing commercial, you understand,' he admonished as he nodded. 'A one-act work – rather avant-garde by *popular* standards – set in the Queen's toilet in Buckingham Palace on the eve of an atomic war. I hope that I don't sound *hideously* presumptuous, but it does have an Ionesco quality – a tone.'

Williston managed to guide the conversation back to entertainment needs and tastes in Paradise City, completed his notes and then left to rent a car. He drove the blue Dart to the post office, mailed the two envelopes and picked up the package of questionnaires sent by the Southern Public Opinion Corporation. Then he telephoned the program director of WPAR–TV, who was so delighted to find a social scientist who respected TV that he invited the spy to lunch at the Country Club. Williston was starting his dessert when Carstairs arrived there for his sailing date with Kathy Pikelis. At the trailer camp, Arbolino sipped cold beer as he monitored the Paradise City police radio to determine the pattern of patrol-car movements and schedules. Late in the afternoon, the stunt man locked his trailer, unhooked the panel truck and set out to scout the area for possible safe places to rendezvous.

That night he broadcast – in simple code – the map

coordinates for three rendezvous points designated 'Bob,' 'Mort' and 'Jo-Jo.' It was the elementary plus-two code, with spots that were located at the intersection of B and 3 on the Chamber of Commerce map of the county to be described as D-5. On another broadcast that same evening – the regular 11 p.m. news on the local radio station – the arrest and confession of Sam Clayton were finally reported. The announcement was brief and routine, reflecting the news director's attitude that 'another colored stabbing' was hardly significant. In fact, it had little meaning except to Reverend Ezra Snell, at whose church dance Clayton had been during the time of the murder, Clayton's relatives and a young woman named Shirleyrose, who'd been with the accused from 9 p.m. until noon the next day. Neither the minister nor Shirleyrose knew exactly what to do, each being aware of what the local police might do to people who 'made trouble.'

In varying degrees, just about everyone in Paradise City was afraid of offending the Pikelis organization. It wasn't only the police who frightened people, Arbolino, Williston and Gilman concluded when they met at 'Jo-Jo' – the rendezvous point near the quarry on Route 99 – late on Wednesday night. The thugs employed as collectors by the Merchants' Security Service and other corporate fronts were dreaded even more, Williston and Gilman had learned, had overheard and pieced together from a hundred snatches of conversation. They made their plan for the first operation, and half an hour later – just before 4 a.m. – Gilman relayed the scheme to P. T. Carstairs. Using an infrared beamer whose signals were invisible to the naked eye, he flashed the message onto the wall of the office building across the street from the Paradise House. Wearing the special goggles that looked like standard racing-driver gear, the rich gun collector had no difficulty 'reading' the Morse message.

Thursday: reconnaissance.

Friday: a test run.

Saturday afternoon: the first blow against the Occupation Forces.

At 5:20 p.m. on Saturday, Luther Hyatt entered the lobby of the office building at 129 Fletcher Avenue and took the elevator to the fourth floor. He was the last of three collectors to deliver money to the suite occupied by the Merchants' Security Service. This was a fact; it was seen by trained observers and it fit the pattern of the previous days. In a few minutes, the M.S.S. bookkeeper would close the venetian blinds. The stunt man watching from the panel truck across the street could almost hear Williston's briefing again.

'Nearly immediately after he closes the blinds, he completes the count and gives the money to the fat one . . . two minutes, maybe three. Then the fat man takes the elevator down and drops the cash into the night depository chute at the Paradise Commercial Bank across the street. We won't have much time for this, so as soon as those blinds go you hit the horn twice – long and short. Then you move into position at the loading area in the back alley.'

Arbolino glanced up, puffed on his cigarette and then turned toward the doorway of a nearby shoe store as if he were waiting for someone inside. The streets were crowded with Saturday shoppers and traffic was steady if not heavy. This operation would have to go exactly right, because there couldn't be any quick escape in this traffic.

The blind closed.

He pushed the horn twice, started the truck a moment later.

In Suite 402, a small fussy man in gold-rimmed bifocals meticulously proceeded with his ritual addition. It was almost a religious ceremony, as his solemn voice communicated.

'5,210 . . . 5,230 . . . 5,250 . . . 5,260 . . . 270. Good, it's all here.'

'It's always all here,' the assassin pointed out while he shook his head in exasperation.

Ignoring this irrelevance, the bookkeeper proceeded to make out the bank deposit slips and place them in the two prepared envelopes with the cash. Then he handed the envelopes and the key to the bank's night chute to the fat man.

'Thank you, Beasley,' the assassin said sarcastically.

'You're quite welcome, Luther.'

Hyatt walked out into the corridor, stuffing the envelopes into the pockets of his seersucker jacket as he moved toward the elevator. Inside the elevator, Associate Professor Andrew T. Williston waited. Two minutes earlier, Gilman had taken up his 'covering position' in the fourth-floor service hall and the teacher had stopped the elevator at the fourth floor by simply throwing the emergency cut-off switch. The man from Las Vegas would be watching, holding the door to the stairway half an inch ajar.

Hyatt pressed the elevator button, and the door opened almost immediately. The brief interval reflected the seconds it took Williston to flick the 'on' switch.

As the door opened, Luther Hyatt got a terribly short glimpse of somebody in coveralls and some sort of hat or cap.

Then he got something else – in the face.

Williston raised the can of Mace, aimed for his enemy's eyes and nose.

A four-second burst, and then a three-second squirt to make sure.

The results were exactly as the manufacturer had promised, precisely those seen on television news broadcasts. Hyatt's hands went to his eyes, which felt as if they were on fire, and when he tried to scream because of the pain he found that his throat was all knotted and his chest hurt and he could barely breath. It was awful. He staggered, stumbled and gasped helplessly. He couldn't see anyone or anything.

He slumped against the wall, barely conscious. Gilman hurried up behind him with the hypodermic needle in his hand, and as soon as Williston closed the door the man from Las Vegas pumped the drug into Luther Hyatt's bulging left wrist.

'*Bien fait*,' the assassin heard somebody say a hundred miles away.

He was unconscious by the time they loaded him into the truck. Arbolino had backed it right up against the building's freight and garbage loading door, so no one passing by on the street twenty yards away saw the body. At 5:28, Arbolino guided the vehicle out into the Fletcher Avenue traffic, and Gilman – in the rear compartment with Williston and the prisoner – automatically looked at the luminous face of his watch.

One minute late.

Not bad.

Not good, but not bad for a first operation after all these years.

At 10:50 that evening, Mr John Pikelis, his daughter and the second most eligible bachelor in the United States were proceeding along Central Avenue graciously – in Mr Pikelis' 1970 Cadillac, with driver and stereo – en route to the Fun Parlor. The visitor had expressed some interest in trying his luck 'for a few quid,' and the host was curious as to how P. T. Carstairs would behave in a gambling house. Sometimes you could learn surprising things about men – especially controlled men such as Carstairs – by how they acted and reacted in a casino.

The car slowed, stopped.

A large crowd of people – obviously emerging from the last show at the Central Movie Theater fifty yards away – stood in front of the windows of the Herman Brothers department store. There were so many people that they overflowed the sidewalk out into the street itself, and most of them were giggling. A few were simply gaping or shaking their heads, but the majority were grinning or chuckling.

'What's going on, Tom?' Pikelis demanded.

Before the chauffeur could reply, the siren of an approaching radio patrol car sounded and the crowd started to disperse immediately. By the time the police car arrived, half of the spectators had moved on as if they didn't wish to be associated with or blamed for whatever was in the window.

'Drive up close, Tom. Let's see what this is all about,' ordered the racketeer.

The sound of another police siren – not too far away – cut the night as the Cadillac rolled forward to within a dozen yards of the window. Pikelis took one look, blinked.

'Closer.'

The limousine stopped directly in front of the display that had been attracting so much attention.

It was, to be fair, a rather unusual display that would have attracted attention in any department-store window anywhere. Even the elaborate Christmas extravaganzas staged by Neiman-Marcus couldn't touch this for sheer novelty, simplicity and directness of message. Luther Hyatt was sitting in a rocker in the middle of the window. He was naked, unconscious. His hands were tied together and his feet were tied together, and some wag had placed a curly red wig – slightly askew – atop his large head. His genitalia were also covered, by a heap of crumpled U.S. currency, and a few odd bills peeped out from between his toes and the fringe of the ridiculous wig. In case the intended message wasn't entirely clear, somebody had printed it – in lipstick – on Hyatt's chest.

Doyle, Dane, Bernbach would have loved the whole idea, for that creative New York agency made its name on visually arresting ads with short, punchy copy.

This was certainly lively in visual terms, and the copy couldn't have been much shorter.

It was, in fact, only two words.

Clean, simple, zingy.

Two words – in large print.

DON'T PAY.

CHAPTER SEVENTEEN

Graffiti – that's what it was.

It wasn't scrawled on any lavatory wall and didn't include any of those historic Anglo-Saxon sex words that are now being used so heroically by young revolutionaries in their war against materialism, soulless conformity, racism, imperialism, the meddling *fascisti* of the post-thirty generation and the sadists who run all educational institutions and drugstores.

The two words may not have been offensive in Chicago or Los Angeles or London, but in Paradise City they were plainly obscene. If not legally obscene, they were certainly indecent and calculated to incite a breach of the public peace and order. Therefore it was surprising that the impact of this subversive phrase wasn't reflected on the faces of either the two policemen or the people in the limousine. The officers who'd stepped from the radio car looked vaguely embarrassed, slightly guilty, as if they'd dropped a touchdown pass and let the home team down. Pikelis' driver took one glance, then stared away. The racketeer's daughter studied the bizarre sight thoughtfully and calmly, seemingly unaware that it had any relevance to her father or her life. As for John Pikelis, his eyes were a bit wider and colder than usual, but his big face was empty of any emotion. He was showing no concern, no rage, no reaction at all.

Careful, Carstairs thought.

He's being cool and careful, and I've got to follow that same line.

'What's it all about?' the handsome spy asked.

Pikelis shrugged.

'Hard to say,' he answered.

'Practical joke? College kid stunt?' the visitor tested.

'I doubt it.'

The second police car arrived, and Ben Marton stepped out to survey the scene. After one quick look at the window, he said something to the men from the first radio car and they separated. One officer hurried around the corner – presumably to the store's rear entrance where a watchman might be found

– and the other patrolman strode purposefully toward the front door where he searched for a night emergency bell.

Marton recognized the limousine, walked over to confer.

Pikelis pressed the button that opened the rear window of the air-conditioned Cadillac, spoke first.

'Mr Carstairs – excuse me, Petie – was just asking what this is all about,' the ganglord announced blandly. 'You got any ideas, Captain?'

'Nothing definite, but I'm going to give it a real good look and a real deep think,' Marton promised.

'If this is some sort of consumer protest about the store's high prices,' the spy mused, 'it certainly is dramatic.'

'It's bizarre,' agreed the girl beside him, 'like something out of an avant-garde film.'

Marton shook his head.

'Our consumers aren't that crazy,' he judged. 'This is weird, real weird. It's like some hippie stunt, but no bunch of smart-ass kids could do that to Luther.'

'Luther?' asked Carstairs.

'The man in the window. He's an ex-policeman, no push-over. I dunno.'

At that moment, one of the uniformed men from the patrol car stepped into the rear of the display window from inside the store and began to untie unconscious Luther Hyatt.

'I'm curious about this whole thing, Ben,' Pikelis announced, 'so let me know when you find out who did it – and why.'

Then he pressed the button that closed the Cadillac's right rear window, abruptly terminating the conversation as his totalitarian power permitted him to do. The police had been given their orders, and John Pikelis had no intention of wasting the rest of his Saturday night on this matter. Equally important, he certainly wasn't going to risk exposing his relationship with the Merchants' Security Service to either his daughter or the second most eligible bachelor in the United States. With both these considerations in mind, the racketeer who dominated Jefferson County steered the talk to the Fun Parlor until they arrived there.

As the car swung into the driveway off the main road, the yellow-haired spy automatically scanned the defenses. There was a high stone wall, about eight or nine feet, topped by three strands of naked wire that were probably electrified. There was one guard in the gate house – the window looked thick, possibly bullet-proof glass – and he controlled the heavy metal barrier. Inside, the Fun Parlor itself was set back about 150 yards. Surrounded by pleasantly landscaped lawn and shrubbery and flanked by a large parking lot, the windowless two-story structure resembled a reasonably tasteful bowling alley.

From the outside.

Inside, it was quite another matter.

Elaborate crystal chandeliers, red velvet drapes and deep wall-to-wall carpeting in a dramatic shade of royal blue.

The eyes of the hat-check girl were also blue, and her imposing wig was precisely the same shade of crimson as the drapes. Her skin was a pale powdered ivory, and a large amount of it was showing in the low-cut blue costume. She had a lovely smile, a fondness for stray kittens and instant affection for gentlemen who were generous. She never asked questions, and she was extremely popular.

Willie Dennison, manager of the Fun Parlor, could have explained all this to Carstairs but he was much too busy welcoming Pikelis. It wasn't every night that the man who owned the man who technically owned the Fun Parlor – indeed, the proprietor of the entire county – dropped in to visit. Thin mustachioed Willie Dennison had a great respect for Mr Pikelis, not only because Pikelis had given him this $40,000-a-year job but also because of the executive efficiency and unobtrusive grace – no, *style* – with which he ruled the county. Like the ex-German rocket scientists in Huntsville or the advertising agencies that can cheerfully handle political campaigns for either party, Mr Pikelis was a professional and Willie Dennison – as another professional – respected his competence.

And his tailor.

As he often said.

'Good evening, Mr Pikelis,' he welcomed sincerely. 'And Miss Kathy, it's a delight to see you. Welcome home.'

She smiled – very well – and thanked him.

'You're looking so well, Miss Kathy,' Dennison pressed on. 'So rosy and pretty – you must have enjoyed Europe a great deal.'

'Well, I've had a pretty good time since I returned to Paradise City, too,' she answered.

There was that light in her eyes – that woman light – and the casino manager intuitively guessed that it had something to do with the yellow-haired stranger who stood so close to her. Dennison's glance flickered to the man's familiar face for a moment, and then Pikelis introduced him.

'This is Mr P. T. Carstairs, a visitor to Paradise City and, I hope, a friendly one. I'd like you to treat Mr Carstairs as my personal guest, Willie.'

'Of course. It's a pleasure to meet you, Mr Carstairs. Won't you all come in?'

Dennison knew who Carstairs was, and he knew what it meant when Kathy Pikelis glowed as the handsome celebrity took her arm. Pikelis nodded slightly in paternal approval, pleased that his daughter and the socialite bachelor were getting along so well. Not being a member of the Sicilian-Neapolitan underworld federation that dominated organized crime, he was in no position to marry his daughter off to the son of some *capo mafioso* who controlled 'the family' in Detroit or Boston. Not even if he wanted to – which he didn't. No, John Pikelis' daughter would wed somebody important and legitimate – in a cathedral – and it would be in all the papers all over the country.

It was, of course, premature to think that seriously about P. T. Carstairs.

And it would certainly be immature to discuss this possibility with anyone, so Pikelis quickly protected himself from any such slip by asking the gambling-house manager about the state of business. Aware that Little John Pikelis was informed each week – to the penny – exactly what Fun Parlor income and profits were, Dennison blandly acknowledged that everything was 'going nicely' and complimented Mr Pikelis on his splendid new suit.

'Why, thanks, Willie,' the ganglord answered. 'Remind me to give you my tailor's name and address in New York.'

Dennison smiled appreciatively, conscious that Pikelis would never do so because it simply wasn't appropriate for an employee – even a senior and well-paid employee – to wear the same clothes as the man who ruled Jefferson County. Committed to the appropriate, Dennison continued the pretense and guided these extremely important guests into the 'lounge,' where some thirty couples were dancing.

'She's good,' Carstairs judged as he listened to the blonde singer on the bandstand celebrate a Harold Arlen blues.

'As a performer, of course,' he added as if to reassure Kathy Pikelis.

'Of course,' she agreed wryly while she studied the pretty, vital woman who sang so well.

'A large talent,' Carstairs teased.

'All over,' Kathy Pikelis concurred.

The blonde was big, big-boned and big-voiced and big in the chest, as the bare shouldered dress revealed. She wasn't fat – not even plump – but she had a size and solidity that came through in her strong, sure voice. Judy Ellis was twenty-seven or maybe twenty-eight, the knowledgeable bachelor calculated instantly, and the way she moved her body – subtly and sensually without the slightest trace of vulgarity – told that she was a woman and she enjoyed it. As Dennison seated Pikelis and his guests, the blues ended and the band leader smiled, paused about four beats, and sent sextet and vocalist swiftly into the Beatles' bouncy 'We Can Work It Out.' Like the best of the professional football players, she had an effective change of pace and all the moves. She seemed almost too good for a gambling club in Paradise City.

'Has she been here long, Mr Dennison?' Kathy Pikelis asked.

'About five months. She came with the band. They're very popular.'

'I can see why,' John Pikelis judged.

They ordered drinks, and then Carstairs danced with Kathy Pikelis again and he stopped thinking about Judy Ellis or any other women. The ganglord was still talking with Dennison ten minutes later when they returned to the table, but the casino manager excused himself immediately and Pikelis suggested that they now adjourn to the gambling room.

'You've probably heard about the sin in our city,' he announced with an amused smile as they strolled past the two sturdy young men – plainly security – who flanked the swinging doors to the casino area, 'and here's your chance to see how wicked Paradise City really is.'

'Sin has always been one of my most favorite things,' Carstairs answered. 'Sin and pretty girls.'

'I'll bet,' commented the pretty girl beside him.

'Do you mind, Kathy?'

'I haven't minded that since I was sixteen,' she whispered mischievously as her father led the way.

'You're the most attractive girl here, you know.'

'And you're the most clean-cut dirty old man I know,' she replied pleasantly.

'You're mad about me, right?'

'Hopelessly. It's your shyness that gets me,' she jested.

'Don't forget my sincerity.'

'No, I'll never forget your incredible sincerity. That's what's so sneaky about you – you don't lie,' she explained. 'Girls aren't used to that sort of thing. It isn't really fair, Petie.'

He squeezed her left hand, raised it to his lips for brief connection.

'I never said I was fair – just honest,' he answered. 'I'm the most honest, clean-cut, dirty old man in the world. And the youngest.'

Now they were in the gambling room, and it was much like a dozen others that the millionaire sportsman had seen around the world. It was more attractive than the ones in the Hilton in San Juan but not nearly so elegant as the one he'd visited in Biarritz. The red velvet drapes lent a certain European plushness to the decor, but the miniskirted waitresses circulating with drinks were much more Vegas than Versailles. It was a large room with two roulette wheels, three dice tables and three others where men were playing cards. Carstairs' eyes wandered thoughtfully around the scene, up the walls to the ceiling for a long moment and then back to the tables.

There were no gun ports in the ceiling, so far as he could tell.

Gilman would know for sure, of course.

There he was, Samuel Stanley Gordon Gilman – coolest man in this air-conditioned chamber. He was working the number-two roulette table, calm and efficient and pleasant and doing everything right. He would know about the entire security system and how the gambling casino operated, what the 'house' brand of Scotch was, where the air-conditioning ducts were and which of the $50-an-hour women was considered the best value. By now, his orderly mind would have recorded all these details and many others – analyzed, cross-indexed and filed them for instant retrieval. He was as good with facts and numbers as Carstairs was with guns and women, the celebrated sportsman reflected.

Kathy Pikelis saw her escort looking at the croupier, wondered.

'You know him, Petie?'

'No, but I think he's the sly fellow who asked the bartender at the hotel whether I dye my hair.'

'Do you?'

'I don't even shave under my arms,' Carstairs replied truthfully as he started toward one of the card tables.

'No roulette?' Pikelis inquired.

'A mug's game, sir. Too purely mathematical for a fun-loving and thrill-seeking lad such as myself,' the bachelor explained. 'A recreation for scientists and stock brokers.'

'Not adventurous enough?'

'That's it, John. No adventure and no romance.'

'Are you a romantic, Mr Carstairs?' fenced the racketeer's smiling daughter.

'What? Oh, I thought you knew that. Don't tell me that you really believed I was just another fortune hunter after the fabulous Pikelis pearls?'

For a moment the racketeer was puzzled by the reference to the nonexistent jewels, but then he nodded.

'No, no, Kathy,' Carstairs continued, 'it is you and your pure girlish beau-ty that fascinate me, that send my senses reeling.'

'I'd say that you were probably intoxicated by your own charm, *cher ami*.'

'Cruel, cruel woman,' he grumbled as they reached the dice tables.

'This your game?' tested Pikelis.

His daughter instantly shook her head.

'No, Dad, that wouldn't be for Petie. Too vulgar, right?'

The spy grinned.

'Definitely lower-class.'

'And lacking any solid challenge for a man dedicated to skill and control in his adventure? Too chancy, right?'

Carstairs raised her hand again, kissed it reverently.

'Yes, my dear. You understand me so well,' he confessed.

'You aren't really a gambler at all, Petie?' she accused.

He sighed.

'I have no silly compulsion to lose my money, if that's what you mean, Kathy. I'd rather make money. Your father understands that, I think.'

Pikelis nodded.

'So it's cards?'

'Yes, John. I'll try a few hands. Will you join me?'

They sat down at the nearby '21' table, and the dealer hesitated uneasily for a moment before he pointed out that they had no chips. Carstairs extracted ten $50 bills from his wallet, glanced at the ganglord. Pikelis coolly added five $100 bills to the heap, and some ninety seconds later they had chips and the game began. Pikelis watched guardedly, and Carstairs played boldly. Boldly but intelligently, the racketeer observed. In forty minutes, the wealthy bachelor was $370 richer.

'So twenty-one is your game?' Pikelis speculated as a pretty waitress – she was about fifteen pounds overweight but in the right places – set down the drinks they'd ordered.

'Not really. I prefer poker.'

'He would,' the girl standing behind him said. She was near and warm and smelled subtly of promise. 'Of course, he would. Poker is a more combative game, isn't it, Petie?'

'I have no secrets from you, honey,' the second most eligible bachelor in the United States replied.

Her perfume was marvelous, and her body heat seemed to magnify its effect.

'I like poker myself,' announced the graying racketeer in carefully measured tones.

He finished the Scotch, looked his question.

'Why not?' Carstairs replied affably.

The two men rose, collected their chips and started to the next table where the poker contest was in full swing. By the end of the third hand, Pikelis realized how correct his daughter's judgment had been. Carstairs played poker the way he stalked tigers in the Burmese jungles – totally, craftily and ruthlessly. It was a kind of war all right, and the handsome millionaire obviously enjoyed it immensely. It was a very special sort of war, very personal – a duel. It wasn't that Carstairs was out to get Pikelis in particular; he meant to defeat them all – every player at the table. He meant to win. Pleasantly but totally, he was committed to conquest. He joked, he smiled, he bluffed, he tested, he calculated – and he won. He won three out of every four hands, sometimes with daring and sometimes with cunning but always with a cool grace.

Pikelis studied him, trying to figure out the man and his game.

Both were effective, tough, admirable and difficult to define.

'You play like a professional, Petie,' the racketeer announced in a voice of guarded compliment.

'I like to think of myself as the most professional of the amateurs, John,' Carstairs answered.

'In everything,' judged Kathy Pikelis.

'Is that a proposition or a put-down?'

She hesitated a moment before replying.

'That's just a woman's intuition. I'm really saying the same thing as Daddy, you know. You play to win.'

The second most eligible bachelor in the U.S.A. managed to nod, shrug and smile simultaneously.

'I need the money,' he fenced, 'and I enjoy the action.'

John Pikelis shook his head.

'*Everybody* in this room likes the action and the risks and the feeling of importance that a man can get when he lets people know that he can afford to gamble,' the practical old ganglord disagreed. 'And I saw a doctor on a TV show once – couple of years ago – who said that many guys who gamble are so mixed up they want to lose. But you're like me, Petie. You want to win, and that's normal for a man.'

The ganglord liked him.

That was promising.

'See, I told you I'm a normal man,' Carstairs chided the girl. 'You're right, John,' he continued as he turned to her father. 'I only play the games I like – the games I'm good at – and I play to win. You play pretty damn good poker yourself.'

It was true. Carstairs was ahead some $3,100, but Pikelis also had more chips – perhaps $500 or $600 more – than he'd bought at the start of the game. In addition, the racketeer had some further ideas about this yellow-haired stranger who was – ever so gracefully – wooing his daughter. Petie wasn't spoiled, soft, smug or simple or any of those other things that the magazine writers and gossip columnists had indicated. Polished and smooth and strong – like stainless steel, that was P. T. Carstairs.

Some people, some men, some fathers might have found that combination disturbing.

John Pikelis didn't.

He found it interesting, perhaps admirable.

He wasn't sure yet.

There was something – not exactly criminal but very clearly outside the normal rules of society – in P. T. Carstairs. It wasn't just the arrogance of wealth and influence; it was something more – and more difficult to define.

'One more hand?' the racketeer suggested.

The other players nodded. The handsome celebrity shrugged again, played smiling again and won again. He was now $4,300 ahead and bored. He glanced at his watch, realized that Arbolino and Williston might not be finished yet back at the hotel.

'I suppose that it would be lousy manners to walk out on the game when I've got so much of your money, gentlemen,' the tough, smiling bachelor announced casually, 'so I'd better give you demon gamblers a chance to get even.'

The losers beamed.

Carstairs had style and manners as well as money, Pikelis approved as he signaled the dealer to resume the play. Kathy Pikelis arched her eyebrows, wandered away to the roulette table to watch the action there. She couldn't help but notice the stickman's cool expertise and subtly superior patter. Gilman smiled at her pleasantly, approvingly and the least bit distantly. He was a professional all right, keeping her at arm's length as a sensible stickman should do with a patron, especially a pretty woman. She guessed that he was somebody new from some other place, but she knew nothing more than his speech and poise communicated. He knew a lot about her from the dossier that Williston's R and A team had provided, but he focussed on the role of playing the perfect croupier and he played it perfectly. Only infrequently did he permit his mind to wander to Arbolino and Williston, and when he thought about it he wasn't really worried. After all, the 'recon' and the gear and the plan were all carefully integrated, selected, right for the operation.

It wasn't *that* complex or dangerous an operation, nothing comparable to the assault on the 5th Panzer Army's main fuel dump or the assassination of Colonel Detzler by rigging his desk lamp with a bomb that looked exactly like a light bulb. It was cool – almost too cool – in the gambling room, Gilman noticed as he raked in some chips, but he was too busy to ask anyone to adjust the air-conditioning.

It was much warmer in the alley behind the Paradise House. As a matter of fact, both Williston and Arbolino were sweating in the white cotton coveralls. Each man carried a tool box marked ACE EIEVATOR in his right hand and a silenced .32

pistol in a sling under his left arm. As they entered the rear of the hotel, a black man in a waiter's uniform – obviously sneaking a quick smoke between duties in the cocktail lounge – looked up and smiled from the doorway.

'Freight elevator?' the professor asked in an accent as Southern as he could counterfeit.

'That way. Left at the end of the corridor.'

The black man didn't ask whether anything was wrong with the elevator. Negroes weren't encouraged to ask questions in this town, and it wasn't any of his business anyway. The spies followed his directions, found the freight elevator and ran it to the top floor. Then they found the steps leading to the roof, not the area that was occupied by the Pikelis penthouse but the rear corner where the bulk of the building's massive air-conditioning plant thrust its functional tower into the sky. The man who ruled Jefferson County would have preferred to have his suite at the highest point – the top – but Pikelis had grudgingly accepted the economic realities with the proviso that his quarters be screened from and isolated from the big cooling machine. Dozens of potted plants and shrubs had been aligned to comprise a solid green wall some seven feet high to separate the penthouse and its terrace from the air-conditioning gear.

Williston and Arbolino knew this, having studied the photostats of the building plans and the newspaper clipping about the opening of the hotel and the aerial photographs that P. T. Carstairs' money had persuaded a certain Jacksonville charter pilot to take for a certain nonexistent advertising agency's imaginary brochure. The Columbia professor and the stunt man had also listened to Gilman's own scouting reports on the building, so they had no hesitation in heading directly for the door marked 'AIR CONDITIONER – ROOF.'

'Alarm,' Williston reminded.

Arbolino nodded, found the alarm device exactly where Gilman had described it and then carefully disconnected it. The door opened easily. As they stepped out onto the roof, Williston rechecked the luminous dial of his wrist watch again. The man from Las Vegas had calculated that the operation should require between four and a half and six minutes, seven at the outside. If they stayed more than eight, they were probably in trouble and if it took ten minutes or more the odds were that they'd have to fight or shoot their way out of the penthouse. The penthouse surely had guards outside in the foyer – at the door of the private elevator – and there could be other armed men or perhaps servants inside as well.

The stunt man pointed to the metal steps running up the side of the tower, opened his tool kit and took out a nylon ladder with hooks at either end. He climbed a dozen rungs up the side of the tower, attached the hooks securely to the metal step and then swung himself out and over the wall of shrubbery. He dropped lightly and – quite mechanically, like some veteran trapeze artist – swung the nylon ladder back up to where Professor Andrew F. Williston of Columbia University was waiting on the side of the tower to catch it.

Williston repeated the process, studied the green walls warily until he found the barbed wire concealed so neatly and hooked the end of the nylon ladder to a branch that was free of electrical alarms or other hazards.

They were on the terrace.

So far, so good.

Elapsed time from leaving the freight elevator: one minute and fifty seconds.

The two invaders slipped on the special goggles, flicked on the infrared 'pen lights' and moved warily toward the French doors that led into the penthouse itself. A brief examination revealed no alarms, so Williston turned the knob and the two men entered. It was the living room, as big and grand as Carstairs had described. The furniture was all where he'd said it would be, the three couches, the grand piano and the enormous marble coffee table. Williston would have expected John Pikelis to have one of those chic glass-and-chrome tables, and for a second he wondered.

Then he heard the sound.

Both of the spies dived for cover, one behind a couch and the other in a gracious fall of drapery near the window. The door opened. One of the liveried Negro servants entered, looked around for a moment before strolling to the bar and pouring himself three fingers of John Pikelis' best cognac.

In a paper cup.

He had brought his own paper cup; he'd leave no traces.

He sipped the Remy Martin V.S.O.P. appreciatively, crushed the cup and put it in his pocket. He smiled. It wasn't the smile of a thief or the smile of a bitter servant or even the smile of a sly Uncle Tom. It was the open look of a man who recognized and enjoyed fine brandy, whose conscience was as pure as his taste. At the door, he hesitated and stopped by an end table to move an ashtray – it might have been an inch out of place – before departing.

There was probably a lot of social or psychological significance in what they'd just seen, the professor thought wryly, but it had cost them nearly two minutes. One minute and forty-two seconds to be precise, and that time was more important than any possible implications of the act. There was only one thing that mattered anyway – the mission. It was just like The Old Days.

The mission was simple. The equipment that it involved was complex and sophisticated, but the mission itself was simple. They were going to plant two subminiature electronic devices in this penthouse so that they could listen to what Pikelis and his associates said. Ordinary 'bugs' – the standard little FM transmitters – wouldn't do. If the racketeer had his quarters periodically 'swept' by technicians equipped with gear to detect FM transmitters, such broadcasting devices would be found. No, Gilman had secured something much newer and more ingenious – equipment that listened and relayed sound on command and without broadcasting. It was called the infinity transmitter. It was small, fantastic.

Williston pointed to Pikelis' office, and as Arbolino started in that direction the professor turned toward the racketeer's bedroom. There was an unlisted direct-line telephone in each, and in each of those instruments they would place a tiny infinity transmitter. Moving silently in rubber-soled sneakers, the professor entered the bedroom and swept his 'black light' around until he found the telephone.

He unscrewed the mouthpiece, inserted the tiny device and screwed the mouthpiece back into place. As he returned to the living room, Arbolino flashed a thumbs-up signal from the opposite doorway and pointed to his watch. Both infinity transmitters were in place, and the spies had more than a minute left for escape according to Gilman's timetable.

Of course, the timetable for the operation had not – indeed, could not have – provided for *all* eventualities. It had been based on the known, the logical, the predictable. Actually, the intruders had only about thirty-four seconds left to depart without being detected. Despite Carstairs' delaying efforts, Kathy Pikelis had pried him from the gambling tables and ever so sweetly – subtly promisingly – persuaded him to bring her home. They had just emerged from the big limousine in front of the Paradise House, were moving arm in arm through the lobby toward the private elevator to the penthouse. Williston and Arbolino had no way of knowing this, of course.

Not until they heard the elevator door open and Carstairs laugh.

Loud and clear and charming, it was meant to alert them.

It succeeded.

They hurried to the terrace, carefully locked the door behind them and sprinted for the nylon ladder. Time – it was a question of seconds now. They had to move swiftly, and it was up to P. T. Carstairs to do what he could to buy them extra moments. As soon as the door to the penthouse foyer closed behind them, Carstairs put his hands on the girl's bare shoulders. She didn't resist, simply looked up at him questioningly.

'You're a very attractive man, Petie,' she said quietly, 'but you're not quite the man described in those articles.'

'Less? Are you disappointed?'

She was very close, her body heat almost magnetic.

'No, not less. More.'

Outside, Arbolino swung the ladder back and swooped over the green wall back to the air-conditioning tower. He caught a rung with one hand, retained his grasp on the nylon with the other. Panting, he sent the ladder back to where Williston crouched on the terrace.

'More what?' challenged Carstairs as he gently framed her neck in his hands.

'More complicated, and I'd bet more trouble.'

He leaned down, kissed her.

'Don't play games with me, Petie,' she advised several seconds later. 'I'm a big girl and I don't like to play games very much.'

He kissed her again, felt her stiffen and then press closer in woman response.

'I'm not playing games, Kathy.'

She held him tightly, stared up with a look that was almost grim.

'I know you play games and I know you play to win,' she warned, 'but I'm the wrong girl for those games. I'm no innocent virgin, but it would be a large mistake for you to play casual games with me.'

His hands moved down her back now, and she shivered in further wanting.

'You're probably just passing through town, aren't you?' she whispered as her hips began to move.

'Probably.'

They kissed a third time, even harder and more hungrily.

Eighteen yards away, Professor Andrew F. Williston raced back to the edge of the terrace and swung himself on the nylon ladder across to where the stunt man waited. They unhooked their equipment, coiled it in one of the tool kits and returned to the freight elevator. As it neared the street level, Williston glanced at his watch.

Five minutes and twenty-one seconds.

Not bad.

Not really good, but not bad after all these years.

'We could have done it in under four minutes if that brandy-hound hadn't barged in,' Williston boasted.

'Maybe.'

Arbolino eyed him soberly, sensing the excitement and elation that his scholarly partner was trying to conceal.

'I'm sure of it, Tony. *Four* minutes – and *clean*.'

'Save it for Gilman. He may be impressed. I'm still tense and sweaty, and we're not home free yet.'

The elevator reached the ground floor. They stepped out, scanned the corridor in both directions. Approaching at the end of the passage on the left was the white-jacketed bartender, three bottles of Haig Scotch whisky under his right arm and a set of keys in his left hand. He was obviously replenishing his supplies for the drinkers in the nearby cocktail lounge.

'They're really sopping it up tonight,' he announced.

Williston calculated, realized that the liquor store room must be off this corridor.

'Giving out any samples?' suggested the teacher.

'Sorry, boys, but the management would be annoyed something fierce if I did.'

He noticed their coveralls, the inscriptions on the tool kits.

'Elevator grief?'

'Not really,' Arbolino answered easily. 'Control box overheated a bit. Nothing any kid couldn't fix with a jackknife.'

Without waiting for any reply, he led Williston out into the alley where the truck was parked in the shadows. The stunt man slipped behind the wheel and drove two blocks before he stopped at the traffic light at the Braden Avenue intersection. A police car cruised up beside them, the blue-suited officers eying them automatically. Then the light changed and the truck swung west. It was another minute before Williston saw the telephone booth at the Texaco station, smiled and pointed.

It was time to test the infinity transmitter.

Arbolino parked the truck beside the booth, drew the small metal cylinder from his coverall pocket. It was a whistle, a special whistle. It was a sonic whistle that issued a sound no human ear could hear, and that silent sound was the device that would make the infinity transmitter 'live.'

'You blow it, Tony,' invited the professor.

'No, you blow it. I'm tone deaf anyway.'

'It doesn't matter, Tony. Nobody will hear it anyway.'

So Tony Arbolino blew twice on the whistle and Andrew Williston entered the phone booth and dialed one of the unlisted numbers – one that served the instrument in Pikelis' bedroom. There was no one in that chamber, but the door to Kathy Pikelis' room nearby was open and there were two people in that room. They were making love. Her moans and sighs were audible over the ultra-sensitive transmitter. Now the Sledgehammer agents could dial either of the unlisted numbers from any phone and listen. The telephone in the penthouse would not ring, but it would serve as a microphone to transmit – over the phone line – everything being said in the room.

'You bastard, you handsome bastard!' the girl groaned as P. T. Carstairs did one of the four or five things that he did so well.

Williston didn't want to, didn't have to listen to anymore.

He returned to the truck, climbed in and closed the door.

'Well, Andy?' questioned the man behind the wheel.

The teacher nodded.

'It works, Tony.'

Arbolino grinned.

'Beautiful. Just beautiful,' he rejoiced as he started the truck.

Williston didn't know what to say, so he simply nodded again.

Up in the penthouse, a very honest girl who spoke excellent

French and who knew that P. T. Carstairs wasn't entirely to be trusted was naked, gasping and arching helplessly under the weight of her strange new lover.

CHAPTER EIGHTEEN

Sunday in Paradise City, the sabbath in a community where nobody ever said that God was dead but quite a few people suspected as much – and felt relieved. The town wasn't exactly Peyton Place or Sodom on the Sea, but a substantial percentage of the population cheated on their wives, taxes and golf scores and many others routinely violated the Ten Commandments with a skill that could only come from long practice. Nevertheless, almost everybody dressed neatly on the Lord's Day and went to church and hoped that He'd give them a break because their transgressions were 'only human.' There was a policeman outside every place of worship – at least in the white neighborhoods – to direct traffic, so that you knew that if God didn't strike you dead inside the church no passing car would finish you off as you left.

A number of people – some of them prominent residents whom you might even call society folk – did not attend services that Sunday. The late Dorothy Parker – or was it Che Guevara's psychoanalyst? – once said that in California any girl who finished high school was Society. Well, almost all of those who missed the services in Paradise City that morning had finished high school and a number of them had also completed rather substantial breakfasts in addition. Mrs Ben Marton and Mayor Ashley were not in that group because they were both still drunk – in their own and separate homes – but Captain Marton had a full belly and a certain amount of information. Both of these facts were obvious as he reported to Pikelis in the hotel penthouse.

'Mace. I think it was Mace, John,' the chief of police announced.

Pikelis sipped his coffee, considered, rejected.

'I think you're crazy, Ben. Either you're crazy or you're trying to crap me with some story so you'll be in the clear. Don't crap me with any talk about Mace.'

'It was Mace, John,' Marton insisted.

The racketeer shook his head. 'Mace is police stuff. Cops use it on rioters, on niggers.'

Mr Pikelis, who was not running for elective office or

expecting to be interviewed by any TV network news crew, could afford to use such old-fashioned epithets when he wished. Mayor Ashley spoke of 'our Nigra citizens' and Marton referred to 'colored folks,' but they sometimes talked for public consumption and were therefore instinctively a bit more tactful. Such niceties were not necessary for the man who ruled Jefferson County, who had the power and controlled the mass media. He never made statements to or dealt with the working press.

'You're right, John. Of course, you're right that Mace is police equipment,' Marton agreed, 'but they used Mace on Luther.'

'Where'd they get it?'

'I don't know. There's plenty around.'

'You don't buy that stuff at Sears or J. C. Penney,' Pikelis challenged.

'No, you don't. But they got it somewhere.'

Pikelis brooded for fifteen or twenty seconds.

'The money? What about the money?'

'They didn't take a dollar. I don't understand that. Nossir, I sure don't figure that at all.'

The ganglord glanced at his watch. His daughter should be up soon.

'Ben,' he said slowly, 'I don't like it. *They* knew where and when to jump Luther and *they* had this Mace and *they* staged this crazy scene in the store window, and *they* didn't keep any of the money. Who are *they*?'

'I don't have the goddamdest idea, John,' Marton admitted.

'And *why* did *they* do all this?'

The porky policeman shrugged.

'John, if we knew *who* they were we could probably reckon out *why*,' he reasoned carefully.

Marton wasn't terribly imaginative, but he was more practical than most and more ruthless than almost anybody. That combination, which if otherwise applied could have made him a vice-president at any major movie company or lieutenant-governor of a medium-sized state, also made him a useful junior partner in the Pikelis organization. But Marton probably aspired to a full partnership, the racketeer sensed, and that was impossible. Pikelis would give him more money, but he would never share the power. It was the power – the authority – that counted.

'You don't think that it was any policemen – maybe some of yours, for example – who used that police Mace on Luther?' Pikelis speculated.

'No. No, it wasn't anybody connected with any kind of police or law outfit. It wouldn't make sense.'

Pikelis nodded. Right. It wouldn't make sense.

'Some out-of-town mob? How about that, John?'

'No, that's just possible but I don't see how that makes sense either. I get along pretty well with the syndicate boys, and this doesn't have the Mafia feel to it. They'd have killed Luther, gunned him on the spot.'

Pikelis saw the police chief eying the mahogany humidor on the desk, gestured an invitation to take one of the Partagas. The racketeer didn't mind sharing the smuggled Cuban panatelas, for he got a box every week, and it amused him how the deluxe illicit cigars seemed to please Marton. The police chief took one, bit off the end, lit it and puffed happily.

'John,' he began. 'Oh, thanks for the cigar. John, I don't mean to dispute you but don't you think it wouldn't hurt to check with New York and Chicago and Miami just to make sure that it isn't somebody connected with the Mafia?'

'It can't hurt. Meanwhile, let's keep it quiet around town,' Pikelis ordered. 'I've already made sure that the paper, the radio station and the TV news boys won't say a word. Officially, it never happened.'

'People saw it, John. There'll be word of mouth, talk.'

'About what? About something that never happened. I say it never happened. Let's give people something else to talk about, to think about. How about that black girl who got cut up? A nice juicy murder should keep people interested.'

The police chief puffed on the cigar again.

'Could be. We got the bastard who did it. One of those smart-ass colored boys who was so friendly with the civil-rights agitators we ran out of town. Truck driver named Sam Clayton. Meaner'n hell, but he confessed the whole thing.'

Pikelis smiled.

'I've really got to hand it to you, Ben,' he complimented ironically. 'The way your men track down criminals and get them to confess – mighty fine detective work. I suppose he raped her too?'

Marton peered and squinted, obviously puzzled.

'I don't know about that. Maybe,' he hedged.

'Of course he raped her, Ben. I'm sure that our brilliant coroner will find that he raped her. Yes, a nice juicy rape-murder,' Pikelis calculated aloud. 'That's just what we need right now. Something rough and dirty to grab everybody's attention. A real quick and sensational trial – that's the ticket. Shouldn't be any problem, I'd imagine.'

'No problem at all. In the meanwhile, my boys will keep working on this crazy thing that happened last night,' the police chief pledged.

'It wasn't crazy, Ben,' his master corrected. 'It was very neatly planned and very neatly done by some very tricky people who had some very goddam special reason for it. You've got to keep that in mind every second if you're going to stop them.'

'Stop them? You think there's more coming?'

The man who ruled Jefferson County nodded.

'I'm so sure that I bet your badge on it, Ben,' he warned.

Marton didn't like the threat, but before he could answer the door opened and a smiling Kathy Pikelis entered the room. Her elegant robe looked good, but the young woman who wore it looked even better. Her radiance communicated that she'd either had a wonderful dream or a superb lover the night before – or both. Conscious that such matters were none of his business, the beefy police chief hesitated for only a minute's amenities before making his exit.

John Pikelis also recognized the look on his daughter's face, and he wondered.

'Quite an evening,' he probed ever so casually after they exchanged morning kisses.

'I enjoyed it, Daddy,' she replied in tones that told him nothing.

'You seem to be getting along pretty well with Petie.'

She looked thoughtful, pleased and not quite sure.

'Yes, Petie Carstairs is an extremely attractive and interesting male – very male and very slick,' she answered as she reached for the coffee pot on the side table.

'He plays a helluva game of poker. I'll say that, honey.'

She poured herself a cup, added sugar.

'I'd bet that he's good at a lot of games,' she agreed cryptically.

'You think he's just a playboy, one of those phony jet-set creeps?' Pikelis asked uneasily.

'He's no playboy. He's for real, Dad. No line, no phony charm – and an honesty that's so outrageous that I'm a little afraid of him . . . No, don't look so worried. He was a perfect gentleman. Just perfect,' she repeated with a mischievous animal grin.

'You like him?' Pikelis questioned paternally.

She laughed, and it was the laugh of an adult, knowing woman.

'I could fall in love with him,' she acknowledged between sips of coffee, 'but liking him might be more difficult.'

'Why? What's the problem?'

'I'd like a man who needs me,' she explained softly, 'and I'm not so sure that a man like Petie – a man who has everything – really needs anybody.'

Then she changed the subject – quite openly – and asked what the police chief had reported on the strange event of the previous evening. She listened to his reply with far less interest than Professor Andrew Williston, who was eavesdropping on the infinity transmitter and carefully taping the entire conversation. This tape – and the others that would follow – would be mailed to a certain postal box in Miami, where they would be picked up by an employee of the Southern Public Opinion Corporation who would place them in a safety-deposit box rented under the name of still another company. Williston listened until noon, then left for his meeting at rendezvous point 'Bob,' where Gilman and Arbolino would be waiting.

They would discuss the next operation.

Little Johnny Pikelis had been absolutely right.

There was a lot more coming – soon.

Someone else in Paradise City had also made the same guess. As the three infiltrators shaped their plans that Sunday afternoon, that someone else was dropping quarters into a pay telephone outside a roadside hamburger stand nine miles away. He was speaking to a man in Atlanta, a man with an unlisted telephone number and a number of armed associates and a great curiosity about conditions in Paradise City.

'Bud, this is Freddie,' said the man who wasn't Freddie to the Atlantan who'd never been christened Bud. 'Something's going on here. Something we hadn't bargained for . . . No, I'm not going into it all over the phone. I'll send you a picture postcard . . . All I can say right now is that it looks real weird . . . Listen, if I knew what the hell was going on I'd let you know . . .

No, I don't even pretend to know what the score is. I'm not sure what the game is, Man, or even who's playing, so how can I tell you what the score is . . . Yeah, yeah . . . I think it's going to get rough around here and the hunting season may start about thirteen weeks early this year . . . Am I getting through to you, Buddy Boy? . . . Your concern about my health and welfare is touching, definitely touching . . . How bad is it here? Well, only yesterday a former policeman was *kidnapped* and robbed and stripped naked and left bare-assed in the window of a department store. Now if that ain't a sign of the moral decay of our times, Buddy Boy, I don't know what is. Why, that's a Federal offense! No . . . no, but I'm starting to feel a little lonely and it might be nice to have a family reunion down here soon . . . I'll let you know when the weather's right. It's warm right now, and I don't think we ought to wait till it's too damn hot . . . Buddy, I just *know* it's going to get hotter in the immediate future . . . People will sweat and tempers will get frayed and I wouldn't be surprised if there were a number of serious accidents, domestic disputes and loud noises in the night. You had better tell that to the family . . . Read my next letter to Uncle Jed; he'll understand. He's got that wonderful warm feeling for people, like Vito used to have . . . Well, I thought it was funny.'

Then he hung up the telephone, stepped out of the hot booth and mopped his wet brow with a handkerchief. The bell on the instrument rang, and he knew that it was the operator calling to ask for another thirty or forty cents for overtime. It rang and rang, and he listened, smiling. It was dishonest and illegal to ignore the demand for proper payment, and that was why he smiled. He took a perverse pleasure in the thought that he was illegally beating a large organization out of such a ridiculous sum. He was getting tired of rules and large organizations and violence.

As he drove back toward Paradise City in his yellow '67 Mustang, he listened to the two-o'clock news on the car radio and wasn't at all surprised to hear nothing of the bizarre hijacking. Pikelis controlled the paper and the broadcasting stations, reflected the man who telephoned Atlanta almost every Sunday, but that wasn't going to stop the people who'd pulled this job. They had designed it and worked it like a military operation, like a trained commando team. But they hadn't done it for the money.

Publicity.

They wanted publicity. That had to be it.

They *wanted* everyone in town to know that they were there and that they had no fear of the Pikelis organization.

It was more than that.

They were showing their contempt, publicly humiliating a well-known Pikelis thug in an open challenge.

'Jeezus,' the man in the Mustang said as he realized the implications, 'this is a declaration of war.'

The people in Atlanta and the people who controlled the people in Atlanta weren't going to like that at all. The plan hadn't called for any war, and if the previous night's incident was any clue it was going to be a wild and weird war indeed. The unknown and uncounted invaders might do anything, hit anywhere at any time with any tactics and any weapons. There was absolutely no way of predicting what they'd do or guessing why they'd come, but if publicity and defiance was their immediate goal the next attack would be soon and spectacular.

'Wednesday night,' Williston announced as he, Arbolino and Gilman pored over the drawings and photos in the shaded isolation of the rendezvous point in the woods. The smell of the green trees was strong, but the three men were focussed entirely upon the next strike.

'We go Wednesday night,' the psychology professor explained, 'because we want to keep the spotlight, to shake up their organization and to show that we're not a one-shot group. We've got to maintain our momentum, and we've got to keep the initiative if we even hope to build a Resistance here.'

'Even if we keep hitting them, Andy,' Gilman warned, 'it's going to be tough to get any significant Resistance movement going here. This is a pretty complacent town. As long as nobody gets mugged on Main Street and the *Reader's Digest* arrives on time every month, I doubt whether these people are going to get mad enough to risk their necks.'

Williston nodded.

'We need an issue. That's obvious. We need an issue around which enough people can or will rally,' he agreed. 'In the meanwhile, we've got to keep kicking around and embarrassing the Pikelis organization until their own people get shaky and the rest of the town realizes that these hoods aren't invulnerable.'

'Any ideas on what our issue might be?' wondered the stunt man.

The teacher shrugged. 'Maybe John Pikelis will give us one,' he joked hopefully.

Williston had no way of knowing that this most unlikely possibility was, in fact, already moving toward becoming a reality.

CHAPTER NINETEEN

Late that afternoon, Miss Kathy Pikelis received about $50 worth of roses – the large long roses – in a box delivered personally by the proprietor of Barton's Blooms, Paradise City's most expensive florist shop. Most people would have some difficulty in arranging for such a delivery on a Sunday when the store was closed, but five $20 bills passed to a hotel desk clerk – even one who looks like a dead Nazi named Gindler – can work more wonders than two bottles of Bayer aspirin or three hours of silent prayer. Not that P. T. Carstairs would ever put down prayer or nationally advertised headache remedies, but he had worked out his own ways of coping – especially with women – and he saw no reason to change his methods after all these years of success.

There was a card with the roses.

'Compliments of a friend – P. T. C.,' it read.

Kathy Pikelis stared at it, smiled fleetingly, and then sighed.

Friend?

He was a bastard all right, a perfect gentleman and a perfect lover and a perfect bastard. She had no ideas as to what to do about him, or what he meant to do about her. She didn't realize that America's second most eligible bachelor – so perfect in so many ways – wasn't quite sure either. That annoyed him. He realized what he ought to do and had to do, and he would do it – he told himself. But he was still annoyed, with the girl and with himself. Gilman and Williston had masterminded all the research and planning with great care, but neither of them had told him that this girl would be so vulnerable. He could handle her, of course, and he did. He was absolutely charming – with just the right amount of warmth and the barest smiling promise of tenderness – when he took her water skiing that afternoon. He was very good at that too, very strong and skillful without being the least bit exhibitionistic. It reminded her of the way he'd made love to her the night before, and that visceral recollection started tiny shivers deep within her that she had to struggle to control. The heat of the July sun didn't help her a bit; nothing did. The bikini that she wore was small, but when this man looked at her she felt absolutely naked – and she didn't mind. No, she minded but she didn't care.

She wanted, and the wanting made her look even more attractive.

Carstairs told her how desirable she looked when they returned to the Paradise House, and she knew that he wasn't lying. But he wasn't really committing himself either. Even after they had the iced vodka drinks in his suite and he kissed her and they made love again, even after she held him tight and tears diffused the glow in her eyes and he reassured her, she sensed – as a woman can – that there were reservations, things left unsaid because he couldn't or wouldn't speak of them.

'It would almost be better if you'd lie to me,' she said with her head on his shoulder.

He looked at her, stroked her hair gently.

'No, I imagine that you've heard all the lies you'd ever need. You're a lovely young woman, Kathy,' he answered, 'and I'd bet that a lot of males have told you a lot of tales and that not one of them ever fooled you for a second. That's not my bag, anyway. Remember? I'm the most honest dirty old man you know.'

'I know you're not a dirty old man either, you bastard,' she announced.

'That's ridiculous. Of course I am.'

This sudden recognition that he wasn't came as an immense relief and release; she smiled and kissed him with an odd spurt of joy. He would say what there was to be said – whatever it was – when the time came. She kissed him again.

'What are you, a sex maniac?' Carstairs jested.

'Weeell, if you don't have *anything else* planned for the next half hour—'

'I'm not talking about any half hour,' the handsome millionaire countered. 'I'm thinking about the long run – say, a week or a month. We may not be compatible. I'm so much older. I'm thinking about the generation gap.'

'I just adore men who talk dirty,' she replied as she drew him down to her again.

Less than one hundred yards away, her father was talking – cleanly and warily – on the telephone to a man named Irving in Miami. To be entirely truthful and grammatical, he was named Irving everywhere – including the files of three Federal agencies where there were extensive reports on the slot machines and other 'gaming devices' sold by Irving's company. The bulk of the firm's product went to casinos and gambling establishments owned by associates of Irving's oh-so-very-silent partner, a white-haired elder statesman named Meyer who had $6,000,000, lot of friends in the Mafia and an inconvenient criminal record that made it useful to have Irving 'front' the company. If anybody in the Mafia or the Cosa Nostra or the American Dental Association or the Girl Scouts of Montreal – it's hard to keep track of what they're labeling the Syndicate these days – was or were or had been meddling in Paradise City, then Irving could surely find out from Meyer because Meyer knew a lot of people everywhere and had a terrific memory. Meyer was also the sort of sensible person who deplored trouble and violence, Pikelis reasoned, and could also serve to negotiate a peaceful and reasonable settlement.

Now none of these matters were said right out over the phone, but Pikelis referred to 'some trouble' with 'people from out of town, I think' and Irving assured his good customer that he'd 'ask around tomorrow' to see if 'anybody had heard anything.' Meyer didn't like to be bothered at home on Sunday because he was having more gall-bladder trouble, but Irving didn't mention this on the telephone because any law-enforcement agents who might be tapping were certainly well aware of Meyer's gall-bladder problems and Irving wouldn't give those lice the satisfaction anyway. Irving was loyal as well as prudent; he was also Meyer's nephew by marriage. There were practically no limits to what Irving would do for his uncle-in-law. Why, he'd even cultivated a taste for veal cutlet parmigiana just to get along with Uncle Meyer's Northern friends when they visited Miami. You couldn't help liking good-hearted Irving, Pikelis thought as he hung up the phone, but yet nobody did.

The next morning's Paradise City paper announced that Coroner Percy Farnsworth had discovered that the late Pearl Delilah Tubbs had been barbarously violated both before and after she'd been stabbed to death, and reported that the rape-murder trial of Sam Clayton would start on Thursday. Judge Ralph Gillis had declared that he'd appoint a lawyer for the accused if Clayton couldn't secure his own counsel. District Attorney Reece Everett piously declined to discuss the case to avoid possibly prejudicing any members of the jury 'in accord with recent rulings of the U.S. Supreme Court,' but confided 'off the record' that the sexual aspects of the trial would make shocking reading. The police reporter who wrote the story didn't quote this, but hinted very broadly that sensational testimony might be anticipated.

The case apparently attracted very little attention in the middle-class white neighborhood where Williston was going through the motions of poll-taking that morning, a ritual that he used to try to feel out the temper of the community and to search for potential recruits for a resistance movement. Nobody mentioned the imminent murder trial, and nobody showed the slightest signs of discontent with the governing and criminal exploitation of Paradise City. One thirty-two-year-old blond housewife indicated some discontent with her husband's performance and implied that Williston needn't hurry away, but nobody talked about the immorality or viciousness of the Pikelis organization. This town didn't even know that it was occupied, Williston brooded, so how could it fight to expel the Nazis?

He had lunch with the mayor at the City Club; Ashley's press secretary had set it up because he calculated that it might make a story for the paper. Roger Stuart Ashley didn't get much publicity because he didn't actually need it – since no one opposed him – but he still had some shreds of ego, and the press secretary liked to show that he was doing his job. The lunch abounded in bourbon highballs, fried chicken, and well-marinated platitudes about the emerging economic boom and cultural explosion of the New South. The mayor also made a few shrewd observations about public tastes and political power, revealing that there was still some intelligence and awareness behind that photogenic face despite all the years of drink and corruption. Degraded but not wholly destroyed, Ashley came through to Williston as a weak, wily man whose commitment to his own comfortable survival would preclude any opposition to John Pikelis.

A photo was taken of the two men, sent with a copy of the mayor's prepared statement on the city's future to each of the local news media. After lunch, the spy resumed his public-opinion survey – edging into the Lowell Square area where the more affluent black residents lived. There weren't that many of them – some lawyers, doctors, insurance men, undertakers, merchants and restaurant and bar owners. It was just off Lowell Square that he saw the First Baptist Church and recalled that

Mayor Ashley had referred to its minister as 'a responsible clergyman who speaks for many in the Nigra community.' It was not a large church and the minister's office in the rear of the building wasn't large either, but Reverend Ezra Snell was big. He was big, ebony-black, slow-speaking and courteous.

'I don't wish to be inhospitable to visitors,' he declared in tones of dignified sonority, 'but I rather doubt that I can answer these questions about the future entertainment market in our community.'

He'd probably taken some courses in oratory – or perhaps in acting – at college many years earlier, and now this barrel-chested man projected both richly and routinely. He had the voice and style of a powerfully effective speaker of the old school, the manner of a natural leader.

'There are some other questions on my mind of a more urgent nature,' the minister continued soberly. He paused, studied the spy for several seconds. 'You are employed by a Miami research firm, is that correct?' he asked.

'Yes, for the past three years.'

'But you're not a Southerner, Mr Warren?'

'No, I'm from Vermont originally. I guess you can hear that in my voice,' the teacher acknowledged. 'I've lived in New York too. Why do you ask?'

The black clergyman hesitated, phrasing his reply precisely.

'I don't intend to embarrass you, Mr Warren, but I find that I have – perhaps because of the difficult nature of our times – I have a tendency to speak differently to Southerners. And I guess that most of them – the whites, I mean – talk differently to me. I don't mean to criticize or complain, you understand.'

'I think so, sir. Of course, there are plenty of Northerners and Westerners – lots of people in all parts of the country – who'd speak "differently" to black people. Our company does work in many states, and I meet such people quite often.'

Snell nodded.

'I have a public-opinion problem of my own right now,' he said quietly. 'One of our church members is going on trial for a murder he didn't commit, and our people are going to be very bitter – very angry and full of hate – when he is executed.'

'You're talking about the Clayton case?'

'Yes. Samuel Clayton did not kill Pearlie Tubbs, and he surely didn't rape her.'

'What makes you so sure, sir?'

'Because no one would have to rape her. She was a prostitute, and she had been for years. Her mother threw this pitiful harlot out of the family home when she was fifteen – eight years ago. Anybody could have had Pearlie Tubbs for a pint of gin or a couple of dollars, any hour of any day of the week. Pearlie Tubbs was a fallen soul, and she'd fallen all the way to the gutter.'

'Maybe Clayton didn't have any money, not even a pint of gin,' Williston challenged.

The old black man shook his head.

'That's impossible. He had his own business, his own ice truck, and he had his own girl anyway. He was at a church dance – I saw him – with his girl until well after midnight, after the murder. A number of people saw him at the dance.'

'But he confessed?'

The minister shrugged impatiently.

'He was beaten into confessing. That is quite common here, and everyone knows it.'

'The witnesses? The people who saw him at the dance – they can testify,' Williston reasoned.

'I doubt that anyone would have the courage to do so. It would mean "making trouble" so far as Captain Marton is concerned, and black people who "make trouble" in this city run the risk of being arrested, beaten, crippled or *disappearing*. I might be considered as "making trouble" myself for even discussing this with you – an outsider. Please don't mention this to anyone.'

'I won't. Is there anything I might do to help, Reverend?'

'If you happen to be the best criminal lawyer in America you could, but you're not and I'm not either. They're going to convict Sam Clayton,' the troubled older man predicted, 'and that's when the big trouble will come. There are men – young black men – who won't let them carry out this legal lynching. They'll get guns and they'll try to break him out, and they'll be slaughtered. That's my public-opinion problem, Mr Warren.'

The idea that had been forming in Williston's mind abruptly took shape, and he recognized the potential instantly.

This could be the issue.

This could be the rallying point for an Underground, a black Resistance that would take the risks and the casualties that the other citizens of Paradise City wouldn't.

'I may be able to get Sam Clayton the best criminal lawyer

in America, an Edward Bennett Williams or a Joshua David Davidson,' Williston said slowly.

'That's fifty or a hundred thousand dollars' worth of legal talent, Mr Warren.'

'I know that. I may be able to help you, if you can help me. I have to talk to somebody about this, and, in the meantime, I'll make the same appeal for discretion and silence that you made. No one – not a single person – must know about my interest, or it could cost my life as easily as it might yours.'

The gray-thatched minister thought, agreed.

'I don't have any idea of what you want, Mr Warren, but if it isn't immoral or criminal—'

'Let's just say that it's unorthodox but worthy.'

'You're being evasive, Mr Warren,' Snell noted.

'Deliberately, but only for the moment. You will have all the facts before you make up your mind,' pledged the lean spy, 'and I think that's a fair offer.'

'Fair enough,' the clergyman judged.

They didn't shake hands, for they hadn't anything worth shaking hands on yet. Williston was at the door when Snell stopped him with a final question.

'You're not Communists or anything like that? Communists have used black people before, and I wouldn't have anything to do with that – we've been used for too long, Mr Warren.'

The former OSS agent shook his head.

'No, we're not Communists or Nazis or anything evil like that, sir. We're the good guys. I think you'll agree that we're the good guys when we speak again. Until then, it would be best if no one even knew that we're in town.'

Shortly before 7 p.m. that night, however, one more person knew. The evening paper carried a photo of Williston and the mayor on page two, and one reader who had seen other pictures of Andrew Williston recognized the man who was identified as Arthur Warren. Good.

Gilman was here.

Carstairs had come.

Now Williston, the one who'd been so bold and fierce and ruthless, had joined them.

The fourth – Arbolino – was probably in town too.

They had answered the appeal in the envelope full of clippings, and they had already struck once. The public humiliation of Luther Hyatt – that had to be their work.

And that was only the beginning, if Barringer had described them correctly.

For several minutes the person who had mailed those clippings considered whether it was time to make contact – to let them know. It was a complex decision filled with intangibles and dangers, certainly not one to be hurried. It would be easy if the invaders needed help, if the Pikelis group knew that they were there or had identified even one of them. The newspaper reader stared at the photograph again, impressed by the teacher's face. He looked so much younger than his years, so much more innocent than his past. It was odd how little you could tell about men by their faces.

After a few more seconds the newspaper reader reached a decision.

No.

Not yet.

CHAPTER TWENTY

The promised letter reached Atlanta on Tuesday morning, approximately an hour and a half before Mr Milburn Pembroke of the prestigious New York–Washington–Paris law firm of Ackley, Pembroke, Travis, Cabot and Hoover telephoned Joshua David Davidson. Mr Pembroke, Harvard Club and Lotos Club and so Ivy League that it was almost necessary for him to be trimmed twice a year, was the senior partner in a very respected and large aggregation of legal talent that served many of America's richest corporations and individuals. He was a former president of the New York Bar Association and played a tigerish game of croquet. Bank presidents and corporate board chairmen practically freaked out when they spoke with Milburn Pembroke; he was that sound and that respectable and that dignified. He had never handled a criminal case in his life, nor had his firm (thirty-two partners and ninety-nine associates). He viewed such work as vaguely bizarre, but he knew that Joshua David Davidson – melodramatic and colorful in speech and raiment – was an attorney to be respected. The Wall Street partner realized that Davidson was a very able lawyer, a brilliant trial man and a genius at murder cases.

Milburn Pembroke, a person of immense discretion if not reserve, said none of these things to Davidson over the telephone. He simply explained that a Negro ice-truck driver named Samuel R. Clayton – R. for Roosevelt – was about to go on trial in Paradise City for rape and murder and that Clayton would be convicted for this crime he hadn't committed because defense witnesses were afraid to testify.

'How do you know he didn't commit this crime?' the long-haired Davidson demanded.

'I can't say that I personally *know*,' Pembroke replied carefully, but I have been so informed – no, *assured* – by my client.'

'Samuel Roosevelt Clayton, a colored truck driver, is a client of Ackley, Pembroke, Travis, Cabot and Hoover?' Davidson asked in a tone that reflected both amusement and incredulity.

'No,' the corporation counsel snapped. 'He isn't an employee of any of our clients either.'

'Well?'

'I beg your pardon?'

'Mr Pembroke, it's nice to talk to you but what do you want?'

'One of our clients has instructed me to secure outstanding and specialized legal representation for Mr Clayton, and since our firm has no experience in criminal matters I'd like to retain you.'

'I suppose Ed Williams is busy and I'm your second choice?' Davidson chuckled.

'That's right.'

So Pembroke did have a temper buried somewhere down beneath all that encrusted cool.

Davidson laughed at the corporation lawyer's bluntness.

'I didn't intend to minimize your ability and reputation, Mr Davidson.'

Davidson laughed again.

'You didn't. I've got an ego like Mount Rushmore, very large and very sturdy. I'm good and I'm expensive.'

'My client will pay your normal fees – or more. Do you have the time?'

'Who's your client and why the hell does he care about Samuel Roosevelt Clayton?' the murder expert parried.

'I am not at liberty to say, but he does care – fifty thousand dollars' worth. Do you have the time – now?'

You couldn't rattle or divert Pembroke, Davidson noted. He had a rather appealing toughness of his own.

'Now? You mean *immediately*, Mr Pembroke.'

'I'm informed that they plan to start selecting a jury within three days and to begin the trial by the end of the week if possible.'

'When was he indicted?'

'Yesterday.'

'That's *goddam* fast justice,' Davidson exploded. 'It's *ridiculous*!'

'It isn't meant to be justice at all, Mr Davidson. I thought that I made that clear at the outset.'

There were several moments of silence.

'Will you take the case?' Pembroke pressed.

'I'm supposed to leave on vacation – tomorrow. My first vacation in thirty-seven months.'

'Then you can't defend Clayton?'

More silence.

'An ice-truck driver, you say?' Davidson asked in a voice that was suddenly grim.

'Yes, although I don't see what that's got to do with anything.'

'And he's being hustled right to the gallows?'

'I believe that is the plan, Mr Davidson.'

'It isn't my plan, Mr Pembroke. No, it isn't my plan at all. This poor bastard is going to get a very complete and careful and absolutely ferocious defense, Mr Pembroke, and the trial may take months. Nobody is going to railroad Samuel Roosevelt Clayton,' the criminal lawyer announced in tones that were edged in raw anger, 'and you may take the word of Joshua David Davidson on that. I *also* give you the word of Nathan Louis Davidson.'

'Who's he?'

'My father, a very great man – a man of high principle.'

Pembroke didn't fathom what the criminal lawyer's father had to do with this, but he didn't care. He had only one concern.

'Then you'll take the case?'

'I'll be in Paradise City tomorrow. Yes, I'm going to cancel the vacation – my wife will be hysterical, which she does very well – to do righteous battle for Sam Clayton. I feel less tired already, exhilarated by the prospect. I don't *need* any vacation . . . But I'll need five rooms – a suite in the best hotel – for myself and my staff.'

'I'm told that's the Paradise House . . . My client has authorized me to advance fifteen thousand dollars in expense money immediately. Shall I have my secretary transfer the money? And what about the fee? Will fifty thousand dollars – that's aside from the expenses – be all right?'

'Fine. I leave all that to you.'

It was hardly what Pembroke had expected. Davidson often received sixty thousand or even eighty thousand for a case, and he wasn't known for his indifference to money. What was so special about this case? Why was he accepting it?

'Mr Davidson, I'm delighted that you'll defend Mr Clayton and I'll so inform my client. He, in turn, will inform Reverend Ezra Snell of the First Baptist Church in Paradise City. Reverend Snell may be able to help you, I'm told . . . Mr Davidson, may I ask you a question?'

'Certainly.'

'What made you decide to take this case?'

The criminal lawyer laughed. 'I'll answer that if you'll tell me who your client is,' he bargained. 'No? All right, I'll find him or her myself. Mysteries! I love mysteries almost as much as I love the combat of a trial. I'm a warrior, Mr Pembroke, like King David in the Old Testament. I was raised on the Old Testament. The path of the just is as the shining light – that's Proverbs Four. Woe unto them that call evil good and good evil – that's Isaiah.'

The man was a spellbinder, evangelist, pitchman and advocate all rolled up into one. With some slight awe and difficulty, Milburn Pembroke of Ackley, Pembroke, Travis, Cabot and Hoover managed to terminate the conversation and sat back to catch his breath. Several miles north in his office on 57th Street overlooking Park Avenue, the criminal lawyer who'd been named after two great Biblical warriors – Joshua and David – was busy barking orders as he prepared to do battle against the Philistines. As expected, his wife was effectively hysterical that evening when he told her that the vacation was being canceled. As expected, she abruptly terminated her noisy reproaches when he explained *why* he was going to Paradise City to defend Sam Clayton.

'You're a crazy man, Joshua,' she announced with tender approval.

'I don't see any choice, do you?' he answered.

'Not for you, Joshua. Not for you . . . You know, if I told anybody this they wouldn't believe me.'

'So don't tell anybody – not till it's finished, anyway. And when it's over,' he promised, 'then we'll take the vacation.'

It was at that point that Mrs Joshua David Davidson began to shout again.

In Paradise City, Andrew Williston and Tony Arbolino were listening to another woman's voice – a much more attractive one. They had come – separately – to the Fun Parlor for a final reconnaissance. They sat at the bar – four stools apart – enjoying the look and the sound of the pretty blond singer, and then they wandered – separately – into the gambling room. The layout and the security arrangements were precisely those that Gilman had sketched and described. They each gambled and lost small sums before they left – twenty minutes apart. Williston returned to his room in the Jefferson at half past twelve, rechecked the drawing once again.

Yes, the briefing had been accurate and the operation was feasible.

It should work, barring unforeseen developments.

And if the man who was always right was right this time, they could pull it off without killing anyone – despite the armed guards.

Williston yawned, looked at his wrist watch.

In twenty-three hours and eleven minutes, they would attack again. After that, Pikelis would have no doubts about the presence of hostile forces in his domain and – as the late *Obersturmbannfuehrer* Egon Gindler had done – he would mobilize every man and gun he had to hunt them down.

It would be open war, just like the Old Days.

No quarter.

CHAPTER TWENTY-ONE

By any form of reckoning – Marxist, new math, existential or folk rock – the next day, Wednesday the twenty-third of July, was a large and lively one in the small and grubby history of Paradise City, USA. It actually had the same number of hours, traffic violations, migraine headaches and air-conditioner breakdowns as July 22, and neither day featured any nuclear tests, announcements of tax reductions or reports of high-school girls seeing visions of the Virgin Mary. On the afternoon of the twenty-third, however, a man named J. D. Davidson – accompanied by two younger men and a rather splendidly contoured brunette whom they all addressed as 'Doll' – checked into five connecting rooms at Paradise House. The desk clerk noted that the woman's legal name was Shirley Dollberg, and the entire Davidson party gave New York City home addresses. It was very obviously the *Davidson* party; the older man with the long graying locks radiated command and authority.

Half an hour after they checked in, Davidson and one of the younger men – a sandy-haired type who looked as if he'd once played strong side tackle for Notre Dame and had – descended and entered a taxi. To the driver's surprise they asked to be taken directly to the First Baptist Church off Lowell Square.

'That's a Nigra church,' the driver pointed out as he started the Dodge.

'That's all right,' Davidson replied with amiable irrelevance. 'Neither of us are Baptists anyway.'

'You fellers government agents?' wondered the man behind the wheel who thought they might be Federal civil-rights investigators or poverty specialists.

'Mr Kelleher, would you please tell our driver,' the criminal lawyer requested, 'whether we work for – or against – the government?'

'Mr. Davidson,' the burly investigator-bodyguard replied truthfully, 'during the nine grand years that I've been privileged – and pleased – to work with you, I have never once seen you do anything but fight the government. You have opposed the Federal, state and municipal authorities with a uniform dedication and ingenuity, with an honorable passion that has always warmed my Gaelic heart. Up the rebels!'

'Easy on that corny music-hall act, Jack,' Davidson advised wryly. 'In another minute you'll be singing those terrible IRA songs, and I'll get all choked up . . . What my associate says is true,' the lawyer explained to the chauffeur. 'We are not government employees, or even sympathizers.'

'What did he mean – up the rebels?' the driver queried uneasily.

'It was that statue of Robert E. Lee we just passed,' Davidson lied with nonchalant grace. 'He's a great fan of General Lee and the entire Confederate army. He's a dedicated admirer of the South, you see.'

Reassured, the taxi operator smiled.

'Glad to hear that. One thing I ought to tell you though,' he confided as he turned west toward Lowell Square. 'We don't consider the Confederates were rebels, not down here. So far as folks down here see it, it wasn't any rebellion but a War Between the States.'

'I'll remember that,' Kelleher promised. 'It was awfully nice of you to mention it, real friendly.'

Either Randolph Scott or Joel McCrea would have loved the bit, but it didn't overwhelm Joshua David Davidson, who tolerated the routine solely because it diverted the nosey driver from asking potentially dangerous questions about why they'd come to Paradise City. Aware that Kelleher was doing this deliberately, the older man stared out the window at the pleasant tree-lined streets of this notorious community. They reached the church, paid off the driver.

'You look tense, J.D.,' observed Kelleher as they started up the walk.

'I was getting worried whether you'd run out of material.'

'Hell, no. I still had my bird calls and all my Polish jokes – not to mention my terrific Pat O'Brien imitation.'

'Please don't mention it . . . Well, here we go. Now you can catch *my* act, Sonny.'

'You'll be great, J.D., just great.'

He was, and graceful and courteous and impressive too. The black minister knew who he was and was pleased that a famous lawyer would come to help, and Reverend Snell was also delighted that Davidson knew the Old Testament so well. They quoted back and forth at each other as Davidson questioned him about the case and the situation, understanding and appreciating each other perfectly.

'Frankly, I never expected you or any other important attorney to take the case,' the clergyman admitted as they prepared to part. 'I didn't think anybody cared about Samuel Clayton.'

'Somebody cares at least sixty-five thousand dollars' worth – and that's quite a bit of caring. You'd be astounded to know just how rich and influential a person is paying for this defense . . . As a matter of fact, I probably will be too.'

Snell peered thoughtfully.

'You mean *you* don't know who's putting up the money, Mr Davidson?'

'Not yet, but Mr Jack Kelleher and I will eventually figure it out, won't we? In the meantime, it remains a minor but probably not too important mystery. I assume that it's the good guys.'

'That's what *he* said,' the minister mused aloud.

'*He?*' Kelleher broke in prankishly. 'I'll bet he was a tall masked man on a white horse, and he had an Indian named Tonto with him – right?'

Reverend Ezra Snell shook his head.

'No, it wasn't the Lone Ranger or any other fictional character. He was a man in ordinary clothes, white, nice-looking and probably somewhere between thirty-five and forty-five years old. He said he might be able to get us a first-class lawyer.'

'Yes?' Davidson pressed.

'And he said that I must not tell anyone who he was because it could cost him his life . . . We were talking rather vaguely about cooperative efforts, joint projects. Now he's kept his part of the bargain by payment in advance, and I still don't know what he wants.'

The lawyer grunted.

'Don't worry, Reverend. You can be certain he does,' he assured Snell. 'At these prices, he knows exactly what he wants and he'll tell you when he's ready. He'll have a whole shopping list, I'd imagine . . . In the meanwhile, if you can get word to Mr Clayton that I'm going to represent him, that might be useful.'

'I'll try.'

'There's one more thing that I'd want you to do,' Joshua

David Davidson announced and then he explained what it was. 'Now if they'll need money for transportation or living expenses, I can put up one thousand dollars at once. They're going to be my strategic reserve in this chess game, and I've got to protect them.'

'Is there anything else?'

'Sit back and enjoy,' advised Kelleher. 'When you see Joshua David Davidson go to work in that courtroom, you'll be amazed, delighted and a little bit awed. I still am – after nine years.'

'Stop that nonsense, Jack,' the lawyer snapped in irritated embarrassment. 'With an ego as enormous as mine, I don't need any flattery from my associates.'

'He's better than Perry Mason, although not so handsome,' the former Notre Dame tackle joshed.

Knowing that Kelleher really meant it only made the praise even more awkward, for the criminal lawyer was secretly proud of his staff's esteem and devotion.

'That's not going to get you the extra twelve-fifty a week, Jack,' Davidson replied in pretended scorn. 'You'll just have to learn to live within your present income . . . I'll see you in the courtroom tomorrow morning at ten, Reverend.'

Close-up of Davidson's hand on the doorknob.

Fast dissolve to the two New Yorkers exiting the church.

Medium trucking shot as they walk slowly through the late-afternoon heat toward Lowell Square in search of a taxi.

'We'll need a car. Rent a limousine, air-conditioned, as soon as we get back to the hotel.'

'Right, J.D.'

'I'll want you to drive it. I don't want any of these big-eared locals eavesdropping, you understand.'

'Right, J.D.'

Tighten to medium close-up of both men.

'And stop that "Right, J.D." routine, will you? I've got enough on my mind without either your clowning or extravagant praise.'

'Flattery's the food of fools, right?'

'Jonathan Swift,' the older man identified instantly. 'Yes, that's about it. Let's just do our thing quietly and efficiently . . . Ah, there's a cab.'

Across town in the Paradise House, John Pikelis was on the telephone speaking with Irving. It was very hot in Miami, Irving reported, and he was suffering with a summer cold. Summer colds are especially annoying, Irving sniffled. When it came to sniffling, Irving was a born leader, Pikelis thought, but when would he get to the point? After enduring several more minor complaints, the racketeer who ruled Jefferson County decided to put the question bluntly.

'Irving, have you heard anything on that matter I asked you to check?'

'Yes, I have.'

'Well?'

'I've asked *somebody* who has *a lot of friends* around,' he began.

That would be shrewd Meyer.

'And *he's* asked quite a few people who ought to know. *Big* people in town here, in Vegas and Chicago and L.A. and Cleveland and New Orleans and New York. *Top* people – you know what I mean?'

'I know what you mean, Irving. What the hell did they say?'

The man in Miami hesitated, pausing to phrase his reply precisely and politely. He blew his nose, apologized.

'In a nutshell, it was all negative,' he finally replied. 'Entirely negative. Not one of them had heard anything about anyone who might want to bother you, John, and not one of them has anything but friendly feelings toward you and your associates. Yes, I think that's an accurate summary of all their comments.'

'I see,' Pikelis muttered as he wondered whether it was true.

Had Meyer told Irving the truth, and were all the Mafia bosses being frank with Meyer? According to the book – going by Meyer's stature and reputation – it should be the truth.

'As a matter of fact, some of these people seem to be having problems of their own,' Irving continued. 'There's one awfully nice fellow all hung up with a deportation case and another has a nasty tax problem, and I suppose you heard about the mess in Brooklyn.'

There had been five killings in the previous seven weeks in a bloody struggle between two Cosa Nostra 'families.'

'Yeah, I read the newspapers,' Pikelis acknowledged flatly.

'It's difficult to believe that men would be so unreasonable – so difficult and primitive – in this day and age,' grumbled Irving. 'Sensible people have tried to talk to them – older and more mature people with business experience – but they're like animals.'

'There's a real breakdown in law and order all right,' sympathized Pikelis. 'No more respect. Well, it's not going to happen here. I'm not going to stand for any of that stuff here, and you can tell everybody I said so. This is a nice, clean, quiet town – and it's going to stay that way.'

'I blame it on those crazy college kids and the hippies, John. They're so disorderly and dirty and violent – fighting with the police and making those hysterical demonstrations on the campuses and in the streets – that they're setting a horrible example for the whole country. You're right about the respect thing, John. It's a disgrace.'

Pikelis assured him again that *it* would *never* happen in Paradise City and asked when the eighteen new machines would be arriving. Irving examined his book, promised delivery by the second of August 'at the latest.' He would *personally* call the manager of the factory in Indiana to make sure.

'Thanks, and best regards to your family,' announced the racketeer.

'I'll tell him tonight.'

That night, Gilman drove up to the gate of the Fun Parlor at 7:55 – just as usual – and waved to the guard, who recognized him and opened the massive portal to admit the croupier's car. The guard looked cool behind his bullet-proof glass, relaxed in the comfort provided by the air-conditioner that was built into the side of the gatehouse. The man from Las Vegas knew that Arbolino would be packing his part of the gear at about this time, checking it again as he'd been trained to do. Gilman was, of course, right. As he stepped out of his car in the parking lot, the stunt man – thirteen miles away – was completing his audit and closing the second suitcase.

In Room 407 at the Jefferson, Willison was studying his watch and waiting for the phone to ring. It came at 9:10, and the caller congratulated 'Mr Warren' for sending along 'the data' so regularly 'on schedule.' A listener would have thought that the caller was an associate at the Southern Public Opinion Corporation. In fact, the voice belonged to P. T. Carstairs, who was reporting that he was back – on time – and would seize the car in ninety minutes as planned.

At 9:25, Carstairs walked into the lobby of the Paradise House and announced that he had returned from Daytona. He picked up his key, stepped into the bar for a Pernod. When the bartender named Harry welcomed him back, the millionaire sportsman thanked him for the salutation, acknowledged that he'd seen a racing driver friend in Daytona to discuss Grand Prix prospects and announced that he was going directly to bed.

'Alone,' he added wearily.

'You can't win 'em all, Mr Carstairs,' sympathized Harry Booth.

'I certainly can, young man,' the second most eligible bachelor in the United States responded in mock indignation, 'only this time I'm too bushed to play. Good night, sir.'

At 9:33, Parker Terence Carstairs entered The Breckenridge Suite and at 10;39 he quietly left it via the rear service door. Four minutes after that, the telephone rang in Room 218 – a small room at the back of the hotel – where Pikelis' chauffeur was sprawled on the bed in his undershorts, watching TV. 'Mr Pikelis wants you to bring the car out to the Fun Parlor right away,' somebody said.

'I'm making tracks,' the driver replied obediently and hung up without asking any questions. Mr Pikelis didn't encourage questions, but he did reward fidelity, so the chauffeur dressed quickly and hurried down to the basement garage where the gleaming Cadillac was housed. The big limousine pulled out approximately sixty-five minutes after Mr Arthur Warren had pulled into the entrance of the Starlight Drive-In Movie on Route 121.

'Can I still see the whole show?' the man in the blue Dart had asked.

The fat woman in the box-office booth nodded, chewing gum and smiling.

'Last show starts in a couple of minutes. First picture's *The Rape of the Zombies* and then the main feature's *Bullitt* starring Steve McQueen,' she singsonged mindlessly.

'I hear *Bullitt*'s pretty good,' the spy chatted as he waited for the change from his five-dollar bill.

'Top-notch, they say . . . Three, four, five. Thank you.'

He drove in and parked at the back. There were at least eighty to one hundred other cars spread across the lot, he noticed with satisifaction. Most of the other patrons appeared to be teenagers, and that was good too. They would be busy groping and panting through most of the evening, and his presence at the Starlight would probably be remembered by the gum-chewing cashier. At 10 p.m., the lights dimmed and

The Rape of the Zombies began – immediately after three slides advertising local roadhouses and stores. He stared at the picture in disbelief, for if it wasn't the worst film of all time it was certainly a major contender. It was a genuine tribute to the 1943 OSS survival course and the more recent riots on the Columbia campus that Williston was able to endure *The Rape of the Zombies* without gagging. Even the two topless scenes of the seminude 'native' girls didn't help. It was a little better when he turned off the sound, but not much.

At 11:05, the mad scientist was hacked to pieces by his own zombies, and the film ended and everybody who still had pants on left the cars for soft drinks and pizzas and Texas-style 'giant hot dogs.' At 11:25, the lights faded once more as *Bullitt* jumped onto the huge screen. At 11:31, Professor Andrew Williston looked around warily and concluded that no one in the immediately adjacent vehicles was interested in his car. He reached down to the floor near the far door, found the half-dummy they'd stolen from the department store and slowly raised it to the seat. Then he opened the well-greased door beside him, slid out as he moved the dummy into position behind the wheel. He closed the door with a minimum of noise, glanced around again. No one was looking. Crouching low, Williston moved off into the shadows and slipped through the trees at the back of the lot. Two minutes later, he found Arbolino in the panel truck on the side road.

They drove five hundred yards slowly before the stunt man accelerated to thirty miles an hour and flicked on the headlights. A moment later, the truck moved into the intersection of Ocean Road – four and three eighths miles from the Fun Parlor. They'd measured the distance precisely during the 'dry run' rehearsal the previous night – studying the route, traffic, timing of the escape.

'I guess I'd better tell you about the picture – in case anyone asks you about it later,' Williston announced.

'I saw *Bullitt* on the Coast a couple of months ago, Andy.'

'I'm talking about the other one – *Rape of the Zombies*. A real stinker, pure – or should I say impure – trash. Listen to this yarn.'

Arbolino listened, laughed.

'Sounds like one of those low-budget exploitation pictures they shot in ten days,' he judged when Williston finished.

'Very low-budget. I think they were using secondhand

zombies. Even the teats on the topless natives were sagging,' the professor complained. 'Oh, here we are. This is where we pull off the road and wait. Shouldn't be long, if he's on time.'

'He'll be on time.'

A mile away, the large Cadillac was rolling smoothly through the night and the driver was enjoying the stereo sound of the radio, humming loudly along with Bobby Gentry's rhythmically plaintive 'Ode to Billy Joe.' Just before the final chorus of the 1968 hit, he stopped enjoying the record – abruptly.

The cold gun muzzle at the back of his neck had that effect.

'Keep your hands – both hands – on the wheel, Tom, and don't look back,' a voice hissed.

He sneaked one instinctive glance at the rear-view mirror, saw that the man behind him appeared faceless. Stocking mask, he guessed correctly.

The gun dug painfully into his flesh.

'Don't do that again, Tom, or I'll kill you. Just drive.'

'You're crazy,' warned the chauffeur. 'This is John Pikelis' personal limousine. You've got to be crazy to try to hijack this car.'

'I'm crazy and you're still alive – for the moment . . . Up ahead there . . . by the two big trees . . . pull off the road, stop and blink your headlights three times. Then turn them off. You got that, Tom?'

'Yeah.'

The saga of 'Billy Joe' ended, and now the genial announcer was praising the merits of Miller's High Life beer. Tom Waugh's throat felt exceedingly tight and dry, a combination induced by fear and confusion and anger. He was furious but not foolhardy, so he obeyed Carstairs' instructions to the letter.

'Good boy. Now no tricks, or you'll be splattered all over the windshield . . . Turn slowly to the right . . . just your head . . . That's it.'

The door beside the chauffeur opened, and Waugh heard the keys being removed from the ignition. A second man. The gun was still pressed against the base of his skull, so there had to be a second man. A few seconds later, the driver heard footsteps and the sound of the trunk being opened. The second man – or men – loaded something into it, closed it and walked back to replace the key in the ignition. Then the door behind the chauffeur was closed, and one of the rear doors opened and slammed. The weight of the car shifted, reflected the presence of one – perhaps two – additional passengers.

'Let's go, Tom,' the voice hissed.

'Where to, *sir?*'

There was an understandable bitterness in that last word.

'Fun Parlor.'

'What the hell for?' wondered the chauffeur irritably.

'To have some *fun*, you idiot. Roll it . . . now.'

The limousine moved back onto the highway, cruised two hundred yards.

'Put your lights back on, Tom. No tricks, please. We don't need any police cars, you know.'

The driver obeyed, moved the Cadillac at a steady forty miles an hour down Ocean Road.

'When we get to the gate, just wave to the guard and show your teeth in your country-boy smile. I'm moving back into the shadows, but this gun is still pointed at the back of your head.'

The pressure of the round hard muzzle vanished, and then the chauffeur heard the sound of metal against metal.

'Silencer, Tom,' explained the invisible whisperer. 'Just put on the silencer. Now I can blow out the back of your head with almost no noise – if you get stupid.'

'I'm not *that* stupid,' Pikelis' chauffeur snapped.

It was eerie. The other passenger or passengers hadn't made a sound, said a word. Their discipline added to the driver's fear, confirmed his belief that these were cold-blooded professionals who actually would kill if resisted. Now the radio was thrumming out one of Chet Atkins' best country records, but even that familiar favorite didn't make Tom Waugh feel any better.

In the back of the car, Williston looked down at the phosphorescent face of his wrist watch and realized that Gilman was taking his nightly 'ten minute break.' He'd be turning over the roulette table to the 'relief' man, strolling back to the male employees' lavatory and then planting the incendiary time pencil in the alarm control box concealed behind the painting in the corridor outside Dennison's office. It would erupt in a single searing flash of intense heat, melting, fusing and destroying all the controls at 11:51. Or perhaps 11:52 or even 11:50 if the timing mechanism wasn't quite perfect; you couldn't sensibly count on it completely.

That was why they were going to strike at 11:49.

'There's the gate, Tom. Slow down and be good,' Carstairs hissed.

As planned, the guard admitted the Pikelis limousine without question. The chauffeur obeyed the whispered instruction to drive the car to the rear of the Fun Parlor – the employees' parking area – and it was there that he was knocked unconscious. To make sure that he stayed that way for at least an hour, Williston injected a small dose of the same drug they'd needled into Luther Hyatt so satisfactorily. The Sledgehammer team propped up the driver to make it look as if he'd dozed off behind the wheel, and then the three spies scattered on their individual assignments.

Williston wriggled through the shrubbery to hide the radio-controlled device just under the gate guard's air-conditioner, and Arbolino found the main telephone cable leading from the casino to a nearby line. He had to struggle with the insulated cutters, but after five tries he succeeded in severing the line at 11:47. Twenty yards away, Carstairs was loading the weapon that was supposed to get them out. It felt odd. He hadn't handled one of these in years, not since they'd led the Maquis attack on the Wehrmacht armored-car column a week before D-Day. Or had it been the raid on Hitler's birthday?

He placed the weapon beside the radio transmitter on the floor of the back of the car, watched Williston and the stunt man return. They all checked their watches. It was almost 11:49 – time to attack.

'Three minutes, and then we'll come out like gangbusters,' warned the taut teacher.

'Your car will be waiting, sir. Although I really ought to go in with you.'

Williston shook his head.

'We've been through all that. You're the best driver, and you're the best outdoors marksman, so you're logical to cover us out here, Petie,' he reminded the sportsman.

Arbolino and Williston picked up the gear that Carstairs had unloaded from the suitcases for them.

'You'd be smarter to take the nine-millimeter Uzi instead of the M-3,' Carstairs grumbled. 'It's got a higher rate of fire – six hundred and fifty rounds per minute instead of four hundred – and it packs a forty-round magazine instead of thirty.'

'This is going to be a raid, not a massacre,' Arbolino observed, 'and these silenced M-3s make a lot less noise.'

'Let's move,' ordered the teacher.

They turned toward the building.

'*Merde*,' Carstairs called out softly in the traditional farewell used by Allied agents before parachuting into Occupied France.

'*Merde*,' floated back Williston's whisper in the darkness.

The two raiders reached the rear door, and the teacher carefully inserted the extra key that Gilman had provided. Inside, one of the guards was seated in a canvas and metal armchair – smoking a cigarette and listening to the music that drifted up the corridor from the lounge where the band was playing Jim Webb's 'Up, Up and Away.' It was a catchy, pleasant tune, made even more familiar as a much broadcast airline commercial. Suddenly, the door swung open and the startled guard stared.

Two men.

Two men in black suits, each wearing a Santa Claus mask.

Two black-suited and masked men, each wearing an Army musette bag over his left shoulder and each pointing a submachine gun at him. The weapons didn't look exactly like the ordinary submachine guns, but the difference wouldn't cover his burial expenses.

The guard froze.

'Not a fraction of an inch, or you're dead,' one of the intruders whispered.

'In red chunks,' added the other.

The guard knew that a .45-caliber automatic weapon could do just that at such short range – five yards. Unlike Carstairs, he didn't know that the M-3 weighed 8.15 pounds, was 29.8 inches long – with the stock extended – and fired with a muzzle velocity of 920 feet per second. He didn't care about those fine points, being aware of the fundamental fact that this piece of hardware could literally dismember him at this range.

'What do you want?' croaked the frightened thug.

'We're looking for a pay phone, you idiot,' Williston replied.

Then he stepped forward swiftly, swung the gun and knocked the guard to the floor. Arbolino drew a can of Mace from his musette bag, sprayed the dazed man in the face for a full five seconds.

Williston glanced at his watch.

11:51. Late, but not dangerously.

At that moment, the incendiary time pencil ignited and burned out the alarm-system controls. Only a tiny wisp of smoke seeped out from the closed and hidden control box, but the temperature inside was nearly 1000 degrees.

The invaders moved down the corridor cautiously, found the curtained passage that Gilman had described and peered through a narrow opening between the velvet drapes. They were looking directly into the gambling room, where several dozen men and women were cheerily and naïvely trying their 'luck.' Gilman was swapping wisecracks with the blond band singer who stood watching the roulette and sipping Scotch on the rocks, and dapper Willie Dennison was standing near the dice table, where seven or eight grown men were totally occupied with two pitted ivory cubes. One of them paused between rolls to pat the rump of his redheaded companion, as if the call girl's plump flank would bring some magic to his throws.

A very ordinary Wednesday night at the Fun Parlor.

'Four . . . three . . . two . . . one . . . *go*,' chanted Professor Andrew Williston of the Columbia University faculty.

Then the raiders charged into the room. Arbolino shifted his rapid-fire gun to cover the door to the lounge, outside which at least two guards were always posted. A moment later, he swung it around in a tight arc to point it at the armed man who protected the cashier's booth. Williston spun on his heel, aimed his machine gun at the other guard who stood by the door to the manager's office. For several moments, nobody noticed them. One of the bettors glanced up from his poker hand, gaped.

A plump woman in an expensive silk pants suit that did nothing for her peered, screamed.

It was a small ladylike scream, but adequate.

Hush.

'Nobody move,' Arbolino ordered loudly. 'You two bastards – you by the cashier and you at the back exit – put your hands behind your necks . . . Now – or you're dogmeat!'

One of the guards hesitated, and Williston put four bullets into the wall about half a foot to his left.

'He'll kill you with the next burst,' the stunt man promised.

Both guards obeyed.

'Now you two lie face down on the floor – over in the middle where we can see you,' he commanded.

They obeyed.

'What the hell do you think you're doing?' rasped Dennison.

'Ho, ho, ho – we're having Christmas early this year, Daddy,' Arbolino answered.

The plan was for Arbolino to do the talking; Williston's voice was known around town from all the interviewing.

'Only this time Santa is taking instead of bringing the presents,' Arbolino continued. 'No, don't worry, ladies and gentlemen, we don't want your jewels or your wallets. Just the house cash, just the bank's money. Just Little John Pikelis' money.'

Dennison was edging backward, and Williston guessed that the casino manager meant to reach the alarm button built into the side of the dice table. It didn't matter. Beneath the hot mask, he smiled at the awareness that the alarm system had been neutralized.

'Get the money,' he whispered.

Arbolino moved swiftly to the cashier's cage, pushed the muzzle of his M-3 within eight inches of the man inside.

'Nothing smaller than twenties, and fast,' commanded the stunt man as he opened his musette bag.

The cashier hesitated nervously.

'Either the money goes out in this bag, or they'll carry you out in another one,' Arbolino promised.

That did it, and within thirty seconds the musette bag was bulging with thousands – perhaps seventy or eighty – of dollars in currency.

'Bug-out time,' announced the stunt man.

'The reindeer are getting restless, so we're leaving now,' he told the people in the room. 'If nobody follows us for three minutes, nobody will get hurt . . . Go.'

Arbolino went, backing out toward the drapes through which they'd entered. Williston followed the same procedure, swiveling his eyes and machine gun like the rotating radar antennas atop a warship. It was going perfectly, perfectly.

'Dennison,' a husky voice off to the left warned softly.

Just as he'd been trained so many years earlier, he swung the machine gun and simultaneously picked out his target. The casino manager had drawn a .32 automatic from somewhere, was raising it furtively. The instantaneous burst from the M-3 slashed at his upper right arm and shoulder, punching three holes in his dinner jacket and slamming Dennison back against the dice table as if he'd been hit with a baseball bat. The casino manager slumped over the green felt, now spotted with red-brown from the wounds.

'I'll take your head off next time, Willie,' whispered the gunman who'd once been known as Marie Antoinette.

'Son of a bitch . . . son of a bitch,' moaned the casino manager.

Williston swept the machine gun back and forth twice, but nobody moved.

'Just stay where you are, ladies and gentleman. This isn't your money or your war,' Arbolino told the patrons. 'Give our regards to Pikelis, Willie.'

Dennison cursed again; the pain was terrible.

Suddenly, they were gone. They fled up the corridor, pausing only to throw three tear-gas grenades that flooded the passageway behind them with choking, blinding fumes. At the door, they ripped off the masks and fled into the night. Carstairs was waiting in the Cadillac, holding the magnetized metal box out the window. While Williston covered the door of the building with his automatic weapon, the stunt man crammed the musette bag into the metal box and locked it as he sprinted swiftly to Gilman's parked car – one of thirty in the employees' lot. Arbolino crouched down slammed the magnetized box into place under the bottom – midway between the front and rear wheels – and raced to the Cadillac.

'Let's go, let's go – dammit,' urged the second most eligible bachelor in the United States.

They opened the front door on the right side, pulled out the limp chauffeur and dropped him on the concrete. When Williston and Arbolino jumped into the rear passenger section, slamming the doors as Carstairs put his foot down on the gas pedal. The teacher reached down, found the radio-control device, raised the small transmitter to his lap. It had to work, or they'd never get through the gate.

He flipped the switch and stared through the moonlight at the guard house at the entrance – perhaps 120 yards away. A moment later, the cylinder he'd placed began to spew yellow nauseating gas which the air-conditioner intake sucked into the guard house. That ought to take care of the sentry. Now it was up to Arbolino to cope with the heavy metal gate.

It barred their exit – 100 yards ahead.

'Ready, Tony?' Carstairs asked over his shoulder.

'Ready . . . stop.'

The millionaire stopped the car, Arbolino raised the weapon and took careful aim – and fired. The bazooka rocket flamed through the night, struck the gate and blasted it open.

'Groovy,' exulted Carstairs, who'd suggested the anti-tank weapon as a key to the exit.

The Cadillac roared through the ruined gate at fifty miles per hour, swept down around the curve along Ocean Road for two minutes before the wealthy racing-car enthusiast slowed it to a less ostentatious forty. 'One minute and fifty-five seconds to the truck, clock it,' he challenged. The men in the rear were busy peeling off the black jackets, cramming those garments and the machine guns into a suitcase along with the masks and the radio-control device. Williston put on a blue and white cord jacket, clip-on gray bow tie; Arbolino was busy ripping off his gray shirt to expose the gaudy green-and-yellow sport shirt beneath.

'One fifty-three, two seconds under,' Carstairs boasted as he pulled the limousine off the road and flicked off the headlights. He hurried out, raised the hood and placed another incendiary time pencil inside before closing it. Then he peeled off the gloves that he'd worn to avoid leaving any fingerprints, sighed. Arbolino and Williston were loading the two suitcases into the back of the truck.

'It was beautiful, wasn't it?' Carstairs demanded.

'I'll tell you all about it as soon as Tony gets this truck rolling.'

Williston and the millionaire jumped into the rear compartment of the panel truck, and the stunt man immediately swung the vehicle back onto the highway. In three and a half minutes, he stopped and banged on the partition behind him. Williston leaped out, vanished into the trees on the dead run. The truck rolled on a moment later, heading toward Paradise City. Arbolino would let Carstairs out near the entrance to the alley leading to the Paradise House garage, and the millionaire was to make his way back up to the Breckenridge Suite by the service stairs. Then Arbolino would drive 'home' to the trailer camp on Route 121. It was unlikely that he'd meet any police road blocks, for (1) they'd knocked out the gambling casino's phone lines; (2) Crowden's Caravan Camp was far from the Fun Parlor – on the opposite side of Paradise City.

Williston paused at the tree line, looked. He recognized the scene on the screen; there were still at least twenty minutes more of *Bullitt* to come. Crouching low, he moved back to his car and slipped in – pushing down the dummy to the floor. Then he leaned back, pointing his eyes at the screen as if he cared. It had gone well, remarkably well. Gilman's plan had worked. That business with Dennison had almost . . . well, the whispered warning had saved him. He tried to remember who'd been standing nearby, who'd alerted him in time.

He was still thinking about this when the film ended, and then he drove out in the herd of other cars. As he guided the blue Dart out onto the highway, he saw a flash of distant flame in his rear-view mirror. The time pencil had ignited, and now Pikelis' Cadillac – with any evidence of fingerprints – was burning. He heard the sirens of two police cars, saw them race past in the direction of the Fun Parlor a few moments later. The police paid no attention to the stream of vehicles eddying out of the Starlight Drive-In, reckoning that none of these cars could have been involved in the hold-up. Yes, it was going along according to plan. The man from Las Vegas, who'd played the major role in designing the operation, had been right again.

Williston drove along in the caravan carefully, maintaining the same speed as the other recent alumni of the Starlight's sex-and-violence course. It had been a fairly ordinary evening at the Starlight, if you took the larger view. A fat girl named Beverly had had relations with three teen-age boys in the back of a green Ford, but that wasn't unusual for Beverly, and the Arden sisters had 'fooled around' with a couple of fellows who'd starred on the football field for Jefferson High. That wasn't extraordinary either, since the sisters' fondness for both athletes and 'fooling around' was well known. The cashier would report that business had been about average for a Wednesday night, and sales of pizzas and hot dogs were nothing exceptional.

At the Turner Traffic Circle, the cars split out in various directions, and Williston found he could pick up some speed. Two more police cars swept past as the sound of a distant blast echoed, announcing that the Cadillac's fuel tank had exploded. The limousine would be a total loss, the ex-OSS agent thought happily, and this would add to Pikelis' humiliation. Now he'd know that *they* were here, that there were several of *them* and *they* meant to *fight*. Near the city limits, the teacher began to look around for a place to dispose of the dummy. It wasn't until he reached the London Boulevard section that he spotted a pair of garbage pails on the sidewalk. He stopped the car, found one of the pails empty and dropped in the dummy.

'Out hitting the hot spots?' joked the sallow desk clerk as Williston entered the lobby of the Jefferson ten minutes later.

'I wish I had.'

'If you're looking for a piece of tail . . .' suggested the clerk.

Williston yawned, shook his head.

'Some other time. I'm going to try to sleep off the effects of that show at the drive-in.'

'I heard *Bullitt*'s pretty good,' countered the clerk.

'You're right, but the other one – *Rape of the Zombies*, a real stinker.'

'*Rape of the Zombies?*' chuckled the balding man behind the desk. '*Rape of the Zombies?* Hot damn!'

The spy shrugged wearily, took the self-service elevator to the fourth floor. Later – after he'd undressed and washed and listened to the radio – he realized that it was 2:13 and Arbolino might be broadcasting in half a minute. He tuned his set to the proper frequency, waited.

'Please repeat the message, Charlie. Please repeat the message, Charlie,' he heard Arbolino say.

The key word was 'Charlie.' Everything was all right. The stunt man had dropped off Carstairs and returned to the trailer camp without incident. That was fine, but Williston was still troubled by the question of the unknown helper who'd saved him at the Fun Parlor. Who would want to – dare to – assist the enemies of brutal John Pikelis? He turned off the radio, leaned back on the bed and closed his eyes. For the tenth time, he struggled to recall the faces of the people who'd been standing near him when Dennison reached for the gun.

Suddenly he remembered, and then he guessed who it was.

Yes, he recognized the voice now.

It was the shapely deep-throated blonde who sang with the band.

Judy . . . Judy something . . . Judy Ellis.

Yes, it was Judy Ellis.

Now why would Judy Ellis do that? Why would she risk so much for masked strangers?

It didn't make any sense, unless – so far as Judy Ellis was concerned – they weren't strangers at all. This realization left Williston even more puzzled, for he had no recollection of ever meeting her or even hearing her name. He would have to ask the others, and they would have to decide what to do about her. They couldn't ignore her, for if she knew them she was dangerous.

That, at least, was certain.

Who she was or who she was working for remained an annoying mystery, one that continued to trouble Professor Andrew Williston until he finally surrendered to sleep.

CHAPTER TWENTY-TWO

'I know the rates are higher during the week, but I didn't think this ought to wait till Sunday, Bud,' announced the man who called Atlanta each week. 'Anyway, it's me who's paying, not you . . . No, I didn't telephone because I'm lonely or because I miss my Teddy bear either. I'm calling because of what happened last night. In concise if not quite elegant terms, the fit has really hit the Shan . . . That's an old joke, Bud. If you don't know it, I'm not going to tell it now at these prices. I'm not made of quarters, you know.'

He glanced out of the booth at the yellow Mustang that was baking in the morning sun.

'Bud, those people I wrote about are getting very energetic and creative – with tommy guns,' he continued. 'And fire bombs. No, I'm not *pulling your leg*. I'm not *jesting* or being *prankish* either, you imbecile . . . Bud, this is getting much too rough for such cutesy language. This is developing into a Chicago-style war, and if you're too young to remember that try on the Gallo-Profaci vendetta a few years back . . . Yeah, Brooklyn. Listen, last night these cowboys hit the Fun Parlor with submachine guns and a lot of fancy hardware. Gas bombs – all sorts of fancy crap. I heard one story that they had *silenced* tommy guns, and even *we* don't have *silenced* tommy guns.'

It was only 9:50 a.m., but it was already burning hot and he mopped his brow in the steamy atmosphere of the telephone booth.

'This is a big-league group, Bud,' he continued, 'and Pikelis has a large rough organization too and I don't like the possibility of being caught in the middle – alone . . . Of course I'm scared. I'm not Lee Marvin or Richard Burton or Jean-Paul Belmondo, and nobody's showed me the final script yet. For all I know, maybe I'm supposed to be "hit" in the last reel and I'm too young to die . . . *Cool?* It's easy for you to tell me to stay cool; you're a couple of hundred miles out of range. Maybe not. Maybe these new boys have guided missiles too. Nothing about this outfit would surprise me . . . No, that's a lie. Everything they do surprises me – and that scares me too. I hate surprises . . . No, I don't know how many of them there are, but I'm only one and the odds are lousy. I'd feel better if I had nine members of our family around – with mortars and cannon. Fourteen would be even cozier – with air support . . . yeah, tell that to the boss. You tell him that I need help . . . Bud, *that's* not my problem. Getting laid is no problem in this town. I'm a very popular and charming guy, and besides I know of at least seven cat houses in town.'

He paused, looked at the parked Mustang again. The seat would be scorching, absolutely sizzling.

'No, no corpses yet but it's only a matter of time,' he warned. 'Bud, these boys are out to demolish John's entire organization and he isn't about to let them . . . You better believe it. Listen, get me some muscle down here or I may get very weepy. I'll spell it out for you. H-E-L-P – that's all in capital letters, with an exclamation point at the end . . . *Very* funny; you're breaking me up . . . Listen, Groucho, you wouldn't be so goddam comic if *you* were down here alone.'

It was at that moment that the conversation was interrupted.

'Seventy-five cents more, please,' drawled the operator.

'I'll check in again on Sunday, if I'm still alive,' the man in the phone booth promised as he ended the call.

He stepped out, heard the church bells chime ten.

'Hear ye, hear ye, the Superior Court of Jefferson County is now in session,' Clerk Arnold Tibbett singsonged eight miles away in downtown Paradise City. 'The Honorable Ralph M. Gillis presiding, *please rise*.'

'Here come de judge,' predicted Kelleher.

The high-ceilinged courtroom was crowded with officials, police, reporters and spectators who'd come to enjoy the sensational trial. It was going to be dirtier than a Swedish movie, if the rumors were correct. In this throng of more than 160 people, nobody paid any particular attention to the three white men who sat beside Reverend Ezra Snell in the eighth row. Judge Gillis, triple-chinned and solemn behind his gold-rimmed bifocals, entered in his flowing gown and marched to his high-backed chair as everyone stood up respectfully.

There was a low buzz of anticipation – for about five seconds.

Judge Gillis gestured, and the clerk responded automatically with a loud request for 'Silence in the court!'

Gillis nodded, looked over to the prosecutor's table where Jefferson County District Attorney Reece Everett sat – quite splendid in his new gray silk suit – waiting with two crew-cut young assistants. The judge could see that 'old Reece' was just rarin' to go, full of the wonderful energy and rhetoric that the prospect of publicity always seemed to bring out in him. Gillis could hardly blame him, having been the DA himself before being elevated to the bench eight and a half years earlier. The judge leaned back, let his eyes wander over the room and blinked when he saw the man beside Snell.

Oh my.

Oh my, oh my, oh my.

Yes, it was *him* all right. Judge Gillis recognized the long gray hair, the big famous head that he'd seen on the TV news so many times.

It was *him*, and he sure wasn't here sightseeing. Not *him*. He was a tiger, tough and cunning and plump on the flesh of the dozens of eager prosecutors whom he'd consumed. He was a man eater, that one. It was going to be one helluva trial, and for a moment the judge considered calling 'old Reece' to the bench to warn him. No, 'old Reece' was getting mighty big for his britches and Gillis decided to let him find out for himself. It would be a painful education, Gillis thought, but it was time for 'old Reece' to face some realities after years of soft living in the artificial protected atmosphere of Pikelis' well-managed empire. Let 'old Reece' take his legal lumps and grow up, the judge thought maliciously.

Everett, the mayor, Marton and John Pikelis himself were all in for quite a surprise. Judge Gillis would do his best to move things along, as they expected him to, but the realistic man on the bench knew that with *him* in the case the trial might take many weeks and if – no, when – the Nigra was convicted he'd fight the appeal to the U.S. Supreme Court. It was a rather exciting prospect; none of Ralph Gillis' cases had ever gone up to the U.S. Supreme Court. The U.S. Supreme Court – that was *something*. They said that *he'd* never lost a murder case appeal to the U.S. Supreme Court – a remarkable record.

Oh my, oh my, oh my.

Judge Gillis almost purred, fought down the accompanying smile.

He nodded to the clerk.

'People versus Clayton,' chanted the civil servant.

'Please bring in the defendant,' ordered the judge sharply. 'Can't start the trial without the defendant.'

The clerk signaled to the uniformed man in the side doorway, and ten seconds later four policemen escorted Sam Clayton into the room. Another buzz from the spectators, another judicial gesture and another command for silence.

'Mr Clayton,' began the judge. A number of those in the room were somewhat surprised by this as black people were generally addressed by their first names in Jefferson County, and they didn't guess that Gillis was being meticulously courteous and correct because the judge wanted the trial transcript to look good when it reached the U.S. Supreme Court. 'Mr Clayton, are you represented by counsel?' Gillis asked piously. 'I don't see anyone at your counsel table, and if you don't have an attorney under state and Federal law, I'm obliged to name one for you.'

The district attorney listened contentedly. It was all arranged. The judge would appoint Norton Woodhouse and Woodhouse knew what was expected.

'If it please the court,' somebody said from the spectator benches.

'Here we go,' Gillis thought. 'Yes?' he asked aloud.

A number of people – including the defendant – turned to look at the stranger. He was a well-dressed graying man with a dramatic air, big-headed and clear-voiced.

'May I approach the bench, your honor?' he asked.

'Does this relate to the question of the defendant's attorney? If it does, you may,' the judge announced curtly. 'If not sit down. I'll have no interruptions or nonsense in my court.'

Everett beamed. You could count on good old Ralph Gillis to run a no-nonsense trial. The district attorney didn't notice Clayton staring at the black minister beside the stranger, didn't see Reverend Snell's meaningful nod. The Northerner – his speech identified him – strode down the aisle, stopped ten feet in front of the elevated podium.

'What is it?' demanded Gillis.

'It will not be necessary for the court to appoint counsel, Your Honor,' the man said. 'I am Mr Clayton's attorney.'

Reece Everett frowned at this unexpected development, and Shelby Salmon – the correspondent covering the case for WPAR–TV – swallowed twice as he recognized the stranger.

'Are you a licensed attorney admitted to practice in this state?' the judge asked with poker-faced innocence.

'I am, Your Honor. I'm a member of the bar in New York and several other states, and – by reciprocity and subsequent application to the Supreme Court of this state – am entitled to practice here.'

'May I have your name, please, Counselor?'

'My, my, 'old Reece' was going to have a fit now.

'My name is Joshua David Davidson,' he replied in a voice that sounded like a trumpet call to arms.

And that tore it.

A muffled hysteria – hushed but palpable – swept the courtroom. The reporters whispered, the spectators stood up to see the famous criminal lawyer and the district attorney of Jefferson County blossomed in a look that indicated that he didn't know whether to cry or wet his pants. Joshua David Davidson – what the *hell* was *he* doing *here*?

'I'll have quiet – or I'll clear the court,' threatened the judge as he furtively relished the anguished shock 'old Reece' was showing.

'Your Honor,' Everett blustered a moment after he jumped to his feet. 'Your Honor, Mr Davidson is a very well-publicized and clever and expensive lawyer. I'd like to know what he's doing mixing into this case. I'd like to know who he really represents – some agitator group?'

'I represent Samuel Roosevelt Clayton, sir.'

The judge turned to the defendant.

'Is this man your lawyer?' Gillis asked.

'Yes, he is, Judge.'

Everett blanched again

'With the fancy fees that this prominent New York attorney charges,' he sneered, 'I can't believe that the defendant could possibly afford him. Why, this boy—'

'If it please the court, I'd like to request that the bench instruct the district attorney not to refer to my client in such a derogatory, contemptuous and improper manner,' Davidson whiplashed back swiftly. 'Mr Clayton is twenty-eight years old and served honorably for three years in the United States Army. He is not a boy. He is an adult, with all the rights and dignity and respect that our laws – state and Federal – provide for adults.'

Gillis nodded thoughtfully. Davidson was going to devastate 'old Reece' before this battle ended. There wouldn't be enough left of Everett to make one good barbecue sandwich.

'Will the court so instruct the prosecutor?' Davidson pressed coolly.

'Your client will get all his legal rights. Mr Everett,' Gillis announced, 'please consider yourself so instructed.'

'There's another point that I think I must raise at this time – before we begin the *long* and *arduous* process of selecting a jury, Your Honor,' the celebrated criminal lawyer continued. 'I'd be very grateful if you'd instruct the district attorney not to make any further remarks about the fact that I'm not a local resident or that my fees are substantial. It seems to me that either might be considered prejudicial by the appellate court later.'

Davidson was laying it right on the line.

He was going to fight every point, every word, every technicality and he meant to go all the way. He wasn't going to give 'old Reece' anything – except ulcers, sweats and insomnia.

'Mr Davidson, would you please come a bit closer?' the judge asked.

'Of course, Your Honor.'

'I have duly noted – as I assume you meant me to – your comment on "the long and arduous process of selecting a jury," ' Gillis said dryly. Davidson smiled. 'And your reference to "the appellate court later" did not pass unnoticed either. I'd been informed by our distinguished prosecuting attorney that this would be a short and simple case, that the defendant had confessed and that the trial would not last more than a few days. I'm planning on going off on vacation in about a week. I'd welcome your frankness on this prospect.'

'I see no reason why Your Honor shouldn't take his vacation,' Davidson answered with elaborate deference. 'After all, this trial won't be over in a week but it won't have started either. I'm about to make a request for a month's adjournment to give me adequate time to prepare the defense.'

'And if I don't grant it?'

'Your Honor, I'm certain that as wise and experienced a member of the bench as you must certainly appreciate what the appellate court would say if a newly retained defense counsel were rushed to trial in a case involving a possible death penalty. They'd reverse on that alone.'

It was true and Gillis knew it, and Davidson knew that Gillis knew it.

'I'd bet that you've got a few more motions,' speculated the judge.

Davidson grinned.

'I'm glad to see that my estimate of Your Honor's wisdom was so sound. Yes, I've got quite a few motions – the complete kit. I'll start with *Miranda* when the trial begins, but that's just for openers.'

The man in the black robe nodded.

'You're a poker player, Mr Davidson?'

'Yes, I enjoy the combat of adversary proceedings, Your Honor.'

The judge could see that Everett was getting edgy about the private conversation, gestured to Davidson to step back.

'In accord with defense counsel's suggestion,' Gillis announced, 'I'm advising the district attorney that it would probably be wiser to omit any personal references to Mr Davidson's home, origins or economic status. If we concentrate on trying Sam Clayton instead of Joshua Davidson, we should move this trial much more quickly – and properly.'

The prosecutor shrugged in acceptance.

'Now can we start the selection of the jury?' he asked impatiently.

'Are you ready, Mr Davidson?'

'No, Your Honor. I've just been retained in this very important and complex case which involves a possible death penalty, and I'm certainly entitled to adequate time to prepare.'

'And what would the distinguished defense counsel consider adequate time?' challenged Everett.

Davidson stroked his chin, as if considering.

'I know that I could justifiably and properly ask for two months,' he began.

'*Two months?*'

Oh my, 'old Reece' was getting shrill and angry already.

'Two months – that's *ridiculous*,' the prosecutor blustered.

'But I won't ask for *two* months, Your Honor,' Davidson continued blandly. 'I think that *one* month will be adequate, and I hereby move for a month.'

'May *I* approach the bench, Your Honor?' Everett demanded.

'Of course.'

The prosecutor walked forward.

'Ralph,' he appealed in low, grim tones, 'we've got to do something about this before it gets out of control.'

It was already out of control, and if 'old Reece' weren't so stupid he would have realized it.

'Ralph, this was supposed to be a fast simple trial. That's

what we were *told*. You know *they're* going to be sore as hell if it doesn't go that way, and *somebody's* going to pay for it.'

It would be Everett, not me, thought the judge. Gillis had less than two more years before his term ran out and he retired.

'Any suggestions, Reece? I'd like to do what I can. You know I won't stand for any nonsense in my court, and I'd sure welcome any suggestions on how to get this moving – any *legally sound* suggestions that won't stir up problems if this fellow appeals as he says he will.'

'Don't give him a month, Ralph. Please don't give him a month.'

He was such a fool. Gillis had told Ashley and Pikelis that Everett was a fool, but they hadn't paid any attention and they'd made him district attorney because he photographed well and took orders even better. Now Davidson would show them – and the world – exactly how big a mistake that had been. Wherever Joshua David Davidson tried a case, wire-service reporters and network TV news crews and correspondents of *Life* and *The New York Times* appeared within twenty-four hours. Let Ashley and Pikelis try to control *them*.

'Mr. Davidson,' summoned the judge as he gestured to the defense lawyer to come forward again, 'I propose to give you three weeks – and then, if you need a few more days, I'll consider such a motion. It'll bring us into the worst heat of late August in any case.'

'I don't mind, Your Honor,' the New Yorker answered. 'As former President Truman once said, if you can't stand the heat, get out of the kitchen. I've tried cases in all parts of the country at all times of the year. Well, this will actually be my first case in August since most courts usually close up for August – but heat doesn't bother me a bit, in court or out.'

He was going to get his month if he wanted it, but saying 'three weeks' should keep Everett happy. Happy? No, but less hysterical.

'Three weeks then,' the judge declared. 'Any other motions?'

'I'd like to request permission for an immediate medical examination of the defendant to determine whether he was beaten or otherwise coerced into signing this so-called confession. Under the Supreme Court decision in—'

Gillis gestured.

'You don't have to cite it by name and number,' he

interrupted curtly. 'You've got a right to it. Whenever you want, any doctor you choose.'

'Thank you, Your Honor. My medical experts will be at the jail in *one hour*. They'll be Dr Halsey Travis of the Tulane Medical School and Dr Avery Brigham of Emory Medical School.'

Smart. He was smart all right. Tulane was in New Orleans and Emory in Atlanta. Instead of using Harvard or Columbia types, he was going with well-known and respected *Southern* medical experts. It was a pleasure to watch this Davidson work; he didn't miss a trick.

'Mr Everett will arrange for them to examine the defendant,' Gillis assented.

Mr Everett looked as if he wanted to arrange for something very different – such as the instant deportation if not demise of Joshua David Davidson.

'I have one more request, Your Honor,' the defense counsel announced. 'If it please the court, I'd like an order authorizing inspection of the jury lists – those eligible for jury duty – in Jefferson County.'

'Why?'

'According to the most recent Federal census, the population of Jefferson County is thirty-one point four percent black, and my client, who happens to be black, is entitled to be tried by a representative jury. Under the Supreme Court decision in—'

'I'll give you the order,' Gillis snapped in pretended irritation.

It was going to be a mess, an interesting mess. Of the forty-odd thousand colored people in the county, fewer than a hundred were on the jury list. What was 'old Reece' going to do about that? What was 'old Reece' going to tell those Federal judges when they raised that interesting point? Of more immediate importance was what he might tell Ashley and Pikelis this morning, the judge realized, for it was entirely likely that 'old Reece' would fabricate some slick yarn to shift the responsibility for the coming disaster to Ralph Gillis. The best way to preclude that was for Gillis to telephone his own version of the situation – the facts – first, which he succeeded in doing rather artfully by summoning the tricky district attorney to his chambers as soon as the proceeding ended and then keeping Everett waiting in the outer office while he called Mayor Ashley from the inner one.

'I understand, Ralph,' Ashley assured him. 'I still remember enough law to realize what a mess this is – and who's responsible. You can be sure that I'll explain it to John accurately – and soon. I'll be talking to him in about fifteen minutes or so.'

Pikelis was already talking – angrily – to Paradise City's beefy chief of police. Ignoring the panorama beneath the penthouse windows, the racketeer was harshly laying down the law – so to speak – to Ben Marton.

'Gas, fire bombs, silenced tommy guns – that's fancy stuff but still basically just hardware and hardware can be bought by somebody, anybody with money and connections,' Pikelis pointed out. 'What I expect from you is the somebody.'

'Somebod*ies*, I'd say, John. At least three, according to your driver.'

'Right, and I want all three of them. There may be more. I want the entire group – fast.'

Marton nodded.

'Dead or alive, John?'

He saw the anger flush Pikelis' face again.

'I wasn't being smart, John,' he apologized. 'I want to know exactly what you want. After all, that's my job – to get what you want done done.'

He was trying to placate the man who ruled Jefferson County, with limited success.

'Don't you ever get smart with me, Ben. You're goddam right that it's jour job to get done what I want, and I'm glad that you know it.'

'I never forget it, John.'

This was the only way to talk to Pikelis when he got crazy-wild.

The ganglord thought, grunted.

'I'd like at least one alive – long enough to tell us who's behind this operation,' he announced. 'Then we'll know where to ship the bodies. That's going to be my first answer to the son-of-a-bitch who figured this deal. Burn my car, huh? I'll burn him – alive.'

Marton had no doubt that Pikelis would do it. He'd done it to enemies before, although not for some eighteen or twenty years.

'I assume that you realize they've got somebody working at the Fun Parlor, John,' the police chief warned. 'Either somebody there or somebody who scouted the place real good.'

'Somebody there. How else could they get in the back door? How else could they know about the hidden box for the alarm system? I'll work on that with Dennison,' Pikelis promised, 'and you find those other bastards. It shouldn't be that hard for your men to find three or four or five strangers who've arrived in the last month or two. They're probably holed up in some cheap hotel, or maybe a motel near town. If they work like most mobs do, they're all together somewhere and I'd bet that the car has out-of-state plates. Anyway, they're yours, Ben. That's your number-one priority job.'

'We'll get 'em. It won't be easy without any descriptions of either the men or the car, but we'll get 'em.'

Pikelis extracted two of the smuggled Cuban cigars from the humidor, bit the end off one and thrust the other at the chief of police.

'There'll be a nice bonus, Ben,' he promised. 'I'll give you ten boxes of these – and ten thousand in cash – ten big ones.'

'The price is right,' Marton admitted a moment before he left.

At the door, he was surprised to face Ashley – but the police chief didn't show it. If it was characteristic of Pikelis not to tell each of his associates about his dealings and appointments with other members of the organization, it was equally typical of lumbering Ben Marton not to disclose his emotions. 'Hope you've got some good news for him,' Marton said with a jerk of his thumb toward the living room.

'Could be better, Ben. Is he in a bad mood?'

'You'll find out, Mr Mayor,' the police captain chuckled.

Ashley entered, waited patiently for five minutes while the ganglord spoke to hospitalized Willie Dennison on the unlisted telephone that was checked for taps each month. 'Two waiters – no, I don't need their names this minute. Go ahead,' Pikelis urged. 'I see . . . Two waiters . . . that redheaded hoor with the fat tail . . . the stick man from Vegas . . . a cleaning woman, those are the people you hired in the past three months – right? . . . Good. I'll look into it. You take care of yourself, Willie. I won't forget what you did last night. Remember what I said, if there's anything you want or need, just order it and have the bill sent over to the company.'

He hung up the telephone, sighed.

'If they were all like Willie,' he said admiringly. 'A real stand-up guy. They had tommy guns – two of them – and Willie went for his little .32 to protect the house money. Some guts. Balls of brass, that Willie. Took three slugs in the arm – for my money.'

'He's a good man,' Ashley confirmed.

'The best. Worked for Meyer in Havana, you know. A solid pro, a real loyal company man . . . Well, what did you want to see me about, Roger?'

Ashley looked tense, worried and badly in need of a drink. That wasn't a good sign, for the prospect of his puppet mayor's collapse into alcoholism – daylong boozing – was an additional problem that Pikelis didn't relish. Drunks couldn't be relied on, and men who needed liquor at 11 a.m. were close to being drunks.

'The incident at the Fun Parlor, John? Does that mean we're in some serious trouble?' Ashley blurted. 'I certainly don't like the idea of shooting and violence. This could ruin our tourist business. Very embarrassing for me . . . for the whole community.'

The man was laughable, pitiful in his notion that anybody actually thought he was responsible for running Paradise City. Well, there probably were some boobs who took him seriously but all the top people – the big merchants, factory managers, lawyers, bankers – knew where the power rested. Still, it wouldn't hurt to soothe his panicky pride.

'Roger, I'm glad that you asked about this and I certainly see why such an incident might disturb you,' the racketeer answered. 'As the head of our municipal government, these matters are your concern. But the Fun Parlor is beyond the city line, so it isn't your problem. As for serious trouble, I can tell you – confidentially – that there is some difficulty, but it isn't that serious. It should be settled in a few days.'

'A gang war would be very bad, John,' Ashley muttered.

'Couldn't agree with you more, but that's most unlikely. Anything else on your mind?'

The mayor glanced at the liquor cabinet for a moment, fought down the impulse and told Pikelis about the call from Judge Gillis. 'I'm not so sure that the idea of this trial was such a great one, John,' Ashley concluded weakly. 'I'm not blaming you, but it was sort of risky – with a district attorney like Reece Everett at the helm – wasn't it?'

The ganglord smiled, just as if he didn't want to smash this pretentious ruin of a man.

'Maybe so, Roger. Bread and circuses used to work pretty well for those Roman emperors, I hear, and that's what we've been using ourselves for years. I thought it should still work,' he explained.

'Maybe times are changing, John.'

'Maybe so. I'll talk to Everett and Ben Marton about this situation, and that'll leave you free for the bigger problems of running our fair city. Okay? Fine. Say, Roger, I'm afraid I haven't been very hospitable,' the sly racketeer declared with man-to-man affability. 'How about one for the road?'

Ashley hesitated guiltily.

'It's a bit early, isn't it?' he mumbled.

'Nearly noon. One won't hurt you,' urged Pikelis, who knew that the mayor would be semiconscious before three o'clock.

Roger Stuart Ashley gulped down a double bourbon, smiled happily and left without the slightest suspicion that Pikelis was already thinking about possible new candidates for the mayor's office in the next election. Indignant citizens of São Paulo, Brazil, had elected a hippo or a rhinoceros as mayor in a write-in protest against the hack candidates of the major parties, Pikelis recalled from a TV news broadcast, and the man who ruled Jefferson County could replace this arrogant alcoholic with an alligator or even that idiot Reece Everett if necessary. After he'd settled with the invaders and solved the Clayton problem in a couple of weeks, Pikelis would shape his plans for political regrouping. If worse came to worse, Mayor Roger Stuart Ashley could always be found – dead and drunk – in his wrecked car out near the swamp. Cheered by this prospect, John Pikelis picked up a pad and pen to make a list of the recently hired Fun Parlor employees for Luther Hyatt to check. Two waiters, the fat-assed redhead, the stick man and the cleaning woman – not too big a list at all.

That afternoon at 4:10, Tony Arbolino entered the Paradise City Public Library to return a book of Tennessee Williams' plays. After the routine exchange of amenities with Miss Geraldine Ashley about the fact that this very day – July 24 – was the birthday of 'the great French novelist, Alexandre Dumas, the Elder,' the stunt man left with a copy of *The Count of Monte Cristo* under his arm and a song in his heart. The song was 'Maria' from *West Side Story*, a matter of minute moment since it was inaudible to anyone except a very well-equipped cardiologist. Arbolino was (1) longing for his wife;

(2) pleased with the success of the gambling-house raid; (3) collecting the 'mail.' His 'postal box' was one of the invaders' blind drops, a hollow space behind a loose tile set low in the wall of the library's men's room. Half an hour later, he reread Williston's message and made the telephone call to the union headquarters in New York. As the professor had requested, Arbolino pretended to be a newspaper reporter when he asked the question and, as Williston had predicted, he got the answer.

It was a total surprise.

Total.

The stunt man checked his watch, realized that the communication schedule required Williston to be in the phone booth – the far-left booth – in Hammer's Drug Store at 5:05 on Tuesdays, Thursdays and Saturdays. This was a Thursday, so Arbolino dialed the number at 5:05.

'Simon says,' announced the voice at the other end in the agreed recognition signal.

'Robespierre here,' answered the stunt man, using the code name he'd carried in France long ago.

'Go.'

'Not go. Wow. I made the call to AGVA, and the key word in this cipher is a large loud wow.'

'Translation?' Williston demanded.

He looked out toward the soda fountain, noticed the meaty blond waitress smile and wondered whether she'd been told a funny story or fondled again.

'Two words, *mon ami*. Talleyrand's sister. Now how does that grab you?'

Wow.

'I'm thoroughly grabbed,' Williston answered. 'Talleyrand's kid sister, that figures. None of us had it figured, of course, but it figures. I'll try to reach the Math Wizard; he can get her address.'

'Don't do anything rash, *mon ami* – and let me know how it goes. If you want company—'

'I'll keep in touch,' the lean professor promised.

Talleyrand's baby sister.

That grabbed all right.

'Our big sale starts next week,' Mr Hammer announced pleasantly as Williston started for the door. 'Now don't you forget that, you hear?'

'I'll remember.'

'Sun creams, men's colognes, barbecue grills, folding chairs, breath refreshers, insect repellant – fine savings,' chanted the pharmacist proudly.

'I'll remember. Wild butterflies couldn't keep me away.'

Williston slipped on his sunglasses as he stepped out into the glare of the street, started slowly through the steamy heat toward the bar where Gilman was to check in at six o'clock. The teacher made his way in stages, pausing to study the lobby display at the Central Movie Theater and the Jefferson before dropping it at Ray's Records to listen to Dylan's 'country' album titled 'Nashville Skyline.' He heard one side, made his way through the tangle of teenagers and bought the disk. It wasn't a very practical purchase – not for the moment – because his phonograph was in that New York apartment, but he felt that the twenty-odd minutes he'd enjoyed and the future listening made the expenditure a little less silly. Now I've got another motive for surviving, Williston thought as he walked out with the parcel under his left arm.

At ten to six, he saw Lucky's Den up ahead and carefully studied both sides of the street. He circled the block once, entered the tavern and winced under the impact of the air-conditioning. It was a long, low room, with the usual dark wood bar and a few formica tables filling the front and eight slot machines in the back. Lucky Len Lassiter made quite a bit from these one-armed bandits, enough so he didn't mind giving two-thirds of the coins to a Pikelis-owned firm that supplied and maintained the equipment. Their service men were quick, even faster if you were foolhardy enough to try to hold back any cash. Two or three men would be around within a day; in such cases they used the tools on the bar owner instead of the machines. Such incidents were all but historic, however, for it had been years since anybody required that sort of 'mainten-ance.' As long as Games Inc. got its 66⅔ percent of the take, the tavern proprietor didn't have to worry about anything – including the police. As a matter of fact, a husky Paradise City sergeant – in uniform – was feeding quarters into one of the slots as Williston sat down at the fare end of the bar.

'Beer,' he said to the man in the white apron.

'Comin' up.'

The spy sipped the cold liquid, listened idly to the three baseball fans nearby debating the strength of Baltimore's pitching and watched the door reflected in the big mirror that faced him. Six o'clock. A street walker wandered in, exchanged greetings with the police sergeant, downed a gin and tonic, left. Now it was ten after, and Gilman was late. That wasn't the least bit like him, Williston brooded. When his watch showed 6:20, the former OSS agent realized that something was probably wrong and got up to leave. This was standard operating procedure. If the other agent didn't make the contact at the rendezvous point within twenty minutes of the assigned time, you were to leave immediately and get out of the area as quickly and unobtrusively as possible – hopefully before the Gestapo cordons sealed it off completely.

They'd be moving in vans to block all the intersections, pouring out men with those nasty MP40 machine pistols. Nine-millimeter parabellum, thirty-two round box magazine, 500 rounds per minute, fully automatic – he remembered the weapon perfectly. All this ancient and useless information had been flooding back into his consciousness since he'd gunned Dennison, surfacing at unpredictable intervals in a random series of increasingly disturbing jolts.

They'd be fanning out now, covering the alleys and deploying squads over the roofs.

In a minute, the Germans would be at the door.

He blinked, shook off the fear and reminded himself that it was only one of the old nightmares from long ago.

As he stepped into the heat of the street, he saw Gilman across the street up near the corner. The man from Las Vegas was walking away from the bar, and he had an unlit cigarette in his mouth. He stopped, drew his lighter and flicked it three times before it ignited. Danger. Stay away. The alarm signals were even more familiar than the weapons, Williston realized as his eyes swept the area behind the stick man. Yes, there was the follower – not nearly as good as the surveillance specialists the Vichy Milice had used but still dangerous. Mr Pikelis had moved impressively quickly to start checking on the gambling casino's recently hired employees, quickly but not surprisingly, for Gilman had predicted just this tactic. Now the clever planner would have to live with the surveillance for a week or two until the Pikelis organization lost interest and wrote him off as 'clean.'

And Marie Antoinette would have to find the address of Talleyrand's sister without his assistance.

The teacher returned to his hotel after dinner, watched some television and systematically rechecked his room for any signs of search or hidden eavesdropping devices. Nothing, not yet. They – Pikelis and his group – weren't bitter or desperate enough to investigate *every* lone and apparently legitimate individual at every hotel – not yet. It would be interesting to see how badly they'd have to hurt before they resorted to such measures. At 11:30, Williston left the Jefferson and drove to a dark block two streets away from the First Baptist Church. He kept to the shadows as he made his way to the small house behind the church, studied it cautiously for several minutes before he walked across the grass to the side window where the lamp shone.

'I've been waiting for you,' Reverend Snell announced quietly.

He was sitting in a rocker on the back porch, a black man invisible in the darkness of this cloudy night.

'Would you like to come inside for a cold drink?' invited the minister.

'If you've got another rocker I'll just join you on the porch. Could be more convenient if I have to leave in a hurry.'

He made his way to the porch, settled into a worn but comfortable slatted wood rocker. He swayed back and forth without speaking, waiting. After forty or fifty seconds, the clergyman broke the silence.

'You paid in advance, sir,' he declared. He was canny enough not to use any names. 'And a substantial price. If anybody can save my friend, it's that man you hired – as you said you could. He said you committed sixty-five thousand dollars and he also said he didn't even know who you were . . . No, I didn't tell him. I keep my promises too.'

'I was sure you were a man of discretion, Reverend.'

'I hope so, although I'm not sure that a man of discretion would make this sort of blind bargain with – if you'll pardon my melodramatic phrase – a mysterious stranger. I think it's time you told me who you are and what you want.'

Williston considered the request for several seconds.

'I can't tell you who I am . . . who *we* are . . . but I can say that we're a group of men who want to free Paradise City from the criminal Pikelis organization and its political allies. We are committed to the destruction of that organization – by various means. We need the help of local people who want to clean up this community, your help.'

'So *you* can run Paradise City?' challenged the wary cleric.

'No, we'll be gone twenty-four hours after Pikelis is smashed. It can be done, you know. He's not impregnable, not invulnerable.'

Then the spy explained how he hoped to use Snell's congregation and friends as a vast intelligence network, pointed out how – in the language of black novelist Ralph Ellison – the Negroes were 'invisible men' who moved almost unnoticed in this community.

'That's all?'

'I may ask for more later,' Williston acknowledged, 'and you'll be free then to decide whether you want to go along. There may be additional risks, greater dangers involved.'

'I'd say that there are considerable dangers involved in what you and your . . . your group . . . are attempting here . . . dangers for you . . . dangers that seem unreasonable if you really don't mean to seize this city for yourselves.'

'We were trained for this sort of work. We're professionals, in a sense.'

'Federal agents?'

'No . . . I can't tell you any more. Think it over. If you're with us, run an ad in the classified section of Monday's paper offering a blue bicycle for sale at fifty-five dollars. If you'd rather not, advertise a green bicycle at sixty-five dollars.'

'And what happens to Sam Clayton if I'd rather not?'

Williston stood up, grunted.

'We're giving you Sam Clayton's life as a bonus gift in any case, part of our special introductory offer. It's like those book-club deals,' he announced. 'If you sign up, we'll throw in the complete works of Ronald Reagan and an illuminated world globe. Let's get one thing straight. We're not promising to emancipate the black population of Paradise City or desegregate your schools or housing. That's up to you and the Federal Government and your fellow citizens here.'

'We might have a better chance when Pikelis is gone though?'

'You might. That war is your war, and all I can give you is our best wishes plus any leftover stationery we might have when we leave.'

'Thank you for your frankness . . . Good night,' said Reverend Ezra Snell.

'Good night . . . Will the same people be escorting me back to my car?'

The clergyman laughed softly.

'So you saw them on your way back here?' he asked.

'I said we were trained professionals, didn't I?'

Without waiting for a response, Williston strode the two blocks to the parked Dart and started back toward his hotel. He had done what he could with the black minister. Now he had to find Talleyrand's sister.

CHAPTER TWENTY-THREE

'Don't scream,' the voice said, and as she opened her eyes somebody put a gentle but firm hand over her mouth.

'Don't scream – it's me, Williston.'

It was dark in the room, 2:50 a.m. on a moonless night. Usually Judy Ellis would still be singing the last set with the band out at the Fun Parlor, but the gambling casino was closed for repairs and wouldn't reopen until Saturday evening. Beneath the thin sheet, the blonde was naked and frightened.

'I'm going to turn on the lamp for one second so you can see it's me,' the intruder announced.

The light flicked on and off, giving her a glimpse of the face she'd seen only in photographs. The hand moved away, and she sighed.

'You're very attractive,' he said softly. 'I never knew that Talleyrand had such an attractive kid sister. Of course, you were only a baby then.'

'I'm a big girl now,' she answered as she sat up, exposing perfect shoulders and a hint of chest.

'Big enough to mail clippings,' he guessed.

'Yes, and big enough to save you from a bullet last night. Put the light on again for a moment, please . . . I want to look at you.'

He complied, and she sighed again.

'My brother said you were the bravest man he'd ever met – a born hero. I wanted to see what a hero looked like.'

She heard the muffled laugh in the darkness.

'Your brother was the hero, Judy. He saved all our lives, but I suppose you knew that and that's why you figured sending the clippings would bring us here.'

'Something like that. I hoped it would anyway. He said you'd come even if the others might not. He said you weren't afraid of anything.'

The bitter chuckle sounded again.

'Not anything, *every*thing. I was the most desperate wild-eyed agent who ever jumped into France, little sister. Panic, I was on the knife-edge of subdued panic all the time. I'm still afraid of gray days and unemployed Judy Garland fans and the sounds of cars backfiring. I must have been – we all must have been – crazy. Maybe we still are – to buy this deal. Little sister, you've awakened some ancient devils and passions that I thought were dead forever.

'Don't "little sister" me, dammit!'

'Sorry.'

'And spare me all your psychological clichés and pretended traumas. You came because you wanted to, just as you became a Jedburgh because you wanted to,' she reminded him. 'You were hell on wheels then, and from what I saw last night you haven't changed much. That was a brilliant operation last night, just brilliant. Even Marie Antoinette would have to admit that.'

It was, unfortunately, true.

Unfortunately and fortunately.

'How did you find me?' she asked a few seconds later.

'Finally recognized your voice . . . had Tony phone AGVA in New York to ask whether Judy Ellis was a stage name. The ever efficient American Guild of Variety Artists told him your real name, and that's how we learned Judy Ellis is Judy Barringer . . . Then I just phoned all the hotels and apartment hotels until I got one that had you registered – this one. So I drove over, came up the service stairs – six lousy flights – and quietly picked the lock on your door.'

This time she laughed.

'My, my, so the middle-aged professor is a burglar too.'

'I also earn extra change doing a pickpocket act at bar-mitzvahs and sweet-sixteen parties. Oh yes, they taught us a lot of marvelous tricks such as how to cut off the head of a motorcycle dispatch rider with a cable across the road. I'll do that one for you sometime, if you'll provide the motorcyclist.'

She reached for the cigarettes and lighter on the bed table, revealing more of herself. He couldn't see very clearly in the dim room, but he could make out that she wasn't anybody's little sister any more. This was visible when she ignited the lighter. Illuminated briefly by the dancing flame, she was undoubtedly an adult female – a woman. Williston found himself aware of this, decided that his reactions were immature and walked to the window to stare down into the street.

'What's the matter?' she asked.

'Just thinking, just checking on how I'm going to leave. They've doubled the number of police patrol cars out tonight, according to the amount of radio traffic. I guess Marton's getting edgy.'

'You can stay here, Andy. Is it all right if I call you Andy?'

He smiled.

'Only in America, as Harry Golden would say. Only in America does a girl invite you to spend the night with her – and then ask if she can call you by your first name . . . Yes, you can call me Andy but not in public. I'm Arthur Warren in this town. That's *my* stage name.'

The spy sat down in the big armchair by the window, watched the tip of her cigarette glowing red a dozen feet away.

'I want to talk about your brother,' he announced. 'Do you know who killed him or why?'

'I'm almost sure it was Hyatt, the ape you left in the store window. He's supposed to have some experience with bombs and other kinds of killing.'

'Sort of the Assassin-in-Residence on this campus?'

'That's what they say, Andy.'

Each of them discovered that there was something special about the way she spoke his name, but neither of them said it.

'I suppose we were lucky we didn't know that when we grabbed him,' the teacher reflected.

'You might have killed him?'

'There would have been a temptation to do something stupid like that. Well, there'll be enough violence before this thing is over,' he predicted. 'More than enough to go around – with enough left over to supply programming for a major television network for two years. Do you know why Pikelis wanted your brother killed?'

She hesitated for a moment.

'No . . . he might have thought Eddie was collecting some sort of evidence – that's just a guess.'

She was lying, or at least holding back something. He could sense it, hear it.

There was no point in pressing her; that didn't work with women. They were born with the self-defense instinct, and they gave in only when they wanted to. There were so few things about human females that one could generalize about, he thought, but this was one of them. It was an animal thing.

'Did Eddie have any other enemies here?'

'I never heard of any . . . I don't think he was fooling around with anybody's wife, if that's what you have in mind.'

She sounded angry.

'Just checking all the possibilities, Judy. I've got the responsibility for committing four lives – including my own – and I've got to know what the hell I'm doing. Now, what are you doing in Paradise City? It's no accident that you're here.'

Smoke spiraled from her cigarette in an oddly erotic eddy.

'He asked me to come to help him. He was out to break the organization,' she declared, 'and I was to work inside – at the Fun Parlor. That's why I had our agent – the band's agent – get us this job.'

'You find out anything much?'

'Nothing big enough to send anybody to jail . . . Say, would you like a drink or something? I've got half a bottle of Scotch, and you can run some cold water in the bathroom. Over there, the bottle's on the dresser – see it?'

His eyes had adjusted to the darkness, and he made out the familiar shape of the glass container without difficulty. He picked up the bottle, found the bathroom and flicked on the light over the sink.

'I'll have one too,' she announced.

He poured some of the John Begg whiskey into two glasses, added cold water and turned.

'You can leave that light on, Andy.'

He walked into the bedroom, handed her one of the glasses and returned to the armchair by the window. They drank, talked about the situation in Paradise City and the danger – for her and for Gilman – that was growing now that Pikelis realized a spy had infiltrated the gambling club. They spoke of Clayton and Davidson, and then Williston made two more drinks as she told him what she'd learned during her months in Jefferson County. At 3:35, he glanced down into the street and saw the police car stop a passing convertible to question the driver. They'd be checking everyone and every vehicle out at this hour.

'Maybe I had better stay,' he said wearily. 'I'll sleep in the chair, if that's all right with you.'

'You won't be very comfortable.'

'I'll be okay,' he replied as he took off his tie and put it over his jacket already draped on a straight-backed chair. 'Go back to sleep, Judy. I'll be fine.'

He closed his eyes, leaned back and tried not to think. He tried very hard not to think of Eddie Barringer, Sledgehammer, John Pikelis, all those men who'd been dead so many years and the desirable woman twelve feet away. It was not easy, and it took a long time before he could escape into sleep. Even there he found no peace, however, for the ugly memories of the armored-car ambush and the slaughter of the German payroll escort and how Gindler had died kept seeping up from his unconscious. They were terribly vivid and garish, even more than usual.

'Wake up, Andy. Wake up,' she said.

He opened his eyes, saw her standing nearby – white and almost ghostly.

'You were having a nightmare, Andy. It was only a dream, that's all.'

He nodded.

'No, remembering. No dream . . . it all happened.'

Her hand touched his face, cupped his chin.

'You'd better come to bed, Andy,' she urged. 'You'll sleep better.'

She was naked, near, lovely – very attractive.

Much more than attractive – desirable.

'No,' he said quietly.

It was the compassion that stopped him.

She felt sorry for him – almost maternal – and he couldn't handle, couldn't accept that.

Even if she wanted him too, it wasn't him – not a professor past forty – she really desired. She wanted to sleep with the hero, the young wild warrior who didn't exist anymore. She didn't know Professor Andrew F. Williston nearly well enough for that, and he wouldn't let her give herself to a legend, a romanticized memory, a gilded ghost. It was bad enough that he couldn't escape the past in his day and nightmares, but this would be too much.

God, she was beautiful.

He was either very stupid, very arrogant, very idealistic – or in urgent need of psychotherapy, the psychology teacher realized wearily. She would be warm, tender, everything – everything he needed – but it would be another fantasy and he was already too deeply immersed in fantasy in Paradise City.

If they knew each other it could become a reality, and that would be very good. Would be or could be; it was so difficult to tell. He didn't know her either, but he wanted to. He ought to tell her that, he brooded.

All these thoughts flooded through his consciousness in a few seconds.

'No, I'm too restless and I'd keep you up all night,' he evaded.

It was so hard not to reach out, not to touch her.

'Do you want to talk?' she asked gently.

'Tomorrow.'

She went back to her bed, accepting but discontented. She lay there for some minutes, wondering about this man who was so near and so remote. She listened for the regular breathing that would signify he was sleeping again, but it was not there.

'Judy?' he said suddenly.

'Yes?'

'Judy, I'm glad I found you.'

'Why?'

He hesitated again.

'I think we might . . . well, we might get along – well. You're so lovely, warm, maybe even wise.'

'No, not wise. You're wise enough for both of us – maybe too wise.'

Then she laughed softly.

'I'm glad you found me too – I think,' she said in the darkness. 'You're a serious man, and I could use a serious man, Andy. Do me a big favor and stay near, stay alive.'

Now he chuckled.

'Staying alive is one of the things I do best,' he answered, 'but staying near sounds very attractive too. I don't want a mother, though, because I don't feel the least bit filial.'

'I don't feel very maternal at the moment, Andy. I want to help, but not as mommy or sister or nurse. I owe you at least that much. Don't forget, I got you all into this.'

She heard him sigh across the room.

'You must be as crazy as we are,' he judged.

'I sent the clippings,' she insisted.

'Yes – and we'll get you for that. If the others don't, I'll get you myself.'

He was teasing, but his voice held something more.

'Can I count on that?' she challenged.

'Of course, I'm compulsive. Now go to sleep, woman.'

There was something good about the way he said 'woman' – something that let her smile, relax and begin the descent into unconsciousness.

Out at the trailer camp, Arbolino was awake – for the third time that night. He was thinking of his wife and children again, and he was wondering – again – about why he'd left them for this dangerous mission. An honorable man paid his debts, of course, but did vengeance justify *this*? This wasn't like the war, no matter what Carstairs and Williston said. It was different. Things that had been so right in that war didn't really make the same sense now. He was older, he reflected, and maybe that made things appear more complicated. Yes, this town was dominated by a Fascist organization, as Williston had said, and somebody had to do something about it, but should four middle-aged private citizens from other states be the ones? What was that thing Andy quoted from Jefferson – or was it the Declaration of Independence? – about the people's right to overthrow tyrannical governments? The stunt man tried to remember that comforting noble justification, tried and failed. 'When in the course of human events—'

No, that wasn't it.

Well, it didn't matter that much anymore.

They were in it now, and they couldn't quit.

In the morning, he'd drive seventeen miles south to Tracy and mail his wife a letter from that small town. There might be mail from home waiting for him c/o General Delivery. That would surely help, he thought wearily, and he could certainly use every bit of help he could get. Tony Arbolino was still struggling to recall the Jefferson quote when he finally fell asleep.

CHAPTER TWENTY-FOUR

Friday, July 25, was – according to your point of view – a very groovy day or a total drag. It was a very groovy day for a couple of imaginary and imaginative people who called themselves Judy Ellis and Arthur Warren, but they stayed in a cozy cool room most of the day and concentrated on the relatively simple task of finding out more about each other. She called down for food and drink, and he found that he liked all the records that she played on her phonograph. In many ways, their tastes were compatible. For example, they both enjoyed George Shearing and neither of them thought that Andy Warhol or Mrs Mao Tse-tung would make a very good President. Of the United States of America, that is. Dizzy Gillespie? Well, he was a big talent not to be brushed off lightly. Yes, Dizz might turn out to be a real 'heavy' President. He had class and experience, and he'd already been cleared for 'security' by both the State Department and the FBI as a prelude to government-sponsored tours overseas. He certainly played a much better horn than Spiro Agnew, the mayor of Chicago or John Wayne.

For Ben Marton, the twenty-fifth was a total drag. A clutch of out-of-town reporters arrived to interview that bigmouthed Davidson, the investigation at the Fun Parlor produced no solid leads and none of his police could find any group of strangers who might be the raiding party. As if that weren't bad enough, Pikelis remained in a grim mood as the initial surveillance reports on recently hired Fun Parlor employees were all unrewarding. Aside from the discovery that the cleaning woman named Inez was stealing a few napkins, there was nothing worth mentioning. That night, Marton sent out a few of his most reliable men to talk to the Negroes whom Clayton had initially insisted could confirm his presence at the church dance at the time of the murder. The idea was to explain *firmly* that it would cause considerable *waste* and *trouble* if any of these good folks were to come to court to testify, because the city already had a cast-iron case against the confessed criminal. Such precautionary warnings weren't usually necessary in Jefferson County, but the chief of police saw no harm in being a bit extra wary in light of the unusual situation. Shortly after ten o'clock, the last of his messengers reported back. Of the seven blacks they'd gone to see, three had left town – without any forwarding addresses. One of these three was the strapping girl whom Clayton had described as his fiancée and night-long companion, Shirleyrose Woods, who had never been out of Jefferson County before. Her brother said that she'd mentioned getting a job in one of those Miami Beach hotels, or trying to get one, or something.

'I think the three who took off were just scared, Chief,' Sergeant Wallace reported. 'Too scared to stay let alone show their ugly faces in court.'

Maybe. Maybe not. Probably, but could you be sure?

Marton brooded, decided not to mention the uncertainty to Pikelis, who was already extremely irritable. Ashley wasn't helping much by stepping up his drinking, and Reece Everett was fussing and fuming and pouting like some nervous high-school girl afraid that her mother might find out what she'd been doing with the swimming coach. To add to all the unpleasantness, Mrs Marton was on the Southern Comfort again – in which case anything might happen. When the extra patrols and the informers and the brothel keepers produced no clues about the faceless invaders, Marton shrugged as if he weren't bothered and passed the word to keep looking. All his experience told him that there was no reason to be bothered, for the enemy would make some mistake – some tiny error that would identify them as outsiders – and then he'd wipe them out as he had other intruders in the past. But he was bothered, for the sophistication and boldness and ingenuity of this group wasn't at all similar to that of the others.

There was something different involved.

These people didn't even kill; they cut like surgeons.

There was no way of predicting where they'd cut next, so the corrupt captain could do little but watch and wait.

Saturday – nothing.

Sunday – nothing.

Nothing that anyone reported, anyway. Andrew Williston – furtively but very gracefully – met Judy Barringer and drove her out to a secluded beach for a picnic of cold chicken and white wine, Niersteiner.

Monday – nothing, nothing that anyone in the Pikelis organization noticed. There was nothing to attract their attention to the newspaper advertisement offering a blue bicycle for $55 that was buried in the second column of the classified section, no reason to tap Reverend Snell's phone that afternoon or to follow him to the rendezvous where Williston laid out the details of the intelligence-gathering operation. There was no way of guessing that the invaders now had an additional two hundred pairs of eyes and ears working for them, that the information was being funneled through the minister of the First Baptist Church to a psychology professor who carried a silenced M-3 submachine gun. Black porters, waiters, delivery boys, maids, bootblacks, taxi drivers and tavern owners – all so familiar and anonymous that nobody noticed them as they moved through the city on their normal routine duties – had joined the secret war.

Now the Sledgehammer team was no longer a quartet; it was an army.

It was everywhere and yet it was invisible, almost like the Viet Cong. In accord with Williston's instructions, Snell recruited selectively and cautiously – picking only the cleverest and most trustworthy members of his congregation. None of them knew who the other agents were; the network was organized with the same rules and security procedures that SOE and OSS had learned – the hard way – in developing their *réseaux* in Occupied France. By Thursday, useful information was beginning to pour in at an accelerating pace.

It was put to good use. When the big trailer-truck delivered the eighteen slot machines on August 1, the OSS alumni knew when and where it would arrive and Arbolino was able to film the unloading with a concealed motion-picture camera from a roof across the street from the Games Inc. warehouse at the corner of Prince Street. The name of the company and the street sign were easy to read, and the faces of the men and the licence plates of the truck were equally clear in the excellent prints that were delivered two days later to (1) CBS, NBC and ABC news headquarters in New York; (2) the FBI in Washington; and (3) the office of the attorney general in the state capital. If the pictures weren't plain enough, the unsigned letters that accompanied the film filled in the details.

Interstate movement of gambling devices raised a Federal question, and the violation of state law prohibiting slot machines was even clearer. The FBI immediately began its usual thorough and careful investigation, while the state attorney general talked to the governor about what to do. One of the assistant attorneys general knew exactly what to do; he told the senator from Jefferson County to warn Pikelis. That message reached the ganglord at 6 p.m. on the fourth, the same evening that the film was shown nationally on both the CBS–TV Walter Cronkite show and NBC's Huntley-Brinkley news stanza.

Most of the adult population of Jefferson County saw it on the Cronkite telecast that WPAR–TV regularly carried, and dozens of members of the state legislature watched that same news show in the capital. There were a number of calls to the governor and the attorney general, both of whom lost their uncertainty as to what to do approximately eight seconds after they realized what could happen to their own political futures if they didn't move with righteous vigor. The will of the people was an awesome thing, and CBS even worse.

'Poor John,' muttered the attorney general sympathetically as he picked up the phone to call the superintendent of the state police.

A dozen men – including five off-duty police, one a sergeant – were already sweating at the warehouse as they hurried the machines into two trucks. Neither Williston nor Arbolino was perspiring on the nearby rooftop, where the teacher and his machine gun protected the stunt man as he took still pictures with an infrared camera that needed no telltale flash to shoot in the dark. All the illegal machines were gone by the time the state police arrived at 9:20, but at noon the next day prints of the infrared stills were delivered by Western Union messenger to the network news bureau in Miami and to the city desks of the key Atlanta and New Orleans dailies. Each picture was neatly captioned with an explanation of who was doing what, where and why.

That night, David Brinkley made some terribly witty and cynical – if not snide – remarks about law enforcement in Jefferson County as he showed the sixteen stills, and a CBS correspondent named Evans arrived in Paradise City on the same flight that brought in a *Life* writer-researcher-photographer team and an Associated Press correspondent. A number of practical politicians in the state capital and Washington made statements – for publication and broadcast – about the need for immediate action to clean up this shocking situation. On Sunday, fifty-one ministers and fourteen rabbis in various parts of the country put aside their prepared texts on Vietnam and the Generation Gap and preached ringing sermons on the decline in morality reflected in the Paradise City corruption.

On Sunday, the man who drove the yellow Mustang made his usual phone call and explained that he still didn't know who was behind the uproar or what might happen next. Nobody outside the Pikelis organization could say where the machines were hidden, and Mayor Ashley was limiting his public remarks to pious pledges to newsmen that 'the entire matter is being checked out by our hard-working police.' The piece of film recording this pap really bombed when it reached CBS News on West 57th Street in New York, and since the story didn't seem to be going anywhere – 'no visuals, dammit' — one top executive began to think of recalling the crew from Paradise City to move on to the strike in Birmingham which promised some wonderful riot footage. But at 5 a.m. on Monday morning, a black bellboy allied with Reverend Snell slipped a note under the door of the CBS correspondent's hotel room, banged twice and fled.

Fifty-three minutes later, the network news crew – all bright-eyed and bushy-tailed and full of histamines aroused by the prospect of a 'beat' – drove up to the large handsome house at 1818 Gardenia Drive. As promised, there was a large handsome truck parked directly in front and when they obeyed the unsigned note's instruction and opened the vehicle's rear door they saw the slot machines. They didn't know that the Sledgehammer army had stolen the gambling equipment in a 3 a.m. raid on Pikelis' waterfront depot, but they were happy enough with what they did know.

(1) The film would look great and New York would be delighted.

(2) The owner and resident of 1818 Gardenia Drive was Mayor Roger Stuart Ashley. They took special care to get the small sign with his name – the metal plaque on the manicured lawn – into as many shots as possible.

Let NBC and that smart Brinkley chew on that, the earnest truth seekers rejoiced as they considered the bonuses and promotions that might follow. To make sure that these benefits followed, the decent God-fearing CBS correspondent took the trouble – as a responsible citizen should – to telephone the state police in the capital. That was 7:10 on a bright, hot August morn, a nice clear cloudless day that was excellent for filming with a 16-millimeter Auricon sound camera. Who said

God is dead? Just before eight o'clock, two cars carrying troopers of the state police rolled up Gardenia Drive and stopped smartly on either side of the truck in front of 1818. Noting the TV crew, the officers did an absolutely bang-up job of searching the truck, finding and officially seizing the slot machines. It was so emphatically bang-up and noisy that the front door of 1818 Gardenia Drive opened right in the middle of Lieutenant Stanley Gregory's interview, and the CBS team got quite a nice long shot – and then a zoom close-up – of Mayor Ashley in his paisley bathrobe and matching hangover.

The United Press and *Newsweek* chaps arrived the next day, and that afternoon somebody asked the President of the United States a question about Paradise City during his press conference. Being a Republican he unhesitatingly denounced the disgraceful situation in Jefferson County – which had given him only 19 percent of its votes in the 1968 election. It was being looked into very carefully, he assured the American people, and the possibilities of sending in a Federal anti-racketeering task force were under 'serious study.' This came as a minor surprise to the head of the U.S. Department of Justice, but the Washington *Post*, the Chicago *Tribune* and *The New York Times* responded so favorably with editorials that he told an assistant attorney general to start the ball rolling. In Miami, Irving suddenly developed a nervous stomach and an eye twitch – his left eye – causing Uncle Meyer to suggest an immediate three-week vacation in Aruba, where a former associate was running a casino.

'It will be good for your sinuses too,' Meyer predicted as he handed his distraught nephew the airline tickets, 'and Gloria could use the change.'

Arizona would have been even better for his sinuses, but Arizona was U.S. and Federal subpoenas could be served there. There was an FBI bureau in Phoenix, but none in Aruba. Meyer was a veritable encyclopedia of such practical information and legal lore, and people said he could write a whole book on the fine points of the Fifth Amendment to the U.S. Constitution. When it came to avoiding self-incriminating testimony, he was an acknowledged authority in certain circles.

On Wednesday night, the *Life* correspondent was taking a shower before dinner – he was clean, alert and thoroughly resourceful – when somebody slipped into his Paradise House room and left an envelope in the pocket of his freshly pressed poplin jacket. He discovered this when he dressed, was delighted to find that he was the owner of a list of addresses of eight brothels – all within two miles of where he stood. His photographer and the girl researcher – the Japanese-American beauty who wore Vassar T-shirts and knew Harold Pinter terribly well – were ready to go into action, but there was the problem of evading the policeman who was watching them. Marton had assigned plainclothes detectives to keep track of all the nosey journalists, to trail them and subtly obstruct their snooping. If this fellow saw the *Life* trio photographing one of the whorehouses, he might smash a camera or two 'accidentally' or ram their car with his own. At the very least, he'd alert the other bordellos and the tough chief of police. It was worth a try, however, even if all the *Life* trio could do was to drive past the houses on a general reconnaissance.

After dinner, the three of them piled into the Plymouth sedan and set off on what they hoped would appear to be a casual sightseeing drive around town.

'That bastard is right behind us,' announced Gillian Daifuku as she turned the car toward City Hall.

She not only knew Harold Pinter, but she drove very well – which was not too surprising since she was also on very close terms with Sterling Moss and Lyndon B. Johnson as well as both Simon and Garfunkel. In view of all this, her occasional lapses from gentility could hardly be taken seriously.

The two men in the sedan glanced into the rear-view mirror, spotted the unmarked police car that was following them. Neither of them noticed the blue 'compact' coupe half a block farther back, and neither did Marton's plainclothesman. He was focussed on the Plymouth, which headed west on Acorn, then north on Magnolia and east on London Boulevard. He began to make the same turn onto the boulevard.

Then P. T. Carstairs leaned out of the right window of the blue Dart, took careful aim with the long-barreled Smith and Wesson K-38 target pistol and blew holes in both of the police car's rear tires.

'Home, James,' he said grandly to the professor behind the wheel.

'You're pretty good with that thing, aren't you?' Williston asked as he swung the Dart toward the center of town.

'One of the best. I'm nearly as good with guns as I am with women.'

The millionaire sharpshooter slipped the K-38 under his jacket, smiled contentedly. Aside from the question of what he'd do about Kathy Pikelis, everything was under control and the operation was moving nicely. Three blocks away, the Plymouth sedan was also moving nicely – without any police car that could block the tour of the brothels. The *Life* trio succeeded in shooting four of the whorehouses before another patrol car – alerted by police radio – raced toward them on the 900 block of Wayne Street.

'Gillian, head back downtown,' the correspondent ordered. 'Let's quit for tonight before the local fuzz suspect what we're up to.'

'What about the interiors? I want to get some shots inside,' pleaded the photographer. 'I can do it with the little sub-miniature job.'

'Tomorrow night, Stu. Take your time, baby, and you'll stay out of jail – or the hospital – long enough to get all the Minox snapshots you want.'

It took three nights, but the two men both succeeded in visiting several of the whorehouses, and the story they got was a sensation when it appeared in the August 14 issue. It ran as the cover story, and since the Arab guerrillas were taking that week off and there were no riots at any colleges and no major-league pitcher tossed a no-hitter it attracted a great deal – maybe a disproportionate amount – of attention. Johnny Carson made several jokes about it, Adam Clayton Powell denounced it as an example of 'Charlie's hypocrisy and corruption' and Simone de Beauvoir blamed it on the 'same evil that produced the immoral American invasion of Vietnam.' The Vice President of the U.S.A. assured a surfers convention at Waikiki that the Administration was moving vigorously to wipe out such organized crime, student violence and the tragic problem of bedwetting in the ghetto. A massive program of outdoor calisthenics, rose growing and safe driver instruction was about to be launched, he disclosed, and organ lessons were also planned.

On the fifteenth, the desk clerk at the Paradise House told all the irritating journalists that they'd have to leave on the next day because their rooms had been reserved for other guests – and when the press checked with other hotels in the city they found not a single bed available. In case the message wasn't clear, the CBS truck was set on fire, *The New York Times* man hauled off to jail on a drunken-driving charge and *Life*'s Gillian Daifuku was arrested when a detective blandly swore she'd approached him in the street and offered to commit an unnatural act for $20. The AP correspondent was fined $150 because he was operating a vehicle without functioning tail lights, a malfunction that had been simple to arrange. A United Press photographer fell – or was pushed – down a flight of stairs, breaking his left ankle and his camera in the process. The entire NBC team became violently ill after dinner at the Dixie Mansion, leaving them retching for two days and suspicious that some sneaky son-of-a-bitch had tampered with the fried chicken or the shrimp jambalaya.

Mr Pikelis was counterattacking on a broad front.

The press fell back under the veiled violence, some leaving and some publicizing the indignities and some retreating to motels just outside Jefferson County. Every day, police cars waited to harass them on the roads to and from Paradise City. Every night, the irate journalists planned new forays and scouting missions into the 'denied territory' – like U.S. Special Forces teams probing the jungles near the Cambodian border.

The Sledgehammer quartet was continuing its own war. On the nineteenth – the day that Judge Gillis grudgingly granted Davidson a final postponement until the twenty-fifth – Sergeant Leroy Beggs of the Paradise City Police and two of Pikelis' gunmen set out to collect the week's profits from the recently reopened brothels that were running full blast now that the state troopers had left. A maid in one of the houses had notified Reverend Snell that Fat Florence and her sister madams were back in business and that the schedule called for the collection on that night. The sergeant and his two escorts were properly wary as they emerged from Fat Florence's, glancing around and scanning the street before they started down the steps toward their parked car. Seeing only an aged invalid in a wheelchair – he was apparently blind as well as infirm if the dark glasses were a clue – being pushed down the street by a shambling white-haired servant who seemed nearly as old, Beggs descended and began to walk past them. As they drew abreast, the hunched codger in the wheelchair spoke.

'I'll take the money,' he announced.

There was – suddenly – a .32-caliber revolver in each hand, with a cylindrical silencer fitted to the muzzle of each gun.

The sergeant stiffened, clutched the airlines' bag in near panic. He wasn't about to surrender the proceeds of seven houses, but Williston persuaded him. The spy pointed his weapons, shot the collector through each arm with a precision that a skilled dentist might have admired. The twin 'pops' – louder than a champagne cork but not much – were followed by Beggs's gasp, and he dropped the bag.

'*You'll* get it in the belly,' the disguised invader promised one of the hoodlums.

The man instantly picked up the bag, thrust it forward. Arbolino, who'd been pushing the chair, reached out and took it.

'Truck,' ordered Williston.

The stunt man ran twenty yards down Merrill Avenue, started the stolen diaper-service truck and drove it up to where the twin revolvers still covered Pikelis' trio.

'You're dead,' predicted the wounded sergeant grimly as he fought down the pain. 'Nobody shoots a cop in this town. It's suicide. You're all dead. Your luck can't hold out forever you know.'

'Into the truck, Baby,' the spy replied in the same croak that disguised his voice so simply.

They climbed into the rear compartment, which Arbolino locked as Williston jumped out of the wheelchair. A moment later, the teacher ripped off his glasses and disguise and climbed up beside Arbolino in front. The white wig slid off the seat onto the floor as the truck picked up speed, but that didn't matter. All that counted was swift flight from this neighborhood and an uninterrupted drive to tree-lined Mercer Lane, where they parked the vehicle and made their escape. Twelve minutes later, an anonymous telephone call informed the duty nurse at the Mercer Lane Hospital emergency room that a wounded policeman required assistance only two blocks from the hospital – in a diaper truck of the Kuddly Kiddee Company.

Word of this latest raid – they'd called them *coups de main* in that other war against those other Nazis – spread through the city quickly. Well, it didn't reach every dental technician and CPA by morning but the news did get to most of the bartenders, whores, police, taxi drivers, public officials, journalists (local and 'foreign'), tavern customers and assorted stay-ups in town. Early that next afternoon, the man with the unlisted Atlanta number was told of the incident and informed that the Paradise City Police had found two fingerprints on the abandoned wheelchair.

'I understand that they mean to send them to the FBI for identification,' reported the Mustang owner. 'Don't you think that's funny? . . . No? Well, you never had much of a sense of humor. I'd give a dollar forty and my three Goldwater buttons to find out whose prints those are, Buddy. John would probably pay even more . . . maybe sixty thousand. That's what I hear the Apaches took last night . . . All right, maybe they're Comanches who feel alienated. They were much too smart and slick to be SDS, and they didn't call a press conference afterwards . . . The local cops are intensely bitter now. Nervous too. Last night – maybe an hour after the hijack – a patrol car spotted a couple of perfectly respectable businessmen who were perfectly respectably intoxicated and looking for a perfectly respectable cat house named Amy's – and the police beat the stuffings out of those clean-cut taxpayers on the theory they might be the heist artists. One of those clobbered is a prominent member of the Chamber of Commerce. He's in the hospital, semiconscious and wholly unhappy . . . Buddy, this is turning into a very bad scene, very fast. I doubt that our own plans are feasible any more . . . That's just too damn bad . . . Yeah, I'll keep my ear to the ground and nose to the grindstone and my eye on the ball – but I'll have my car keys in one hand and my gun in the other . . . No, I kid you not – so don't try to kid me. Okay, *Ciao*.

On the twenty-first, the president of every women's club and every clergyman in Jefferson County received a letter containing $20 – his or her 'share of the brothel profits.' The note thanked each of them for the 'years of loyal support for our local whorehouses, one of our outstanding industries.' Similar cash-laden missives went to all seventy-four members of the state senate and the governor, none of whom were amused. As expected, a number of the recipients had small fits or medium-sized attacks of heartburn or even seizures of the lower conscience. The ladies turned an interesting assortment of the latest high-fashion colors, duly noted by their affluent lawyer-merchant-doctor-banker husbands who caught the psychodelic backlash. The chairwoman of the Paradise City chapter of the Daughters of the Confederacy – Miss Geraldine Ashley – didn't have a husband, but she took it up with her brother as soon as her flush of faintness subsided.

Hackles were rising, tempers were flaring and a number of long-dormant senses of morality began to torment usually sensible citizens. The Catholic bishop and a leading Protestant cleric in the state capital added fuel to the situation with ringing statements that won instant support from several rabbis and social critics; people even began to talk about the mess on a number of golf courses, including the one at the Paradise Country Club. Nobody was ready to take the responsibility – or risks – of doing anything significant about it yet, but there was promise in the fact that the situation – the evil – could no longer be ignored.

Neither John Pikelis nor Ben Marton was ignoring the situation. The chief of police was pushing his men harder and harder, and he kept telephoning Washington to inquire whether the FBI had identified the owner of the fingerprints. Each time he was assured that they were still checking. He would have been extremely surprised and disturbed if he'd known that the FBI was not telling the truth. After all, the Federal Bureau of Investigation is respected for its sincerity, integrity, neat clothing, passion for conscientious law enforcement, efficient staff work, scientific detection and reliable cooperation with local police. Like Swiss-air's cutesy Heidi, the FBI never lies.

But it was lying to Captain Ben Marton this time.

Somebody high up in the Bureau – very high – had ordered this.

He had his reasons for not informing the Paradise City P.D. that the prints belonged to a former OSS agent named Andrew Williston who'd won two Silver Stars and a Distinguished Service Cross. Agents were assigned to check on Williston's wartime records in the OSS files, a task that required the cooperation of the Central Intelligence Agency, which controlled the still-classified archives of its predecessor. Other agents were assigned to find out what had happened to Lieutenant Andrew Williston since he left the Office of Strategic Services in 1946. Still others went to work on Williston's family, friends, wartime associates, sex life, political affiliations and personal hygiene.

The result was a very complete and informative report.

'You'd better send a summary – by hand, not teletype – to MacBride,' ordered the very high official in Washington. 'He'll know what to do with it.'

He did.

About a dozen hours after MacBride began to do, Andrew Williston sat in the blond singer's hotel room waiting for her to return from her night's work. She arrived shortly before three, smiled when she saw him.

'I've been drinking,' he announced as he took another sip from the glass in his left hand.

'My liquor, no doubt.'

'I brought you another bottle to replace what I've consumed. You know, this John Begg is starting to grow on me. Will you have one?'

She nodded, put down her purse.

'I might have two or three,' she warned.

'You deserve it after slaving all night over a hot microphone,' he reassured her.

He prepared the drink, nodded as she took the first drink.

'Hard night at the gambling casino, dear?' he asked in mock solicitude.

'Harder than it used to be before certain people held up the place in such a noisy and colorful fashion, sir. A very uptight atmosphere prevails.'

Williston shrugged.

'Those certain people have problems of their own,' he pointed out as he finished his own whiskey-and-water, 'and you could say they're somewhat uptight themselves. But, unlike certain busty blond beauties, they never complain. They cope.'

'You're wonderful.'

'That's true. Wonderful, capable and pragmatic,' he agreed while he refilled his glass.

'And awfully handsome – for an older man.'

'I think you're putting me on, dear.'

'And I think you've been putting me off, Professor,' she answered truthfully.

She was wise all right.

'I'm trying to cope – intelligently,' he explained.

'It won't work. Even if you got Gilman to plan the operation down to the last detail, you couldn't cope with a woman that way – and you damn well know it.'

He nodded.

'If you stopped figuring all the angles and worrying about those footnotes in the pscychology textbooks, you could cope in about two minutes,' she predicted.

Her estimate was somewhat optimistic. It actually took him seventeen minutes. During that period each of them had an important belief confirmed. He discovered that she wasn't anybody's little sister, and she found out that he was the hero she'd wanted for so many years. Dreamless and warm, they slept all night in each other's arms.

CHAPTER TWENTY-FIVE

By the time the Clayton trial resumed, Paradise City was almost as well known to the U.S. and world public as Lidice, Czechoslovakia, or Selma, Alabama, or Disneyland. French and British and West German radio and newspaper reporters arrived with ample funds and the special enthusiasm that always buoyed them at the prospect of showing how rotten the rich-powereful Americans actually were. The London journalists set up their headquarters in a trailer, while they parked just outside the county, and the resourceful French worked from a chartered cabin cruiser, which they anchored a little up the coast at Calloway's Marina. The foxy West Germans had cleverly tricked the Hotel Jefferson into providing three rooms by making their reservations in the name of a touring rock-and-roll group that didn't exist, and once they checked in they tipped generously and hinted they'd call their ambassador in Washington if they were not treated 'correctly.'

As Davidson entered the courthouse at 9:50 a.m. on the twenty-fifth, cameras were flashing and reporters were buzzing but this clamor didn't prevent him from noticing the steely-eyed young man with the briefcase. Joshua David Davidson recognized him as one of the capable attorneys of the NAACP Legal Defense Fund staff, and he was pleased that the sober National Association for the Advancement of Colored People was taking an interest in the case. The NAACP wasn't the noisiest of the civil-rights groups, but its lawyers were excellent and utterly practical. The chief counsel was an old friend as well as an authority on the Constitution.

'Give my regards to Jack,' Davidson told the NAACP counsel to let him know that the criminal lawyer recognized him.

'I'll do that . . . Hot day, isn't it?'

'Going to get hotter before October,' Davidson prophesied with a grin.

The NAACP attorney eyed him thoughtfully.

'You think it'll take that long?'

'Maybe longer. I've got a thousand questions and motions,

and we won't even get to that until next month after we've picked a jury. That is, if we *can* assemble a proper jury in this county.'

The younger lawyer nodded.

'You're going to do the whole number – *everything*?'

'*Everything*. I don't believe in stinting – not at these prices. I'm going to give them everything in the book, and then I'm sending half the fee over to your outfit as a tax-deductible gift.'

'You serious?'

'I never joke about money,' Davidson answered as he walked on with Kelleher and his other assistant.

They entered the courtroom, saw that it was crowded with press, police and journalists.

'SRO,' commented Kelleher.

'I like to play to a full house. It brings out the best in me,' Davidson replied as his eyes swept the chamber. He recognized Everett, two of his assistants and another face that he never expected to see in Paradise City. He sauntered down the aisle to the third row, smiled.

'This isn't El Morocco, Petie, so what the hell are you doing here?' he asked.

'Nothing much else to do in this town, Joshua,' answered the blond millionaire.

'At ten in the morning? You sick, or bloodthirsty for a sensational trial?'

Carstairs shook his head.

'Neither, just expanding my horizons – as they say in the poverty program.'

'Didn't know you'd lost your money.'

The rich sportsman grinned.

'Not my money, just my mind. Love of a good woman. Get up early and stop wasting life. This is the good woman, Joshua.'

The brunette seated beside him was small, glowing, lovely.

'Kathy, may I present a fellow who once saved a rather hot-tempered cousin of mine from the electric chair?'

'Gas chamber,' the lawyer corrected. 'California uses gas.'

'Okay, the gas chamber. I'd like you to meet Joshua David Davidson, bard of the bar and a keen student of both the Old Testament and the penal code . . . Joshua, this extraordinary female is Miss Kathy Pikelis, daughter of one of Jefferson County's most prominent businessmen.'

She was quite pretty, even if not as glamorous as the girls usually associated with Carstairs.

'Happy to meet you, Miss Pikelis,' Davidson acknowledged politely.

He wasn't going to say a word about her father, not a word.

'I'm pleased to meet you, Mr Davidson . . . I didn't realize that Petie knew you.'

The lawyer shrugged.

'Petie knows almost everybody, although I've never seen him with a young lady as nice as you. Maybe he's growing up – at last.'

'You're a worse flatterer than he is,' she scolded.

'No, better. It's one of the few things that I do better than Parker Terence Carstairs.'

'She knows all about that,' countered the mischievous bachelor.

Kathy Pikelis almost blushed.

'He's got a lot more growing up to do,' she judged.

'And I've got a case to try. Please excuse me, but there's an ice-truck driver who's counting on me to save his life. Will you be in town for a while, Pete?'

Carstairs hesitated, nodded.

'A while. How about you?'

'Quite a while. Let's get together for dinner some night. If you bring this attractive lady along, I'll buy. Where are you staying?'

'Paradise House.'

'So are we. I'll phone you. A pleasure to meet you, Miss Pikelis,' Joshua David Davidson announced with a toss of his gray mane.

Up front speaking with Everett, Marton watched and wondered why the second most eligible bachelor in the U.S.A. – perhaps all North America – and Pikelis' daughter were chatting so pleasantly with the enemy. John ought to talk to her about that tricky Yid lawyer, Marton brooded. Of course there were a lot of things Little Johnny *ought* to do, things Ben Marton would do if he were running Jefferson County. Maybe John was getting a bit soft after all these years of uncontested power and riches; maybe a firmer hand was needed.

The judge entered, and the trial began. When Gillis recessed the proceedings at 4:45 that afternoon, not a single juror had been picked. Davidson's complete command of procedures and technicalities was awesome; he'd made the district attorney look like a flustered, furious first-year law student trying desperately to cope with a cool, wise professor. The next day wasn't much better, and it wasn't until 3:50 that the first juror was named.

'You're not in any hurry, are you, Mr Davidson?' Gillis asked at the recess.

'Can't rush justice, can we, Your Honor?' the lawyer answered with an ironic half smile. 'By the way, I forgot to ask, how was the fishing?'

'Just dandy. I wish I was still at the lake.'

The famous criminal lawyer sighed.

'I'm sorry, Your Honor,' he apologized. 'I'll try to make it up to you by making the defense as interesting as possible.

'You're off to a pretty good start, Counselor,' Gillis answered wryly. 'It's quite interesting to watch you teach our distinguished prosecuting attorney the latest points of trial procedures. It would cost him at least one hundred and fifty dollars to take the course at the Practicing Law Institute.'

Davidson suppressed a grin.

'No charge, Your Honor. I love to educate district attorneys. My father wanted me to be a teacher, you know.'

'I didn't, Mr Davidson,' the judge admitted, 'but it doesn't really surprise me. Quite a number of the best legal minds enjoy teaching.'

'And others are judges.'

Now it was Gillis who fought down the smile, for the graceful flattery was difficult to resist. Yes, 'old Reece' didn't have a chance with this man. On the twenty-seventh, only one more juror was picked, and that night the program manager of WPAR–TV tipped off Mayor Ashley that CBS News was working on an hour 'special' about Paradise City. It was the same evening that eleven FBI agents in Miami and seven in New Orleans received orders to join MacBride; they would all travel separately so that no one would notice them as groups. On the morning of the twenty-eighth, hundreds of Paradise City businessmen found copies of an extraordinary leaflet when they opened their office doors. It listed the crimes, scandals, indignities and collaborators of the Pikelis organization and called for all decent men to fight against the racketeers. It was signed by the Committee of 100 to Free Paradise City. Black janitors and cleaning women had delivered the leaflets in the small hours of the night.

On the night of the twenty-ninth, about one-fifth of Jefferson County was watching the Jackie Gleason show as usual when Arbolino cut into the cable near the transmitter and jammed the audio – for one minute. During that period, viewers watching the leggy June Taylor dancers doing their synchronized high kicks were astounded to hear a spokesman for the Committee of 100 urge them to join in a citizens' crusade to 'clean up our city. If you believe as we do,' the voice urged, 'let everyone know by writing the number one hundred on walls, in washrooms, on cars, in public buildings – anywhere. Be careful that no one sees you, because these thugs are close to panic and they won't hesitate to use illegal violence. Write one hundred. Write one hundred. Write one hundred. Further instructions will follow.'

And then the voice ended and the blaring music came up in time for the final chorus of the big production number. Nobody knew whether to take this seriously until printed copies of the appeal were found in some two thousand prayerbooks at various churches the next morning. People glanced at each other uncertainly and said nothing, but by Tuesday the number one hundred began to appear on walls in various parts of the city. On Wednesday night, a college freshman home on summer vacation was seen by a policeman as he finished whitewashing the Resistance symbol on the back of the bus terminal. The officer fired one shot, shouted a command. When the nineteen-year-old son of Paradise City's most prominent Episcopalian clergyman started to run, the policeman squeezed off two more rounds that killed him.

Nobody could suppress this news, for the victim and his father were too well known. Nobody could buy the official story that Ben Marton put out either, for everybody realized that Terry West simply wasn't the sort of young man who'd steal a car or assault an officer. It was a lie, another lie, another proof that the brutal dictatorship of the Pikelis organization could not be tolerated any longer. Now Sledgehammer had a genuine martyr, and the blunt question of 'Who Murdered Terry West?' made an effective slogan. The discontent was spreading, growing, festering, seething.

It was almost tangible by September 5 when the Clayton jury was completed and the trial began, but any hopes that the trial might divert public opinion were shattered when Judge Gillis called Marton into his chambers at 5 p.m. and confided that he didn't think there was much chance of a conviction.

'Davidson has Reece completely outclassed, Ben, and he's going to shoot his case so full of holes that it'll be damned hard for even the most loyal and friendly jury to convict. Besides, he's going to raise the *Miranda* ruling and argue that Clayton was denied prompt access to an attorney, and even if you win by some miracle,' Gillis predicted, 'you'll lose on appeal. He's going all the way to the U.S. Supreme Court with this, Ben.'

Marton shook his head grimly.

'What do you suggest, Ralph? Any bright ideas?'

'I didn't get you into this, Ben. It wasn't my idea, so don't get salty with me.'

'Any bright ideas?' the police chief pressed.

Gillis thought for many moments, shrugged and promised he'd try to figure out some legal solution. By the time Everett finished presenting the prosecution's case on the ninth, the judge was even more skeptical. That night, Marton heard about the informer's report that the three missing blacks – the witnesses who could provide Clayton's alibi – had been smuggled back into the city and were being hidden until Davidson was ready to put them on the stand. All through September 10 and 11, dozens of police went through the Negro neighborhoods in a house-by-house and room-by-room search but failed to find even one of the trio.

'They're going on the stand Monday, John,' Marton predicted after he gave Pikelis the bad news. 'I'd bet anything that Davidson's going to spring them as surprise witnesses on Monday. If that happens, we'll never hang Clayton.'

The ganglord puffed on his cigar, considered the implications.

'It'll be a defeat,' he judged.

'A bad defeat, John. It'll make us look real shaky. With all this other trouble we've got and all the bad feeling about that West kid—'

'That was one of your trigger-happy morons,' Pikelis snapped.

'A mistake. Yes, a dumb move – but don't forget that my

men have made thousands of smart moves that helped plenty, helped you and the organization plenty over the years. It isn't fair to rip my boys up for one dumb move, John. We've paid our freight.'

The racketeer sighed, gestured for Marton to continue.

'We've got to get out from under, John,' the police chief warned. 'We can't afford to lose this Clayton thing.'

Pikelis' eyes narrowed, and suddenly his face wore that old look of the waterfront hoodlum he'd been thirty years earlier.

'I don't lose, Ben. Little Johnny doesn't lose.'

'Right. That's right. Clayton has to go, but Ralph says there's almost no chance of hanging him. Ralph has thought the whole case out very carefully, and he says we're bound to lose the legal fight.'

The man who dominated Jefferson County paced the big living room restlessly, calculating the odds and the possibilities.

'Ben, if the public executioner won't hang Clayton and we need to get rid of him,' Pikelis reasoned, 'then Clayton may just have to hang himself.'

'Exactly what I was thinking. A nice tidy jailhouse suicide – the perfect solution.'

It made sense.

It would end the entire embarrassing mess, and leave them free to concentrate on this out-of-town group and the goddam Committee of 100.

'Tomorrow night. Late tomorrow night, after midnight,' Pikelis decided. 'Take care of it, Ben. Don't screw up on this.'

'Not a chance. Consider it done,' the police chief reassured him.

'Good. Next week I want to talk to you about Ashley. He's juicing too much for his health – and for ours too.'

Marton laughed.

'Maybe Luther could give him some driving lessons, John?' He chuckled.

'We'll talk about it next week. I'm not sure yet, but it might come to that. He's got no guts anymore, and if anybody leans on him – if things get rough and he's scared – he'd sell us to save his own ass. That's my hunch, anyway.'

'He's a weak sister all right. It's up to you, John. Luther's been itching for work since he took care of Barringer. I'd say it ought to be out of the county, though, maybe out of the state,' the porky police chief advised. 'We could send Roger off on a vacation – or some mayors' convention – and then they'd find him five or six hundred miles away. Less stink back here.'

Pikelis nodded.

'I'm not completely sure yet,' he concluded, 'but let's give it a think.'

Professor Andrew Williston, who'd been eavesdropping via the infinity transmitter, was already thinking. There was only one solution. He telephoned Crowden's Caravan Camp and left word for Mr Antonelli to meet Jo-Jo at four o'clock. Arbolino received the message, relayed the assembly call on his radio. When the Sledgehammer quartet assembled at rendezvous point Jo-Jo at 4 a.m., Williston broke the news and explained what he calculated they ought to do about the situation.

'It's kind of short notice,' Gilman observed. 'An operation like this should be planned very carefully, and we ought to give it a dry run. I don't like it much, Andy.'

'There's very little time, but we've already collected pretty good intelligence on the set-up. Petie was inside last week when Marton invited him to use the pistol range in the basement, and Petie can fill in the details.'

P. T. Carstairs could and did. When he was finished, the man from Las Vegas still grumbled but went ahead to outline several possible plans for the operation. Shortly after 5 a.m., they settled on one that seemed most plausible – a complex scheme that would require all four of them, considerable technical equipment and skill and a reasonable amount of luck.

Seven p.m. on Saturday night.

'I don't want to be a party pooper,' Gilman warned as they prepared to separate, 'but this is still a hastily conceived and inadequately scouted operation. There are too many things that could go wrong. It's very risky, very amateurish from a professional point of view. If we make a single mistake or get one bad break, we're all dead. That's too much to gamble on any one operation.'

'You're right, Sam,' Williston agreed, 'but I don't see any choice.'

None of the others – not even Gilman – did either.

As Williston drove back into Paradise City, he reflected on the negative estimate they'd just received from the man who was always right. Well, maybe this time he'd be wrong. Maybe not. In fourteen hours they would know. That should please Gilman, for it was a mathematical certainty.

CHAPTER TWENTY-SIX

'We've come full circle – right back to where all this started,' Williston reflected to the woman beside him in the bed.

It was nearly three o'clock in the afternoon, and the blond singer felt safe and silky with her lover so close.

'What are you talking about, Professor?' she asked.

'Full circle – another jail delivery raid,' he repeated.

'You're a very great and groovy man, Professor, but I don't have the slightest idea as to what you're talking about. Maybe it's because I haven't done the required reading.'

She rubbed her head against his shoulder, and the scent of her perfume reminded him of their passion at 5:30 that morning. He took her in his arms, kissed her and then explained what they were going to – had to – do.

'You're crazy, Professor,' she gasped. 'It's a crazy scheme, and you'll all be killed. I've heard some wild ideas, but this is the living and dying end. I want a live hero, not a dead one.'

He stared up at the ceiling, reviewing the plan and visualizing how it would work.

'I don't want to be a widow before I'm a bride, dammit,' she protested.

'Who said anything about marrying you?'

'I did and you will. We make such a lovely couple, especially when we couple – or hadn't you noticed?'

He nodded.

'I noticed,' he admitted.

'And I cook up a storm. I'm terrific at emptying ashtrays too. My teeth are in perfect condition and I've already been analyzed. Think of the money you'll save. What's more, I earn good money, three hundred and fifty or four hundred dollars a week. There'll be no problems in having babies either,' she recited triumphantly, 'because my gynecologist says I've got a great pelvis.'

'I noticed.'

She cuddled closer.

'You like the idea of babies, Andy?'

'Absolutely. I used to be a baby myself.'

She swung back her arm to slap, but he caught her wrist and drew her head down onto his shoulder.

'Please, Andy, find another plan,' she pleaded. 'This is like something out of a TV series – maybe "Mission Impossible" or the clowns from Uncle. It doesn't work in real life.'

'It has to, unless you've got a better plan that we can put into operation in the next nine hours.'

She sat up, shivered.

'Andy, there's something I've got to tell you. I know why they killed Eddie. I lied to you about that.'

'I knew that.'

'Listen, you smug bastard, I'm saying something important. He was just like you. He knew it all. He was always figuring the angles, working out tricky schemes. He committed suicide, just the way you want to do.'

'No, Luther Hyatt put a bomb in his car,' Williston corrected.

'Eddie asked for it. He leaked word that he had evidence that could break the whole Pikelis syndicate,' she answered bitterly.

'Did he? And why would he leak word?'

She was crying now.

'He didn't have any evidence. He had cancer. He was dying, and he didn't want to die for nothing. He wanted them to kill him.'

Yes, that was the sort of thing Barringer might do.

He had the nerve and the righteousness for it.

'So we'd come to avenge him, Judy?'

'That's right, you damn fool! Just because he killed himself you don't have to, Andy!'

She was wrong.

It was too late to back out now.

They couldn't abandon Sam Clayton, even if they wanted to.

'We can't let those Nazi bastards hang Clayton,' Williston announced.

She stopped sobbing, stared.

'What *Nazis*?' she blurted. 'This is an American city, *twenty-five years* later. You're still fighting ghosts in a war that exists only in the history books and American Legion conventions. There are no Nazis here.'

He shook his head again.

'It's the same bunch, only they're Americans instead of Germans and Vichy French,' he said slowly. 'I know where we are and what year it is and what we're doing. I even know that *we* shouldn't be doing it. It's illegal – wrong. I know that this is a job for the government and for the people of Paradise City. But we started it, and we can't stop – not until we've rescued Sam Clayton anyway.'

'You can't, you suicidal idiot!'

He reached out, touched her wet cheek.

'Maybe not,' he admitted, 'but we're going to try.'

Gilman and Arbolino were out planting the charges and rigging the radio-control devices now, the teacher thought as he reached for his clothes, and the tape recording should be ready on the Uher by five o'clock. Carstairs would be preparing the weapons and humming, enjoying the anticipation of dangerous combat. He'd be happy, smiling and happy. All Williston had to do was to relay the instructions to Reverend Snell and then show up at the rendezvous at six for a final talk through review of the timetable.

'Don't worry, Judy,' he said before he left. 'I'll be back before morning, and then we can discuss babies and ashtrays.'

She didn't answer.

At 5:55, the watchman at the downtown Atlas Building looked out the glass front door at the crowds of Saturday shoppers on Clarissa Street and checked again to make sure that the office building was securely locked. There wouldn't be anyone coming into the office building, thank God, and all he had to do was walk through the street floor every couple of hours. That left plenty of time to nibble at the delicious peanut butter and jelly sandwiches his wife had prepared and to study the nudes in the *Playboy* he'd recovered from the waste basket in the Friendly Credit Corp. Inc. suite. Those young Mexican girls were really stacked, he thought happily, and the *Playboy* photographers could be counted on to find the most stacked of all and snap them lying on red sports cars or green silk sheets or white polar-bear rugs. Nossir, you couldn't beat *Playboy* for snazzy color photographs. Even the *National Geographic* didn't come close.

At 6:10, a panel truck carrying the name of the Ace Elevator Company – the letters were bright blue and about two feet high – pulled up to the rear of the Atlas Building. A lean, handsome man in coveralls slid out from behind the wheel, swinging his tool box as he walked toward the back door. He rang the bell, waited. The arthritic watchman grunted, put down the magazine reluctantly and muttered in irritation as he strode stiffly to the rear entrance. Through the small square glass panel, he saw the workman. He paused to wipe the jelly smears from the corners of his mouth before opening the door.

'Yes?' he asked.

'Ace Elevator. Emergency repair service.'

The old man shook his head.

'Keerist, you come to fix that door on Number Two, I suppose?' he grumbled. 'Didn't they tell you it was fixed yesterday?'

Williston laughed.

'Must be something wrong with it again. Your superintendent called us last night about five,' he explained.

'Took you a whole damn day to get here? That's some fast service, Sonny.'

'We're short-handed. Three men off on vacation.'

'Keerist,' the watchman mumbled.

He opened the door, and the spy entered.

'Up that way,' he gestured as he sat down to resume his acquaintance with the splendidly stacked young women of Mexico.

The repairman paused, started to open his tool box.

'Nobody told me you was coming,' complained the old man. 'Nobody tells me nothing.'

He picked up the copy of *Playboy*, opened it.

'Excuse me.'

When the watchman raised his face to reply, Williston sprayed the Mace. The old man's hands clutched at his pained eyes, giving the invader a perfect opportunity to snap the handcuffs on his wrists. 'Keerist, keerist,' the watchman moaned between coughs and gasps. He couldn't see, could hardly breathe. Williston pulled out the two prepared lengths of nylon cord, tied his ankles together and then lashed him to the chair. Then he blew twice on the small whistle; the others began unloading the equipment from the back of the truck. As soon as it was all inside the building and the rear door locked, Arbolino and Gilman carried the dazed watchman – still in his chair – up the corridor until they found a storage room. They left him in there.

'Basement,' Williston ordered.

The green acetylene tank was heavy, but Arbolino handled it easily as they descended into the basement to find the manhole cover. The others followed with the rest of the equipment, Williston pointing the flashlight ahead of them. There it was in the floor in the corner, a three-foot-square metal plate marked SOUTHERN BELL – KEEP OUT. A sturdy lock prevented anyone without the key from raising the plate, unless he had an acetylene torch. Arbolino took out the torch, connected it to the tank and put on the special goggles. Then he burned the lock hasp off, exactly as he'd practiced.

Carstairs jerked up the plate, and the teacher aimed his beam down into the blackness. There was a low tunnel – perhaps five feet high – with heavy insulated cables along the damp concrete walls; it ran off to the left.

'Right, that's it,' the sportsman confirmed.

Williston went down first, signaled the others to hurry. They manhandled the gear down the metal ladder carefully, started up the tunnel cautiously. Their sneakers made almost no sound in the subterranean passage. None of them spoke as they advanced up the telephone company's conduit, for noise could betray them. There was to be no nonessential conversation on this operation. They passed three metal plates set in the ceiling, but each time Williston checked the numbers on those manhole covers with those on his chart and shook his head. At the fourth, he nodded.

If the diagram was accurate, this led into the sub-basement of the Paradise City Police Headquarters. Gilman opened his duffel bag, took out a small box and released the catch. He extracted a doctor's stethoscope, put the twin ends into his ears and placed the black plastic disk against the manhole cover. He listened for ninety seconds, straining for any sound that might indicate somebody was on the other side.

Nothing.

He smiled, raised his hand in the thumbs-up signal.

Arbolino went to work again with the torch. This was a much bigger job that would take much more time, for the lock was on the other side, so he'd have to burn out a large section of the plate itself – two feet by two feet – to let them through. The metal wasn't the tempered steel used in bank vaults, but it still consumed twenty-one minutes to carve out the opening that the plan required.

Gilman checked his watch as the stunt man and Carstairs slipped on the asbestos gloves to remove the hot metal square.

6:33 – one minute ahead of schedule.

They all put on the infrared goggles. Williston – silenced revolver in one hand and infrared lamp in the other – was the first up the ladder. He peered over the top into the darkness, swept the invisible beam slowly around the large room. There was machinery in one corner, a control box on the wall and a heap of boxes on the other side of the chamber. An oil tank squatted beside the bulk of the big machine, and on the far wall he made out a door.

He climbed up, waved his partners a silent command to follow with the gear. Two minutes later, the four men stood panting and studying the machine.

'Main generator,' Gilman diagnosed.

They all nodded.

The man from Las Vegas took three pencils from his shoulder pouch, glanced at his watch again. 6:38. He held up his fingers, indicating that they'd have to wait for two minutes. They all understood, for they all knew that these explosive devices were equipped with settings spaced in five-minute intervals. At 6:40, he set each time pencil for twenty minutes so they'd go off precisely at 7:00. He put them in key spots in the generator. Blowing generators was nothing new to this team.

Snell's people would be moving into the telephone booths in another seven minutes. Twenty-four people with thirty dimes each, that ought to do it. None of them had been told what the operation was or what their contribution would be, but they understood that it was important. They would dial the number – again and again and again until 7:18, and eight of them had been told to dial only once but not to hang up. They'd just feed in dimes to maintain the connection, to freeze the lines. That certainly ought to do it.

The police radio was another matter.

It too would be neutralized, but more subtly.

Williston had pointed out that destroying it would be dangerous because the cars – some of them, anyway – would pour back to headquarters if it went off the air, and that was the last thing that the assault team wanted. The trick would be to keep those cars away, as far away as possible for as long as possible. Gilman had scheduled the assault operation inside Police Headquarters for no longer than four minutes, the get-away for eight. The escape route was all laid out, and if the two radio-control devices worked there should be no problem. There would be chaos, but no problem.

Carstairs pointed to the door, then up. He formed the fingers of his right hand into a child's version of a pistol, smiled. The others who sat on the floor beside him nodded in understanding: the police pistol range was at the head of the stairs beyond the portal. Then another flight of steps up to the street floor where four or five patrolmen, a sergeant or two and a couple of detectives might be expected. Clayton was in Cell 4 on the second floor, Snell had reported when he sketched the layout for the man he knew as Arthur Warren. There was a locked steel door at the entrance to the cell block, another on Cell 4.

Plastic charges.

The new version of that smelly C-3.

Six-second fuses.

It had to work.

If everything went according to plan, shooting wouldn't be necessary, the teacher told himself for the twentieth time.

Then he heard the sound of gunfire.

It was barely audible, but it was there and all four of the raiders guessed what it meant. Somebody was practicing on the pistol range on the floor above. Some policeman was there with a loaded gun, firing live ammunition and blocking their access to the main floor. Surprise would be an essential ingredient in seizing control of that floor; there'd be no surprise if they had to shoot their way through the basement.

Forty-one feet from where they sweated, a heavy man in a tan shirt and gray pants peered at a target and took careful aim before he squeezed the trigger of his .38 Colt Detective Special revolver. It was somewhat incongruous for this marksman to be equipped with that weapon, for he wasn't a detective at all. He was a criminal who'd slain eight – or was it nine? – men for money, a professional assassin. He fired again.

'Nice shooting, Luther,' complimented Paradise City's chief of police.

'Got to keep in practice. Got to stay sharp – especially these days,' Hyatt answered.

He let off two more rounds, both bull's-eyes.

'Now it's my turn,' Marton announced.

'No, I've got three more to go.'

There was no point in arguing with Luther Hyatt, so the captain watched him finish his regular eighteen rounds and then Marton began to shoot. He wasn't nearly as accurate as the assassin at this distance, but he was reasonably satisfied with his score when he finished at 6:50. The two men reloaded, holstered their weapons and started for the refrigerator with cold beer in Marton's office upstairs.

Across town, Judy Ellis was getting dressed before going out to eat. Williston had told her to maintain her normal routine and schedule, to vary no detail so that she wouldn't be suspected of any connection with the attack. She buttoned her blouse, combed her hair in front of the mirror and reached nervously for the lipstick on the dresser. It slipped from her grasp and fell to the floor. Sighing, she bent down to look behind the dresser for the yellow cylinder.

Then she saw it.

Not the lipstick, the face of a tiny black microphone.

The room was bugged.

Somebody had been listening, had heard her lover outline the plan and time of the raid.

Pikelis – it had to be Pikelis – would have men waiting in ambush, and the attackers would all be butchered.

She had to warn them. The singer snatched her purse, hurried down to the street to find a taxi. Four went by – all occupied – before the desperate woman managed to hail one.

'Atlas Building on Clarissa,' she said as she slammed the door.

'I'm in a rush, urgent,' she added.

'Yes, Ma'am. Do my best.'

She looked at her wristwatch. It was 6:54, six minutes to what Williston had jocularly called 'H Hour.' Six minutes to cover twenty-one blocks; it could be done. With luck, it could be done.

At 6:57, Arbolino started toward the door with the lock pick in his hand. He crouched down, studied it carefully and nodded. No sweat. The lock would be easy, a standard model. He opened his musette bag, took out the gas mask and gestured to the others. A minute later, they were all wearing similar respirators. At 6:59, Snell's helpers began dropping in their dimes at two dozen scattered telephone booths and starting dialing PInetree 1-1111. Fifteen seconds later, something unusual happened at the switchboard of the Paradise City Police Headquarters. All the lights were flashing, all the buzzers were sounding, all the lines were busy. Nameless long-winded people – some of them either irrational or drunk – were talking gibberish, asking questions, recounting complex, senseless tales of vague problems or suspicions. Crank calls were nothing new, but such a concentration was extraordinary.

'Every nut in town is calling tonight,' grumbled the switchboard operator. 'Must be drinking early . . . Son-of-a-bitch . . . Yes, police headquarters. What? What's that? What's your name? What are you talking about, lady?'

Every line was tied up; no calls could go out.

No calls would – until 7:18.

In the sub-basement, Williston saw the sweep second hand on his watch move steadily. He raised his left hand, opened and closed the fingers twice.

Ten seconds to go. Abolino raised the walkie-talkie, spoke two words.

When the sweep second hand reached 7 p.m. – straight up, as radio announcers would say – the time pencils blew out the generator and there was no electric power in the building. The air-conditioners in the detectives' squad room, the snack bar and Marton's office all died simultaneously. The police radio transmitter was silenced – for fifteen seconds. Then it resumed again, ordering the various cars to handle assorted emergency calls on the waterfront, at the country club, the airport, the far side of the city. The police moved off quickly and obediently, unaware that these instructions were being broadcast by a compact transmitter in the back of a panel truck parked behind the Atlas Building.

Gilman had rigged the equipment rather ingeniously, but simply.

When Arbolino spoke into the walkie-talkie that was set to the right frequency, the voice-activated transmitter went on and the voice-activated recorder began to play and the tape of the stunt man reading off fake orders – he knew the call numbers after weeks of eavesdropping on police broadcasts – sent the radio cars off on imaginary emergencies far from headquarters. In seven or eight minutes – after finding no such emergencies – the mobile patrols would fretfully radio in their complaints and ask that the address be checked. There'd be no answer until 7:09, when the second part of the tape would send the police cars off on another set of wild-goose chases. As Gilman reckoned it, the second set of orders would divert the radio units until 7:13 or 7:14 and then a few of the brighter police might start telephoning. The lines would all be busy until

7:18, by which time the raiders should be several miles outside Paradise City on Route 121.

It was a good plan, flawed only by two omissions.

It didn't take into account the microcphone in Judy Ellis' room, and it didn't provide for the man who owned the yellow Mustang. Or his armed associates, the people he referred to as his family when he telephoned Atlanta. The plan hadn't included these factors because none of the Sledgehammer team, none of Snell's watchers had discovered them. The man who was always right had been correct when he'd warned that the intelligence was inadequate.

Williston pointed to the lock, and Arbolino inserted the pick. He turned it back and forth four times before there was a click, after which he turned the knob slowly. He pushed the door open, about half an inch. The teacher stepped forward, peered through the crack, raised his silenced revolver. The others followed him through the doorway.

Two floors above, the switchboard operator was cursing and the desk sergeant in the front chamber was explaining to a gaunt, frowsy-haired spinster that he frankly doubted that the space ship that had ruined her gardenias was Russian. He doubted the existence of the craft altogether, but you couldn't tell that to the forty-nine-year-old virgin.

'Miss Devereaux, you really ought to check with the Federal Aeronautics Administration or the Air Force,' Sergeant Morgan advised patiently. He had met Miss Devereaux a dozen times before; she was one of the 'full mooners' – the nuts whose neuroses blossomed each month when the moon was ripe. These unfortunates were standard items for every city's police.

'It isn't a police matter,' Morgan assured her. 'Not within our jurisdiction.'

'Chop suey. That's what I say to you, the old chop suey,' answered the spinster. 'You're just shirking your duty. I've had enough of your disgusting old chop suey.'

'Why don't you get in touch with the Russian ambassador in Washington, Ma'am?'

Miss Devereaux glared.

'I wrote him *five* months ago, Sergeant, and that treacherous Commie rat never answered. That's the kind of vile manners he has. We ought to send him back where he came from, or are you on *his* side?'

The full-mooners were the worst, definitely the worst.

'Miss Devereaux,' Morgan began.

Then he saw the strange look on her face turn even stranger.

'You can't scare me,' she cackled as she pointed over his shoulder. 'Your pinko tricks don't frighten me at all.'

The sergeant turned, and he was instantly (1) stunned, (2) frightened. Two men in white coveralls, white gloves and blue sneakers were standing in the doorway. One carried a submachine gun and the other a revolver with a silencer. As if that weren't frightening enough, they were faceless – like creatures in those science-fiction movies – in gas masks.

'Jesus,' appealed Sergeant Morgan hopefully.

The other two policemen in the room looked up from their desks, blinked.

Now a third gas-masked figure appeared, and Morgan heard still another person dragging something. The submachine gun poked in the air menacingly; the police raised their hands in immediate response.

'You don't scare me,' insisted the spinster confidently.

'Shut up,' advised the sergeant in an abrupt lapse of manners.

The submachine gun gestured, and one of the faceless invaders sprinted across the room to lock the street door from the inside. Miss Devereaux saw this, suddenly realized that the threat of violence was genuine. At that moment, her womanly good sense triumphed over her psychosexual problems and she did something extremely intelligent. She let out a small yip of rational terror, fainted.

Seven blocks away, Judy Ellis leaned forward in the taxi and silently cursed the Saturday traffic. She would be too late, too late to warn them.

Now the third raider raised his submachine gun – two of the strangers had the same weapons – and walked to the squad room, where two detectives were playing '21.' A few moments later, they emerged with upraised arms to join the prisoners near the front desk. One of the raiders took all five of the policemen's guns, removed the cartridges and tossed the empty weapons into a wastepaper basket.

Some forty-five seconds had elapsed, and the invaders hadn't said a word. With Williston in the lead, three of them headed for the stairs while Carstairs remained to cover the disarmed prisoners with his machine gun. At the head of the steps, a policeman was coming out of the toilet when he suddenly found himself facing a submachine gun and a .38-caliber revolver.

Having limited faith in the Jefferson County pension system and a date with a delightfully promiscuous car hop that evening, he sensibly swallowed his professional pride and stood absolutely still. When the teacher hit him three times with the revolver, he fell down. As he hit the floor, Gilman jerked the unconscious officer's gun from the belly holster and scattered the bullets. He dropped the weapon behind the water cooler.

They advanced up the corridor, paused at the turn to let Williston glance around the corner. He looked, waved them on. The two guards at the entrance to the cell block were much too deeply involved in discussing the comparative measurements and talents of Raquel Welch and Sophia Loren to draw their weapons in time, and they both – both the police, not the actresses – lost interest in the idea after they'd been disarmed and Maced. Instead, they concentrated on trying to breathe and/or see as they reeled and staggered.

Keys.

One of them probably had a key to the cell block, or maybe the door was operated by an electrical switch. If the system was electrical, it was dead because they'd blasted the generator. Williston glanced at the two helpless guards, decided that it would be quicker to use explosives instead of searching for the right key.

With the revolver in his right hand, he formed the letter 'C' with his left.

Charge. 'C' stood for charge, a charge of plastic. Arbolino opened the duffel bag, pulled out one of the prepackaged lumps they'd prepared and shaped it on the lock. He took a short length of fuse from a pocket of his coverall, inserted it deftly. Waving the others back, he flicked his lighter.

One . . . two . . . three . . . four . . . five . . . six.

The blast tore out the lock, and the shock swung the metal door back with a loud clatter. Gilman checked his watch. Two minutes and five seconds; half the time was gone. He tapped his wrist urgently, and they charged into the cell block on the dead run. *There* – Cell Number 4. The other prisoners were gaping, muttering, yelling questions, but Sam Clayton simply stared at them curiously. Snell had told him earlier in the day that his friends Tom and Jerry might visit soon, leaving the prisoner puzzled because he had no such friends. Williston stepped up to his cell, handed in the printed note.

'Here to save you from fake suicide police planning. Stand back from door.'

It was signed 'Tom and Jerry.'

The ice-truck driver nodded, retreated to the far corner. Williston raised his hand in the 'C' again; Arbolino responded immediately. Some thirty-six seconds later, the second charge exploded. The lock was smashed, but the door didn't open. Somehow the goddam lock was jammed. While Gilman covered the exit with his machine gun, the teacher and the stunt man pushed and struggled. They stepped back, both hit the door with their shoulders in coordinated impact.

It yielded suddenly, swung wide open.

The two raiders nearly fell in, but they caught themselves and Williston signaled Clayton to hurry. By this time, the other prisoners were shouting and screaming to be let out too. The assault team ignored them, hustled the ice-truck driver up the passage toward the stairs.

Below Carstairs was firing. The sounds of the two explosions had been heard by Marton and Hyatt, had brought them charging out of the chief's office to investigate. Parker Terence Carstairs sent them diving back into the office with two quick bursts, and then he threw in one of the nauseating gas canisters to keep them 'honest.' As he lobbed the bomb, he simultaneously stepped back against the wall and swung the submachine gun to cover the disarmed policemen. A moment later, Williston led the others down and through to the steps leading to the basement. Three shots, then two more, flew from Marton's office, and the second most eligible bachelor in North America replied with another gas grenade. He dropped two more in the front room, leaving the five police gagging and vomiting as he backed out warily.

The passageway was already thick with gas from four canisters Gilman had tossed twenty seconds earlier, but Carstairs made his way through the fog and descended. When he reached the pistol range, he paused to lock the door behind him as a responsible rear guard should.

Three minutes and fifteen seconds, and they were still inside police headquarters. By the time Carstairs reached the sub-basement, Gilman, Arbolino and Clayton had already passed down into the tunnel. Williston was crouched on one knee, his silenced revolver pointed at the door – just in case. He gestured toward the manhole, and then Carstairs graciously waved for him to go first. It was a sort of joke, but it was also ridiculous. There was no time for such games, a point that Professor Andrew Williston emphasized by aiming his gun at the millionaire.

'Temper, temper,' the celebrity thought archly as he yielded to the startling threat.

Three minutes and forty seconds, twenty seconds left.

Carstairs vanished into the hole. Williston looked around, saw the generator was on fire and tossed his last two gas grenades before descending into the telephone company's tunnel. The others were already fifty yards up the passageway, breathing deeply now that they had removed the unpleasant respirators. Clayton seemed to be staggering a little; maybe he'd taken the blast of the plastic charge.

A block away, Judy Barringer-Ellis was paying off her taxi driver in front of the Atlas Building. The streets were still crowded with shoppers, couples in the downtown area for dinner and a movie, kids emerging from double features at the nearby movie theaters. She made her way through, found the alley and ran toward the back of the office building as quickly as she could.

There was the truck.

And there was a policeman beside it.

They were trapped.

She couldn't stop herself, so she kept running toward the panel truck without any idea of what she'd do or say. She didn't have to do or say anything. The policeman turned from the vehicle as he heard her coming, and this made it much easier for Carstairs to knock him unconscious with the butt of the submachine gun. She stood there staring and sobbing, unable to believe it. The policeman, who'd been routinely checking the front and rear doors of office buildings on his beat, would have no trouble at all in believing it. He'd have a concussion and a terrible headache for five days to prove it.

'What the hell are *you* doing here?' Williston asked the singer.

She couldn't stop crying.

'Better bring her along,' counseled Gilman. 'No time to talk.'

And there wasn't. They had only six and a half minutes to get out of the city, perhaps a few more if the other radio-control devices functioned.

‘Get him inside,’ Williston ordered as he gestured toward the black man.

Clayton was vaguely sick, having caught some of the nauseating gas. They’d forgotten to bring a mask for him. As Gilman and Carstairs helped him into the back of the truck, Arbolino and Williston ripped off the twin Ace Elevator signs they’d taped to the body so neatly. The signs peeled off like giant Band-aids, leaving an unmarked 1965 Ford panel truck – with a supercharged 1969 motor. The teacher threw the two signs into the back, boosted his woman into that compartment and followed her a moment later. As he closed the rear door, Arbolino turned the key in the ignition.

The traffic was heavy; the truck averaged only three blocks per green light. Counting the lights carefully, the stunt man waited until the vehicle was eighteen blocks from the police headquarters before he hit his fist twice against the partition behind him. Gilman flicked the first switch on the little transmitter, and five seconds later eighteen scattered fire-alarm boxes in the streets of Paradise City began to sound. The control panel at the fire department’s central station – which the invaders had ‘rigged’ — lit up almost completely; moments later every piece of fire-fighting equipment in town was rolling out with sirens screaming.

Good. That would add to the chaos and confusion, slow down pursuit.

Six blocks farther on the flight out of town, Gilman threw the second switch.

The radio-controlled charge knocked out the traffic-department computer in the basement of the municipal office building, instantly blitzing all the controls that regulated the traffic lights. The lights were all frozen for a few moments, then they all went out. The hundreds of drivers who were beginning to grumble at the sudden flood of fire trucks now found traffic totally snarled; they cursed, blew their horns furiously – and blocked the streets.

That too would delay possible police pursuit.

The panel truck swung onto Route 121 at a proper forty miles per hour, rolling toward the caravan camp where they would hide out in the trailer until darkness. Then Gilman would go off to his job at the Fun Parlor, Carstairs would proceed to his date at the country club and Williston would drive to the marina to pick up the speedboat he’d chartered. At ten, he’d move the boat up near the shore – the beach was only 400 yards from Crowden's Caravan Camp – and Clayton would swim out to make his escape. The craft would put him ashore – in the clothes of a crewman – 310 miles south at a marina near Fort Lauderdale, where a car and driver hired by the Southern Public Opinion Corporation would be waiting.

At 7:17 – one minute before the telephone calls would stop and sixty-eight minutes before sunset would come – Arbolino slowed down to turn off the highway into the trailer park. He backed the truck into its place in front of his trailer, turned off the motor and strolled back to buy a couple of beers from nasty Fred Crowden. The idea was to engage the old man's attention while the others slipped out to enter the trailer unnoticed. There was some risk that the families in the other six trailers might see the group, but they were, unlike Crowden, basically people who minded their own business.

Arbolino bought the beer, chatted with the old widower about the cowboy picture that WPAR–TV had announced for that night and then made his way back to the trailer. As he entered, WPAR radio was reporting the known details of 'the most fantastic jail delivery in state history.' City and state police were throwing up roadblocks on all highways out of the county; Chief Marton was confident that 'these vicious criminals and the escaped murderer' would be apprehended before morning.

'Try the police frequency,' Williston ordered.

The police radio was back on the air now, sizzling with rapid-fire instructions to the patrol cars. None of the commands indicated the slightest suspicion that the fugitives were at the trailer camp on 121.

'Seems okay,' judged the stunt man.

'Maybe,' Williston answered. He repeated what the singer had reported about the hidden microphone.

It was puzzling.

'If they knew we were coming, why didn't they stop us?' Arbolino wondered.

The teacher, who'd doffed his coveralls like the others, shook his head.

'I don't know. Even our mastermind-in-residence, the Great Gilman, doesn't know.'

The man from Las Vegas shrugged, sipped at the beer.

'I know and understand and can predict what's logical, what

figures, what makes sense,' he answered slowly. 'This doesn't figure. It doesn't figure at all. You checked the room for bugs, didn't you, Andy?'

'A week ago, but it wasn't there a week ago.'

Yes, it was puzzling.

They listened to WPAR and the police radio for another ten minutes, until the beer ran out and the stunt man agreed to buy a few bottles more. When he rapped on the door of Crowden's cottage-office, the white-haired proprietor opened the door immediately. It was as if he'd been expecting someone. At this time on Saturday nights, Crowden was usually staring at the color TV set – fantasizing lewdly about the leggy dancers who decorated the Gleason variety show.

'Oh, it's you,' the old man mumbled.

He seemed tense and exceptionally alert for a person who'd been absorbing beer since eleven in the morning.

'Who were you expecting, the Black Hand?'

Crowden giggled weakly.

'That's a good one. The Black Hand, ha, ha . . . Say, what can I do for you?'

'The heat's got me. I could use three more beers, please.'

Crowden's acknowledging smile was as watery as his aged blue eyes, but he produced the bottles without comment. He moved with unusual speed, made change quickly and said nothing that might delay Arbolino's departure. The old man generally talked quite a bit – too much – but tonight he seemed to want to be alone. Maybe he's waiting for some woman, the stunt man speculated as he started back toward his own trailer.

Just as he reached it, he heard the sounds and turned. There was a large green sedan entering the caravan camp, two other cars behind it. A dozen men emerged from the vehicles; Arbolino recognized two of them at once. He jerked open the trailer door.

'They're here. Pikelis' hoods. Three carloads,' he whispered.

Something had gone wrong. The man from Vegas had been right – again.

Carstairs, Gilman and Williston seized submachine guns in automatic reflex.

'Pete, move toward the road. Sam, cover the back. Tony, you get behind the truck,' the man who'd once been 'Marie Antoinette' ordered quickly. 'Judy and Sam – Sam Clayton – stay on the floor inside here . . . Let's go.'

They slipped out of the trailer on the run, moving swiftly. Crouching low, Williston saw one of the enemy – yes, it was that bastard Hyatt – walk to the office, knock softly. He emerged a few moments later with Crowden, and when the trailer camp owner pointed to the Sledgehammer vehicle Williston guessed that it was the old man who'd betrayed them.

The professor's eyes swept over the battleground twice, watched the foe fan out in a wide arc. Some fifteen yards away, Parker Terence Carstairs was studying the 'situation' from behind another car. It was not a good 'situation.' The terrain gave the defenders no advantage, there was no easy 'escape route' and the Fascists outnumbered them twelve or thirteen to four. Gilman wouldn't like this 'situation' or those odds at all, the millionaire reflected coolly.

Grenades.

We could take them quite easily with grenades, he thought.

Thermite grenades would knock out their cars, and either anti-personnel or gas grenades would neutralize the men.

It had been a mistake not to bring grenades and launchers, Carstairs concluded. Then he saw one of the gangsters circling between two trailers, drew the silenced .32 that he was still carrying from the jail raid and snapped off two shots. The first punched a hole in the hoodlum's right shoulder, the second broke his left thigh four inches above the knee. It was almost like skeet shooting, the sportsman realized. The man screamed as the slugs hit him, dropped his gun as he fell.

Williston heard the wounded enemy moan, turned to see the millionaire signal that he'd hit him with the silenced .32. The man's cries continued, and the psychology professor wondered why Carstairs hadn't shot to kill. He'd always done that in the other war. Had he changed, or was his marksmanship faltering?

Luther Hyatt heard the cries, wondered. There had been no sound of shooting, no indication that the men in the trailer sensed they were being surrounded. Uncertain and wary, he gestured to another gunman to check on the source of the moans. As the thug moved out in a low crouch, Gilman rapped softly on the door of a trailer that housed a young couple with two children. There were armed men in the camp, he whispered to the astonished father, and there would soon be heavy firing. They must flee – out to the rear – with the children immediately. The man saw the machine gun, collected his family, instructed them to follow him in absolute silence because their lives depended on it. In a television situation comedy, the wife would have laughed and the young boys would have said something snippy about poor old Dad. When they glimpsed the machine gun, they remembered all those news broadcasts – all that Vietnam film – and they realized that this wasn't funny at all. They obeyed without hesitation, genuinely frightened by the awesome awareness that violence had somehow emerged from the seventeen-inch glass screen to enter their lives.

Gilman was tapping at the door of another trailer when Carstairs spotted the second thug nearing the wounded man. The .32 wasn't actually that accurate, the marksman reflected, and for a moment he yearned for the Smith & Wesson K-38 that was so much more precise. Only for a moment, then his training and instincts took charge. He aimed, squinted earnestly, fired.

Plop.

A low muffled plop, and then the hoodlum spun like some ballet dancer with an intestinal seizure. He lost his weapon, his footing, and reeled clutching his abdomen. A short terrible cry echoed as the man crumpled. Carstairs had heard such sounds many times, but he'd never noticed the awful animal anguish before. It was terrible in some undefinable, primeval way. Surprised by his own reaction, the sharpshooter turned to see Gilman pointing the way to safety for an elderly couple emerging from another trailer. Carstairs wondered why he was wasting his time and attention on such details, for it wasn't like the focussed, purposeful man from Las Vegas to lose sight of the realities of battle.

What the hell was Sam doing?

Gunfire.

Somewhere down Route 121, heavy gunfire.

Automatic weapons. At least two, maybe three or four, Williston identified mechanically. Submachine guns, and not very far away. A mile, maybe a bit less. What did it mean?

Hyatt heard the shooting too, turned to stare in the direction from which the hammering staccato came. He didn't see the line of men emerging from the woods behind the trailer camp; he was looking the wrong way. They were armed – nearly a dozen seemed to carry machine guns – and they were many. Twenty or twenty-five, Williston calculated. With these reinforcements, the Pikelis group outnumbered the invaders so overwhelmingly that the outcome was unavoidably clear.

Paradise City wasn't going to be liberated after all.

Williston took aim at the gas tank of the car behind which Hyatt was standing, ready to explode it as soon as the assassin fired. At that moment, one of the new arrivals raised something wide-mouthed and metallic – something that glittered in the fading sun – to his face.

'This is the FBI . . . This is the FBI,' the electric bull horn boomed.

Hyatt and his men turned.

'This is the FBI,' the harsh voice continued. 'Put down your weapons. The entire area is sealed off. You are outnumbered and outgunned. We are Federal agents. You have fifteen seconds to lay down your guns. That means *everybody*. Fifteen seconds.'

It was a good trick, Williston thought grimly as he stared at the reinforcements spread out in a wide skirmish line like trained infantry. A good dirty trick. The Sledgehammer team would lay down its weapons as instructed by these supposed government agents, and this fake 'FBI' troop would massacre them.

'Put down your weapons. You have less than ten seconds.'

Williston was quite surprised to see Luther Hyatt raise his gun, point it at the man with the bull horn as if to fire. He was even more surprised when the assassin's .38 boomed, and – instantly – submachine guns in the hands of two of the reinforcements destroyed most of Hyatt's head and upper torso.

'Excellent reflex shooting,' Carstairs thought.

'No more free samples,' warned the bull horn. 'The party's over. You've all got five seconds to get smart, or join Luther. Five . . . four . . . three . . . two . . . one!'

The men who'd arrived with the late Luther Hyatt looked at each other and then at the corpse – very briefly – before they threw down their weapons, raised their arms. Gilman stared at the strange scene, puzzled because he hadn't figured on anything like this. It didn't figure – not rationally – at all.

'Good. That's good,' approved the amplified voice. 'Now walk slowly . . . slowly and with no tricks . . . walk slowly with your hands above your heads back to your cars . . . That's it . . . When you get there, face the vehicles and put your hands on the roofs of the cars.'

There had been no sign of the FBI, the troubled man from

Las Vegas calculated. How could anyone expect that they'd arrive like this, like the cavalry in some ridiculously corny cowboy flick?

'Hands on the cars . . . Face the vehicles . . . New Orleans section, cover them.'

The voice was familiar, despite the distortion of the bull horn.

'No tricks . . . no tricks . . . Okay, take them.'

The four Sledgehammer invaders watched, waited, said nothing.

'Groovy . . . Just groovy . . . Now, will the creative types who sprang Mr Samuel Roosevelt Clayton from the Paradise City police headquarters please step forward? . . . *Please?* I'm talking to First Lieutenant, or should I say Professor Andrew Williston, formerly attached to OSS Operational Group 73 and now on summer vacation from Columbia University . . . I'm talking to Sergeant Parker Terence Carstairs, also attached to Operational Group 73. I don't have the names of the others, but I'd be mighty obliged if they would also cooperate . . . This is your Uncle Sam, gentlemen, so come on out without any hardware.'

Williston put down the M-3, started forward toward the speaker.

The others stepped out into the open to follow.

The four walked together to the man with the bull horn, stared.

'Surprise, surprise,' the Federal agent chuckled.

It was Harry Booth, the Paradise House bartender who spoke so glibly and owned a yellow Mustang.

CHAPTER TWENTY-SEVEN

'I'll take a double Pernod,' the millionaire announced as he shook his head in awe-shock.

'Sorry,' Booth apologized. 'I quit that job about two hours ago. It was only temporary. Good enough cover for an undercover FBI agent, but it really had a limited future. The Civil Service money's much better, and if I'm clean and diligent I might get to run a field office like my friend Mr MacBride.'

He grinned, shook hands with Carstairs.

'Aren't you going to introduce me to the professor?'

'Sure. Andy, this is Harry Booth, the sneaky bartender at the Paradise House. Harry, Professor Andrew Williston – our fearless leader.'

They too clasped hands.

'Where's Judy?' Booth asked.

'Back in the trailer. There she is, coming out with Clayton now . . . How do you know about Judy?'

The undercover agent winked.

'Man, I've been taping your romance for several days now,' he explained. 'Put a bug in her room as soon as Washington identified those prints you left on the wheelchair. Torrid stuff. Once we had you identified and discovered that you preferred her hotel to yours, it seemed the logical thing to do. That's how we found out about your jail-delivery scheme.'

'But you didn't stop it?' challenged Gilman.

'Who's he?'

'Sam Gilman. He was with us in France too. So was the big guy. Tony – Tony Arbolino – meet Harry Booth, our friendly neighborhood undercover agent.'

The FBI operative studied them thoughtfully.

'That's the *entire* outfit?' he asked.

'The operational side,' Williston answered. 'We've got an intelligence network of about two hundred.'

'You're kidding. You've got to be kidding. Two hundred people?'

The teacher nodded.

'Fantastic,' Booth judged admiringly. 'Your whole deal has

been fantastic. Who the hell are they? How'd you infiltrate them?'

'All blacks, all local. All friends or neighbors or supporters of Sam Clayton, people who signed on to help us when we helped them by bringing in Davidson.'

Booth calculated swiftly.

'That must have cost you lads a bundle.'

Carstairs laughed – nicely.

'Sixty-five thousand. Easy come, easy go. And we nearly went,' he added a moment later.

'Uncle certainly saved your collective ass,' the FBI man agreed. 'You asked why we didn't try to stop the raid on police headquarters. Well, we did. We tried and tried – until five-thirty this afternoon – to get a Federal judge to sign an order giving us custody of Clayton so they couldn't do the phony suicide and you wouldn't have to pull the raid, but we didn't have any hard evidence – not enough to convince a judge – that anybody was going to kill Clayton illegally and thereby deprive him of his civil rights. I tried and MacBride tried too.'

Booth pointed to a large man who was speaking into a walkie-talkie radio.

'That's MacBride – SAC – Special Agent in Charge of the Atlanta office.'

They all heard the car.

They turned in unison, saw a black air-conditioned Cadillac swing off Route 121 – nearly overshoot the curve – and jerk to a halt some twenty yards from where they stood. It was easy to tell that the big sedan was air-conditioned, for the windows were all closed on this hot August afternoon. The same windows told something else about this vehicle. Three of them were shattered, and so was the windshield. Someone had shot this car up pretty badly. Gasoline was dripping from the fuel tank; half a dozen bullet holes disfigured the left side of the Cadillac and a dozen more marked the trunk.

Five FBI machine guns swung to cover the vehicle, to cope with whoever got out. But no one got out – not for twenty, thirty, forty seconds. It was odd, almost eerie. Finally, the door beside the driver opened slowly and the driver slid out.

No, fell out.

He was white-faced, blood-splattered, seriously wounded.

He was Tom Waugh, Pikelis chauffeur.

On his knees, he made one failing effort to reach the back

door – to open it for his passenger as a conscientious chauffeur should. His fingers touched the door handle for a moment, but then Waugh toppled over unconscious. He lay there face up in the sunset, eyes open and bubbles of blood at the corners of his mouth.

'It's Pikelis' car,' Booth announced. 'That's his driver.'

'Must be the car that tried to run our roadblock,' reported MacBride, tapping the radio. 'Just got word that a big Caddy smashed through the roadblock on 121 a couple of minutes ago.'

Silently, they approached and surrounded the luxurious wreck.

Williston and Arbolino looked in one window, Gilman and MacBride a second and Booth and Carstairs a third. They all saw the same thing. John Pikelis, the all-powerful ruler of Jefferson County, sat in the rear compartment. There was a glowing cigar in his right hand, an impassive expression on his face. His eyes moved from left to right, then right to left as he scanned them all. Shards of broken glass littered his clothes and red seeped from two small cuts on his left cheek and forehead, but he seemed to be unaware or perhaps indifferent.

No one – in the car or beside it – seemed to know what to say.

Then MacBride took another look – a long professional look – and he began to speak.

'Eagle One to Eagle Two,' he said crisply into the walkie-talkie. 'Eagle One to Eagle Two. This is MacBride. We've got your Caddy. Repeat, we've got your Caddy. You boys really shot it up, didn't you?'

'Eagle Two to Eagle One,' answered the section chief a mile down Route 121. 'That's what roadblocks are supposed to do, aren't they?'

Williston watched the ganglord's face, saw the dim gleam in Pikelis' eyes and realized that John Pikelis was listening.

'Eagle One to Eagle Two. I guess so. Vehicle and two men – driver and one passenger – are in custody. Both men badly shot up. We'll need an ambulance and a hearse out here immediately.'

'Eagle Two to Eagle One. Did you say a hearse?'

'One ambulance and one hearse. Repeat, one ambulance and one hearse. The driver's just about had it,' MacBride judged dispassionately. 'Shot to pieces and bleeding badly. Should be DOA before the ambulance gets here.'

Pikelis' eyes moved to Carstairs, stared the question.

The millionaire nodded silently, almost apologetically.

Yes, Tom Waugh was dying in the dust a few feet away.

'Eagle Two, I'll want an escort car with four agents to accompany the ambulance to the hospital and men to stand guard over the wounded *subject*,' the Atlanta SAC continued.

He'd almost said 'prisoner' instead of 'subject,' but had caught himself just in time. Pikelis hadn't been charged with any Federal offense yet, hadn't been arrested. He'd been machine-gunned, but he hadn't been arrested – yet. It was a fine point, but FBI agents are both well trained and disciplined and they respect fine points.

Now the old racketeer's eyes swung to Harry Booth, narrowed.

'Harry?' he whispered as he recognized the bartender.

'Yes, it's me. I guess you got hit going through our roadblock . . . I'm with the FBI,' he added in explanation. 'It was an FBI team at the roadblock. We've moved in on you, John.'

'Bastards,' Pikelis replied coldly.

Then his eyes moved to Carstairs.

'Petie?' he asked uncertainly. 'You FBI?'

The jet-set sportsman was astonished to find that he felt sorry for Pikelis. This cruel, evil man was his enemy, his mortal enemy. It didn't make any sense – this surge of confused, sentimental compassion for the murderous Nazi.

'No, John. I'm one of the people who've been grabbing your money and machines, who broke Clayton out of jail. We're not Federal, strictly private. It may sound crazy, John, but we came for vengeance – to avenge Eddie Barringer. We owed him that.'

The pale-faced gangster nodded.

He could understand vengeance.

It was a savage, primeval emotion that he knew, and this familiarity seemed to give him new strength. Again he scanned the faces of the people who were peering into the car, eying him as if he were some animal in a zoo. There was a lean, handsome man standing beside a swarthy muscular type – both strangers – and on the other side he recognized the face of a stickman who worked at the Fun Parlor. Another traitor, another sneaky bastard like Harry Booth.

Pikelis sat up, his face taut with anger.

He opened his mouth, cursed obscenely.

Then he fell forward, and they saw the two red-brown stains that blotted much of the back of his silk sport jacket. Instinctively, Carstairs reached for the door handle to help him.

'Don't touch him,' MacBride ordered curtly. 'There's nothing you can do – except maybe kill him.'

'He's right,' Williston agreed. 'The ambulance will be along soon, and they'll know what to do.'

MacBride opened the rear door, reached in to remove the cigar still glowing in the unconscious gangster's fist.

'Could set off an explosion with that leaking gasoline,' he announced as he prepared to extinguish the flame. He paused, sniffed at the Partaga and then dropped it to the earth and stepped on it.

'Cuban,' he identified mechanically.

'That's a Federal offense,' Booth declared with dead-pan gravity. 'Importation of Cuban products is prohibited, and the penalties are a possible fine of—'

'Don't be stupid,' the Atlanta supervisor interrupted. 'Smuggling belongs to Treasury, not us . . . Oh, this must be Clayton.'

Williston was the first to turn, to see the recently rescued black and the singer approaching.

'They're FBI all right, Judy,' he said to the blond. 'They're the ones who bugged your room.'

'And saved your lives from the forces of evil,' Booth added righteously.

Parker Terence Carstairs wasn't listening. He was still staring into the Cadillac. Gilman was looking too, counting the Federal agents thoughtfully.

'Twenty-three agents,' he announced. 'You must have been expecting trouble – a lot of trouble.'

'Thirty-two, including the men at the roadblocks,' MacBride corrected. 'We came ready for trouble all right, but you're the boys who've got it. It's going to take a week to add up all the laws you've broken. The sentences ought to run at least three hundred years apiece.'

Williston responded instantly to the threat-challenge.

'Hold it. Hold it and cool it,' he ordered.

He didn't appear to be the least bit afraid.

'First of all,' the teacher pointed out, 'your jurisdiction is limited to offenses that are violations of *Federal statutes*, and I don't think that we've violated many *Federal* statutes. I'm not admitting that we've violated any state or local laws either – that's for a jury of our peers to decide. As a matter of fact, I – we – aren't going to say anything till we see our lawyer.'

Booth nodded.

'You've got a right to consult with counsel, and we're supposed to tell you about it,' he agreed. 'I read it in *The New York Times*, or was it the Washington *Post*?'

Williston stared at MacBride, who blinked his assent.

'According to the Supreme Court, you have a right to talk to a lawyer within a reasonable time after being taken into custody,' he admitted, 'but who said you're in custody now?'

'You don't mean *now*,' corrected the teacher. 'You mean *yet*. Pete, you've got at least thirty or forty thousand worth of credit in your account with one of the hottest criminal lawyers in the country. He's right in town too, and he's your buddy, so why don't you give old Joshua a call – *now*?'

'You mean it, Andy?'

'It's only a dime, Petie,' Williston replied.

Carstairs shrugged, held out his hand toward MacBride.

'You fellows are supposed to supply the dime, right?' he queried.

The Atlanta SAC hesitated, startled at the thought that this multimillionaire was asking *him* for ten cents.

'I'll spring for it,' Booth intervened.

He gave Carstairs the coin, walked with him to the office, where Fred Crowden was cowering. He was also cringing, sweating, salivating excessively and on the verge of tears. They ignored him as the second most eligible bachelor in North America dialed the Paradise House.

'Five cents more, please,' said the operator.

'Another nickel, Harry.'

'I don't have to do this, you know,' the FBI man announced in mock protest. 'The Supreme Court said a dime, not fifteen cents.'

'Cossack,' the blond millionaire sneered. He supplied the extra coin himself.

Twenty seconds later, he was speaking to Joshua David Davidson.

'What's up, Petie?'

'A great deal. I want to hire you to represent me and some friends. I think we're about to be arrested by the FBI, and Mr

Milburn Pembroke of Ackley, Pembroke, Travis, Cabot and Hoover says you're a good criminal lawyer.'

'Son-of-a-bitch, it was *you*,' Davidson diagnosed. 'It was your money he paid me to defend Clayton!'

'Son-of-a-bitch, it was me and my money all right. And it was me and my friends who broke Clayton out of jail so the local cops wouldn't stage a phony suicide.'

'Son-of-a-bitch, a fake suicide?'

Carstairs sighed.

'Joshua, you seem to have a rather limited vocabulary for a brilliant trial lawyer,' he observed. 'I'm not sure that you're the man to defend us.'

Davidson laughed exultantly.

'You're too late. I took the case thirty seconds ago, and besides, I've already got a nice sixty-five thousand dollars relationship with you. I love rich clients. Once I'm finished with Clayton, you're next on the agenda, Petie. By the way, what are the charges?'

Carstairs explained what some of the charges might be, and Joshua David Davidson was properly impressed.

'Fabulous, absolutely fabulous,' he judged.

'The FBI says we could get a couple of hundred years for this, Joshua.'

'Nonsense. You'll get *medals*. Before I'm through, people will want you to run for Congress. Don't pay any attention to those FBI men, and don't give them any statements or sign anything. Nothing, you hear? Just your name and home address, and my name as your attorney. Remember what I said, you're national heroes.'

Carstairs turned to Booth.

'My lawyer says we're national heroes and we'll get medals, Harry.'

'Could I have your autograph, sir?' the FBI agent countered.

'Petie,' Davidson continued, 'tell me one thing. Why did you do all this?'

The millionaire explained.

'Now *you* tell *me* one thing, Joshua. What made you take the Clayton case?'

He listened to the answer, shaking his head in surprise.

'You're not putting me on, are you? . . . No, okay . . . I believe you. Right . . . Lunch tomorrow, one o'clock . . . Right. So long, Joshua.'

The two men walked back to where MacBride was speaking with Williston.

'We've got ourselves a lawyer, Andy,' Carstairs announced. 'He's a bit odd and highly emotional, but terribly confident. He says we're heroes, that we'll never serve a day.'

'Tell him about the medals,' teased Booth.

'Yeah, Davidson – that's our lawyer, Joshua David Davidson – says we're going to get medals for our noble deeds. He also told me why he agreed to defend Clayton – because he drives an ice truck. Davidson's father drove an ice truck on the lower East Side forty years ago; that's how he earned the money to send Joshua to college and law school. Crazy, huh?'

'Crazy,' Williston agreed. 'Bizarre, sentimental and preposterous. Our brilliant lawyer was right about our never serving a day, Petie. As a matter of fact, we probably don't need a lawyer anymore.'

Carstairs was puzzled.

'Are you crazy now too, Andy?'

'Andy had a very man-to-man talk with Mr MacBride while you were phoning,' the blond singer reported, 'and they reached an understanding. We're all going to cooperate with the FBI, and there may not be any charges against any of us.'

'What the hell are you talking about, Judy?'

'Pete,' said the teacher, 'Mr MacBride's top priority target is the Pikelis organization. That's why they planted Booth, to get evidence to clean up the town. With the stuff we've collected – the tapes and the pictures and the rest – MacBride can get Ashley to crack wide open. Ashley can deliver Pikelis, Marton and the rest, and the FBI will get all the credit for destroying this notorious criminal syndicate that no other law-enforcement agency could ever touch.'

'What do *we* get?'

'The Bureau's thanks and my advice to leave Jefferson County within forty-eight hours if not sooner,' MacBride replied. 'Go, quickly and quietly and thank your lucky stars that Professor Williston is such a persuasive salesman.'

'What about me?' demanded Samuel Roosevelt Clayton.

'We'll straighten out your legal problems in a couple of weeks,' the Atlanta SAC promised. 'In the meantime, you'll go to a private cell at the Federal penitentiary in Atlanta. You'll be in our custody until your trial. With Davidson as your counsel, I'd bet on a fast acquittal.'

Handcuffed and visibly depressed, Pikelis' men were being loaded into the FBI cars – two to a vehicle.

'You're damned lucky that you didn't kill anybody in all this fighting,' MacBride observed. 'Goddam lucky.'

Williston looked at Carstairs; it was true. Although neither of them said it, it was also – suddenly – chilling. Frightening.

'We never *intended* to kill anybody,' protested Arbolino.

'No, it wasn't in the plan,' Gilman confirmed.

The teacher looked at him. He hadn't changed at all, despite everything that had happened. Samuel Mordecai Gilman *still* believed in plans.

The Federal agents turned to go.

'Can we take one of the extra cars, one of the Pikelis cars, to get back to town?' Carstairs asked.

MacBride glared.

'That's private property, Mr Carstairs. You've broken or bent enough laws without adding auto theft,' he warned. 'Besides, we'll be impounding those vehicles as evidence.'

'I've got a date with a girl – a very difficult date – at the country club,' the millionaire explained.

'You going to tell her the whole story, Petie?' the singer asked.

'It's my only chance. I can't afford to lie to that girl anymore.'

Williston studied his tense face.

'I didn't know you cared, Petie,' he said.

'Neither did I – it wasn't in the plan – but I guess I do. At my age, I'm growing up – I *think*.'

'What about the guns, Petie?'

Carstairs shrugged, sighed.

'A grown man doesn't need such toys – such ugly toys – I *think*,' he answered.

'I *hope*,' he added a moment later.

A siren sounded somewhere down Route 121, and MacBride turned to speak into his radio once again.

'What am I going to tell her?' Carstairs wondered. 'I mean how am I going to tell her, and what is she going to say? What is she going to say about *that*?' He gestured toward the Cadillac.

'*We* didn't shoot her father,' Gilman argued rationally, 'although he deserved to be shot and hanged and otherwise punished for many terrible crimes. Just tell her the truth – it was an FBI roadblock.'

The blond socialite who was so successful with women looked

at Gilman in disbelief. It was no wonder that the man from Las Vegas was alone; he believed that facts and logic and mathematics really counted in human relationships.

'What do you think, Tony?' the millionaire asked.

The stunt man sighed, thinking of his own wife.

'No rules – you know that, Pete,' Arbolino reproved. 'Get to her and hold her; that's what I'm going to do with my woman as soon as I can.'

He's smart, Judy Barringer thought.

The siren grew louder; an ambulance and a car filled with FBI agents pulled off the road and stopped beside the battered Cadillac. The agents nodded to MacBride, sat silently in their sedan with their machine guns across their knees and their eyes on the white-suited doctors.

'DOA,' a redheaded intern called out in matter-of-fact tones after examining the chauffeur briefly.

He looked around at all the armed men, shook his head in awe.

'You boys had some shoot-out, huh?' he marveled.

'There's a man inside who may not be quite dead yet,' Williston said in tones that were surprisingly loud and harsh.

The intern sniffed, strode to the car and peered inside.

Then he opened the rear left door, reached in and recognized the man sprawled there.

'It's Pikelis!' he announced as if he'd discovered some wonderful new spray deodorant.

'Little Johnny Pikelis,' the young doctor marveled, 'so he finally caught it?'

Then the intern's professional training prevailed, and he told the ambulance driver to get out the litter. While this was being done, the intern began his preliminary examination. He shook his head uncertainly.

'Two slugs – at least two,' he estimated soberly. 'Don't know what the hell we'll find inside. Lots of bleeding – that's for sure. It doesn't look good . . . Say, what happened – if it's any of my business?'

'It isn't,' said MacBride.

'Aw, come on, Marty,' urged the ex-bartender.

It was ridiculous.

'He tried to run an FBI roadblock,' Williston explained bluntly, 'and they machine-gunned the car. Strictly routine, strictly correct procedures, strictly legal.'

MacBride nodded, shrugged.

'Get him out of here, dammit,' the Special Agent in charge of the Atlanta office ordered.

They carefully placed the wounded racketeer in the litter, began to load it into the rear of the ambulance. After some maneuvering, they slid the litter into place and turned to enclose Waugh's corpse in a plastic 'body bag' that they pushed onto the floor of the vehicle. The intern climbed up into the rear compartment, leaned over Pikelis and then turned to stick out his head.

'He just said something. John just said something,' he announced with an odd half smile.

'Yes?' questioned the millionaire.

'He said – quote – bastards . . . You're all bastards – that's what he said.'

'Maybe he's right,' speculated Williston.

The blond singer shook her head.

No, he was wrong.

The intern waited a moment, closed the door from the inside and rapped on the back of the driver's interior window. The white ambulance pulled away, turned onto Route 121 and headed toward the city – with the FBI escort car thirty yards behind.

'What do you think?' the teacher asked.

MacBride hesitated, answered.

'Maybe he'll make it, or maybe he'll be dead by the time they reach the hospital,' the FBI supervisor calculated. 'He's a mean old bastard, you know, and a tricky one. You can't tell about that kind.'

'It might also be better if he died.

Several of the people who stood beside the ruined Cadillac thought that, but no one said it. After a few moments, MacBride and Booth walked away to speak with their colleagues, and Williston yawned in weary, uneasy relief.

'It's over – I guess,' he declared. 'I'm glad it's over.'

Arbolino nodded in agreement.

'Me too. We were lucky, you know, but the luck had to run out. I was starting to wonder about the whole thing anyway,' he confessed.

'The whole thing?'

'You know what I mean, Andy. Whether it all made sense.

I've been trying to remember that quote from Jefferson, the one that explained why we were right.

Williston closed his eyes, tried to recall the passage that he'd used to justify the operation as morally correct.

'I seem to have forgotten it,' he admitted, 'but it was something about men's right and duty to overthrow despots or tyrants – by force, if necessary.'

'The Declaration of Independence said almost the same thing,' reminded Gilman. 'When a long train of abuses and usurpations,' quoted the man with the excellent memory, 'pursuing invariably the same object evinces a design to reduce them under absolute despotism, it is their right, it is their duty to throw off such government, and to provide new guards for their future security . . . July 4, 1776.'

Williston sighed.

That had been a long time ago. It was still philosophically sound in principle, but you could use the same argument to justify the violence of Maoist extremists on college campuses, black militants or armed rightist fanatics. The Constitution spoke of the citizen's right to bear arms, but where did it end? Well, at least Sledgehammer hadn't killed anybody.

'I'll let you know if I remember it, Tony,' the teacher promised.

'Drop me a card if you do. I'm going home.'

'And you, Sam?' Williston asked.

'Vegas, on the next plane.'

'Petie?'

'I'll stick around here – unfinished business.'

Kathy Pikelis.

Judy Barringer smiled, squeezed her lover's hand.

'He's got that ashtray-emptying and home-cooking look,' she whispered.

'What did she say?'

'Nothing important, Petie,' Williston lied. 'Come on, we can all ride into town in the truck and trailer. I'll drive.'

Ninety seconds later, the panel truck towed the trailer out of Crowden's Caravan Camp and Professor Andrew F. Williston pointed the Ford toward Paradise City. The woman beside him was humming softly, but he didn't even try to identify the song. He was thinking of what her doctor had said about her splendid pelvis and child-bearing facility. Maybe, maybe it was possible. If Carstairs could grow up, anything was possible. Williston considered the prospect until the Saturday-night traffic on Route 121 grew so heavy on the edge of Paradise City that he had to concentrate completely on the driving.

He could still hear her humming beside him, and he began to hum with her as they crossed the city line.

To avert crank calls and gastric upsets by the disturbed or confused, let it be clearly stated that this is entirely a work of fiction about imaginary people and places and events. What's more, I made up all the names of the characters too – so please leave me alone.

W.W.